SOME GO HUNGRY

A NOVEL BY

J. PATRICK REDMOND

This is a work of fiction. All names, characters, places, and incidents are the product of the author's imagination. Any resemblance to real events or persons, living or dead, is entirely coincidental.

Published by Akashic Books

ISBN: 978-1-61775-467-8
eISBN: 978-1-61775-492-0
Library of Congress Control Number: 2015960624

First printing

Kaylie Jones Books
c/o Akashic Books
Twitter: @AkashicBooks
Facebook: AkashicBooks
info@akashicbooks.com
www.akashicbooks.com

Also available from Kaylie Jones Books

Unmentionables by Laurie Loewenstein
Foamers by Justin Kassab
Sing in the Morning, Cry at Night by Barbara J. Taylor
Starve the Vulture by Jason Carney
Little Beasts by Matthew McGevna
The Love Book by Nina Solomon
We Are All Crew by Bill Landauer

For J.R.S.

The brain may take advice, but not the heart, and love, having no geography, knows no boundaries: weight and sink it deep, no matter, it will rise and find the surface: and why not? any love is natural and beautiful that lies within a person's nature; only hypocrites would hold a man responsible for what he loves, emotional illiterates and those of righteous envy, who, in their agitated concern, mistake so frequently the arrow pointing to heaven for the one that leads to hell.

—Truman Capote, *Other Voices, Other Rooms*

But in the following instructions I do not commend you, because when you come together it is not for the better but for the worse. For, in the first place, when you come together as a church, I hear that there are divisions among you. And I believe it in part, for there must be factions among you in order that those who are genuine among you may be recognized. When you come together, it is not the Lord's supper that you eat. For in eating, each one goes ahead with his own meal. One goes hungry, another gets drunk.

—Corinthians

PALMER MOTHER RECALLS FINAL CONVERSATION BEFORE SON'S MURDER

By Foster Lawrence
Fort Sackville Sentinel staff writer

FORT SACKVILLE, Ind. — Ruth Palmer will forever remember talking with her son Robbie Palmer the evening of May 2.

Robbie, 18, temporarily returned home from a party to pick up his favorite Levi's, whitewashed denim jacket. "He wore that thing all the time," Ruth said. "I gave it to him for Christmas last year.

"I was sitting in this rocking chair here. After he grabbed the jacket, he bent down and kissed me and said he would see me later.

"I told him, *If you're going to be late, or not coming home, please call*, and he said, *Of course I will. I love you, Mom.*"

She never saw him again.

His decomposing body was found by two boys on three-wheelers fifteen days later, in a ditch off Highway 41 South near Knox Road. The location is about 10 miles from the party at 25 E. 1st Street in Fort Sackville.

Two autopsies failed to determine a cause of death. A police investigation has failed to determine how or where Palmer died.

Ruth Palmer has been critical of police and county prosecutor Dallas Ellerman for not pursuing the investigation with greater professional commitment.

During the two weeks Robbie was missing, Mrs. Palmer and friends searched for him. She learned about the discovery of his body while watching an Evansville, Ind., television station news broadcast.

When the body was found, Robbie was wearing the denim jacket he picked up at home.

A cheap gold-colored chain, according to Indiana coroner Vonderbreck, was worn around his neck.

"Robbie wore that necklace all the time too," Mrs. Palmer said.

Vonderbreck says every death investigation has three parts.

The first part is an autopsy. The second is a police investigation. The third is either a grand jury or coroner's inquest.

Since the autopsies and police investigation have produced no leads on Palmer's death, Vonderbreck thinks it is time for a grand jury.

Mrs. Palmer has questioned the police investigation and allegations that the party her son attended was homosexual in nature.

"People can say anything they want because Robbie is not here to defend himself.

"I had a conversation with Robbie approximately a week before he died.

"He asked me, *Mom, how would you feel if I was gay?*

"I told him I wouldn't love him any less. *I wouldn't tell you to go for it because that is not the way I brought you up.*

"I asked him if he was gay.

"He said, *I've never had sex with a man and I've never had sex with a woman. I do have some awfully funny feelings inside though.*

"In my opinion, Robbie wasn't gay, or if he was gay, he wasn't gay very long."

Ruth believes he got involved with the wrong crowd. "Classmates at school often teased him. I think he was just looking for someone to be his friend," she said.

Chapter One

November

My first Sunday back from South Beach I was greeted by our customers at Daniels' Family Buffet as if I were a long-lost prodigal son. *He's returned to God's country*, it seemed they were saying. I was met with good wishes from many of our regular customers: *welcome back. We've missed you. The place wasn't the same with you gone.*

Our restaurant stood next to the Walmart Supercenter on a three-acre commercial out-lot in a thirteen-thousand-square-foot building with seating for 430 patrons. It had a main dining room where each of the three buffets—hot bar, salad bar, and dessert bar—was located near the kitchen, with an additional banquet room for private parties. On Sundays both rooms were packed. The line to enter wrapped around the north perimeter of the main dining room from the front entrance to the cashier's desk. Customers paid before they entered. Oftentimes the line extended out the door and around the corner. On Sundays it was not uncommon for customers to experience an hour's wait. Daniels' Family Buffet was a well-oiled machine cranking out fried chicken, mashed potatoes, and green beans, along with other meats, vegetables, casseroles, soups, various salads, and desserts, not to mention homemade pies and cobblers topped with ice cream. Our restaurant was the epitome of southern Indiana home cooking and hospitality; waitresses in black slacks, black aprons, and burgundy polo shirts served up smiles and the occasional sarcastic remark in response to randy old men. Most importantly, they dished out platefuls of Midwestern charm complimented by tall glasses of sweet iced tea or ice-cold Coca-Colas.

Managing the restaurant had fallen upon me. Dad's health was declining, Mom was consumed with his care, and my little brother Cameron was attending the University of Southern Indiana. Growing up, Cam had bussed tables and run the cash register, but he never managed the entire operation. He didn't understand it, and he didn't particularly want the job. Neither did I, but I didn't feel I had a choice. Dad had undergone surgery on his left lung only a year earlier, after having been diagnosed with asbestosis, a result of his naval service during the Vietnam War. I felt obligated to stay in Fort Sackville and manage the restaurant for him. Our financial well-being and the fate of the restaurant now rested on me.

A customer I did not expect to see my first day back—one who'd never been a regular, ever—was Daryl Stone. Daryl and his family must have arrived in Fort Sackville while I was on vacation. I hadn't seen him since high school. Now he was sitting in my restaurant with a wife and two kids at a four-top on the opposite end of the expansive dining room. Over the years, I'd heard Daryl had become a born-again Christian while studying theology at Liberty University in Lynchburg, Virginia. I'd heard somewhere that he'd married and had children. I'd also heard he was returning to Fort Sackville with his family to take the position of youth pastor for the Wabash Valley Baptist Church. Apparently he'd become aware of the position during a Christian musical theater conference conducted at Liberty—the same conference one of our bussers, Trace Thompson, had attended. Daryl applied and got the job. Trace, who'd only met Daryl the one time, was thrilled.

A youth pastor at Wabash Valley Church? It didn't seem possible. He was male-model handsome, as if lifted by the Falwellian Empire from the centerfold of a glossy men's magazine and primed for his own Christian television network. Beneath his pomade and polish, however, I could see the athletic teenager I'd once fallen head over heels for—the one that had come to my basement window in the middle of the night. He'd matured from black Ray-Bans, a bare chest, and board shorts to stylish silver spectacles, a turtleneck, and a taupe tweed sports jacket with corduroys. I headed toward his table.

"Daryl!" I said, somewhat startling him. "I heard you were moving back. I haven't seen you in ages. How've you been?"

"Hey, Grey." He stood to shake my hand. "Grey, I'd like you to meet my wife, Rebecca. Rebecca, this is Grey. Grey and I were classmates at Harrison."

Classmates?

Daryl sat down and placed his hand on the back of the chair next to him. "This is Isaac. Over there is Jacob."

Did he really just say classmates?

"Nice to meet you, Grey," Rebecca said. She had plain features, wore little makeup, and was dressed in a conservative consignment shop kind of style. She reminded me of that girl in every high school classroom who blends in with her surroundings. The kind of girl, years later at the class reunion, one never remembers. Their twin boys looked seven or eight years old. They were unresponsive to the introduction. Each had his teeth sunk deep into the dark meat of a fried chicken leg.

"Looks like the boys are enjoying themselves," I said, trying to clear the word *classmates* from my mind. *He could have said, "We were best friends at Harrison," or, "We were best friends once."*

"Oh yes. Chicken legs and noodles are their favorite," Rebecca said.

"So, last I heard, you were living in Virginia," I said to his wife. "Have you adjusted to Fort Sackville? Must be quite a change."

"It's lovely. Everyone's so friendly. The church welcomed us with open arms," she said, taking a napkin from the table to wipe pieces of fried chicken from her twin boys' cheeks.

Our conversation was interrupted by the restaurant's public address intercom telling me I was needed in the kitchen.

"Excuse me. It's the same old grind here. This place keeps me hopping."

Once in the kitchen, I got stuck helping the cooks catch up on frying chicken. The vegetable oil in one of the fryers had burned, which required that the fryer be boiled out and replenished with fresh oil.

Boiling out a fryer was a process and often forced the fry cook to fall behind. He did. I was unable to return to the dining room for some time. When I did, Daryl and his family had finished their meal. He was waiting near the front door for Rebecca and the boys to come out of the restrooms, facing the wall of photographs.

When Dad bought the restaurant from Grandpa Collin, he and Mom began framing and hanging pictures that captured the fifty-plus years my family had been in the restaurant business. Because the restaurant was a prominent patron of the Harrison High School Athletic Society, there were many pictures of high school heroes and local sports moments. Daryl seemed to be gazing at a photograph of Robbie Palmer and himself, both seventeen years old, at a county high school golf tournament sponsored by the restaurant. In the photograph, Daryl and Robbie stood side by side, Robbie's left hand propped upon his golf club, Daryl's left forearm resting on Robbie's right shoulder. Both wore big smiles. The photograph date: July 1985.

Robbie had been in my accounting class at Harrison High. I was a junior; he was a senior, skinny and always smiling. We weren't friends, but we were friendly. Daryl's girlfriend Shanni sat behind Robbie in the row next to mine. She was blonde, with '80s MTV hair and shoulder pads under her bold print sweaters. She was a curious girl, always asking him questions. One spring day she asked Robbie about the necklace he was wearing. He'd turned in his chair to face her.

"Shhh. Come here," he said. Shanni leaned closer to Robbie. "It's from this guy I'm dating."

"A guy? You're dating a guy? Really?" Shanni asked. Talking about homosexuality in the 1980s was a frightening and potentially dangerous prospect—especially at school. In October, Rock Hudson had died from an AIDS-related illness after disclosing he was a homosexual, and Rock Hudson AIDS jokes were rampant in our school's hallways and locker rooms. The nation was swept up in AIDS panic, and local folks referred to it in a barely audible whisper as *gay cancer*. In Fort Sackville, being gay meant one had AIDS, and having AIDS meant one was gay.

"Where's he from?" Shanni whispered, looking around to see if anyone had heard her.

"Greenfield, Indiana," Robbie said.

"Where's that?" Shanni asked.

"Outside Indianapolis. He just finished his freshman year at Fort Sackville Community College," Robbie said. "He's going to stay for my graduation, maybe for the summer. If he can find a job."

"What's his major?"

"Law enforcement."

"What do you guys do?"

"Mostly just hang out at his apartment. There's a party the weekend after his finals. He's taking me to that."

"Have you guys kissed?"

"Shhh. Yes." I sensed irritation in Robbie's voice.

"What was it like?"

"Jesus, Shanni, enough with the inquisition," I said. Robbie smiled, then turned forward in his chair to face our teacher.

Robbie lived with his mother and two sisters on the north end of town near the Wabash River, in a poor neighborhood of square prewar houses—three, no more than four rooms. Dad said some of them still had dirt floors. Robbie was in elementary school when his father abandoned the family. Robbie, his mother Ruth, and his sisters had been regular customers at Daniels'.

Ruth was a craft lady. During the months of October and November, our restaurant served pumpkin pie baked in disposable aluminum pans; our cooks saved the used tins for her. Once a week, she would knock at the restaurant's kitchen door to collect the silver discs in a trash bag. She cut the used pie tins into the shapes of moons, stars, snowflakes, toy soldiers, and other holiday favorites. Manipulating the metal and applying texture, then color, she created unique and popular Christmas ornaments to give as gifts or to be donated and sold at Wabash Valley Baptist holiday fundraisers. Everyone in school assumed Robbie was gay, but he was not 'out.' A handful of hairstylists—hairdressers, Shanni called them—were the only other gay people in Fort Sackville she knew. I concealed my own struggle with my orientation by trying to fit in with the school's jocks, the popular kids. I dated girls. When dating didn't work, I took close female friends to proms or cotillions. I watched the boys, the athletes like my best friend Daryl Stone—he was in Robbie's senior class—walk down the halls of Harrison. I wondered what it must be like for them, for him. I fantasized about having sex with a guy, but I spent my time trying to disguise my feelings, fearful of being found out while also trying to keep control of my raging hormones.

Robbie, at least, seemed to be figuring out who he was. No apologies from him. Yet he did not force his sexuality on his classmates. They, in turn, kept him in his place with their homophobic comments. For the most part he remained silent. Yet he felt safe with Shanni. I understand now he was struggling with the same issues as I was. But I never befriended him, that guy in accounting class, fearing I'd be called a faggot by association.

Too much of my time, it seemed, was spent thinking about the past, my family's past, the restaurant's past, my hometown's past, and Robbie Palmer's murder—replaying various events over and over in my mind, analyzing them, dissecting them. I spent only as much time in the present as required, and rarely did I think about the future. The future scared the hell out of me. The framed photograph in the restaurant was the only reminder, it seemed, that Robbie had ever existed. I often wondered what customers thought when they saw the picture—if they thought of him at all.

Robbie's murder was the biggest scandal Fort Sackville had ever experienced. Folks rarely spoke about it. And if they dared to, the allusion was quick, and whispered, like saying *gay cancer*, or AIDS. Rumors of threats that had been made against his life often accompanied the stories about Robbie Palmer. And now here was Daryl, standing before this photo of himself with Robbie, his face a pale, inscrutable mask. I wondered what Daryl thought. Did he ever think about him?

"Seems like a lifetime ago. I guess many of these are," I said.

My voice startled Daryl. He quickly regained his composure.

"There's quite a history here," Daryl said, turning to me. "I figured you'd have left Fort Sackville by now."

"No. I'm here. Dad's health has been declining. He had a pretty serious lung surgery this past summer. So, you know, you do what you gotta do."

"You *do* what God calls you to do." Daryl's face was stern, the same angry expression his father had worn that summer day, when we got caught driving his Corvette.

Rebecca and the twins reappeared, joining Daryl near the photographs.

Trying to disregard Daryl's pronouncement, I said, "I think we might be coming to church for Christmas service. Trace says he has a solo."

"He's such a good Christian boy. A lovely voice. God has called him," Rebecca said.

Daryl placed his arm around her shoulders. "Yes. We have big plans for Trace."

"He's a damn good worker. I know that. We could use more like him on the floor," I said.

"Trace has a future. He will serve the Lord," Daryl replied.

"Right. Well, I look forward to hearing him sing. It was nice meeting you, Rebecca. You too, boys." Isaac and Jacob still did not acknowledge me. Little brats.

"I'll look for your face in the pew on Sunday," Daryl said before he followed his wife and boys out the front door.

Once a year at Christmas is enough, I thought.

Trace Thompson—a lean sixteen-year-old busboy, blond haired, fresh faced, and one of our best bussers on the floor and in the dish room—was working that Sunday too. Not long after I hired Trace the summer before his senior year at Harrison High School, he expressed his desire to study musical theater somewhere close to New York City. His dream was Broadway. He certainly had the talent. I'd heard him sing with the Wabash Valley Baptist Church youth choir. Folks all around town raved about his voice. He was an intelligent kid whose parents had homeschooled him until his third grade year. When he took the public school placement test, he scored high enough to skip third grade. Now he was the youngest senior at Harrison High School and following the AP and honors track. By the end of fall semester, he said he'd have enough credits to graduate midterm. Not long after I hired him, he asked if I'd let him work full-time in the spring and perhaps next fall, so he could save money for his east coast university dream.

"Absolutely, Trace. Anything I can do to help."

"Well, now that you've mentioned it, I'd like some help with my college applications."

"Sure. Where are you applying?"

"Where aren't I applying?" he asked, somewhat exasperated. "I'm starting with the Boston Conservatory, SUNY Purchase, the Hartt School, and the New School."

"Wow! You're not messing around," I said.

"I'm getting to Broadway one way or another. I'm going to apply to as many musical theater programs as I can. Thing is . . ." Trace paused for a moment. "Well, I need some help with the applications 'cause my parents don't want me to apply. They'd prefer I attend a Baptist college like Baylor, Texas, or even Liberty University. So I'm gonna apply to those, too, just to keep them happy."

"What happens when you get accepted to one of your dream schools? What'll you do then?"

"My plan is to wait until I'm eighteen—then they can't do anything. I really just want to work and save as much money as I can. Mother and Father won't mind if I start a semester or even a year late so long as I'm working and saving money for school. Please, don't say anything to them, okay?"

"I don't want to cause problems between you and your family."

"I won't tell them you're helping me," Trace said, his eyes pleading his case. "I just know you do a little bit of writing, and I thought, maybe you could help me with grammar, punctuation, stuff like that. I want to make sure I don't have any mistakes. All the applications pretty much ask for the same thing. It's my auditions I'm worried about. They've got to be perfect!"

"Well . . . I suppose that won't be an issue. But you need to make sure your parents understand I'm just editing your applications, not suggesting which universities you should apply to. Besides, who am I to stop someone from pursuing his dream? I think it's admirable. God knows I wish I would've pursued mine, whatever it once was. You're going to be great, Trace. I'm more than happy to help. When you feel they're ready, just drop them off."

"Thanks, Mr. Daniels. I really appreciate it."

"Call me Grey, Trace. My dad is Mr. Daniels."

"Thanks, Grey."

Our conversation had taken place several months ago, and Trace was patiently awaiting responses. When the restaurant began receiving university flyers, pamphlets, and such in the mail addressed to Trace, I realized he'd used the restaurant address for his dream school applications. I let it slide. What harm could it possibly do? All teenagers keep secrets from their parents. Besides, I always enjoyed working with Trace. He was tidy and quick. He did his job and didn't play around like the other bussers. He was serious but always smiled. His parents were also regular customers at Daniels', and just from local gossip and observing their manner, I knew they would not be happy with Trace when they found out he was applying to non-Baptist universities. Mr. and Mrs. Thompson had a reputation as helicopter parents, always circling about the high school and Sunday school, keeping an eye on Trace, and more importantly, those who interacted with him. Teachers at Harrison High, I was told, purposely avoided the Thompsons. Yet in spite of his parents' constant attention, or perhaps because of it, Trace began his musical ascent as lead in Harrison High School's glee club, along with the youth choir at Wabash Valley Baptist Church. He sang often at weddings and funerals.

As he cleared a four-top, I asked him to make his way to the banquet room when he finished. "I'm sure they need help in there," I said. He tucked the chairs under the table and looked up with excitement.

"Did you see Pastor Daryl?" Trace asked.

"Yes, yes I did."

"Isn't it cool he's come back here? Our rehearsals at church have never been better. He's got some great ideas for our youth choir. He's even promised more solos for me. Mrs. Boil rarely gave me a solo," Trace said, a gleam in his eye.

"That's fantastic, Trace. I know you'll be great." And with a bounce in his step, Trace then pushed his bus cart toward the adjoining banquet room. Watching him leave, I noted he was one of the few bussers that not only stacked dishes neatly in his cart, allowing for easy unloading in the dish room and therefore less breakage, but he also wiped off the chairs before moving on.

"Grey, you have a call on line one. Grey, line one," the cashier announced via the intercom. Opposite me, on the dining room wall of the restaurant office, above the dinner crowd, hung a silver circular neon clock. Its turquoise glow drew my attention; its hands pointed to one p.m. I knew it was Rosabelle. She called every Sunday at the same time to get the scoop on my Saturday night.

Chapter Two

November

As I walked toward the restaurant's office, I thought about Rosabelle. Both her manner and her style were very dramatic. I always thought she was the embodiment of theater living in a thee-*ater* town. Thee-*ater* is how she pronounced it. She was whip smart and quick-witted. And I loved her southern accent. Her voice was vodka and cigarettes whispered in your ear. High kicks at dinner. Reason at lunch. Her sentences sifted, drawing her words out between breaths. To me she was Bette Davis, Marlene Dietrich, with a dash of Mae West.

Rosabelle was my touchstone, the voice of Fort Sackville reason. She knew the community, what people were capable of. She understood their humanity and their brutality—I learned all of it from her. She often tried to save me from myself. And even though she'd gone to high school with my dad, she and I were friends. I'd known her all my life. Rosabelle was the first friend I told I was gay.

For almost thirty years, she'd lived with Mae MacIntosh. Rosabelle had met Mae on a buying trip in Chicago at a quarterly trade show for retailers. They now operated Bonhomme's Apple Orchard and its only remaining profitable business, Rosabelle's, a gift shop and general store housed in the orchard's former roadside market. Everyone said they were *just roommates*. I'd learned long ago, however, that in Fort Sackville two women could live together without folks taking issue. But when two men lived together, eyebrows were raised and voices were lowered.

When I was in high school, Rosabelle and Mae sold parcels of orchard land for commercial development, and it was on former orchard property bordering Highway 41 that Daniels' Family Buffet had been built after Grandpa Collin shuttered Daniels' Diner, our family's first restaurant located near Main Street on Fairground Avenue.

Rosabelle's phone calls were always the highlight of my Sunday afternoons at the restaurant. I walked into the office and closed the door behind me, sat down at the desk, and picked up the receiver for line one. I could hear Rosabelle talking to someone—I assumed it was Mae.

"Well, you're gonna be disappointed," I said. "I only got home yesterday and spent my Saturday night unpacking."

"Mae, he's there, you were right." There was a pause. "Welcome back, sugar," Rosabelle said. "I wondered if you'd make it to work today."

"And miss feeding the Sunday Christians? Are you kidding me? It's the highlight of my week."

"Mae and I just drove by a half hour ago. The parking lot was full. I couldn't tell if that snazzy sports car of yours was there or not," Rosabelle said.

"I parked behind the restaurant. And yes, we are wall-to-wall up in here."

"So did you have a nice time in South Beach?"

"Of course! Are you kidding? In fact, I figured I'd stop by this week and give you the scoop. Do you want to do dinner one night?

"Things are crazy with the holidays ramping up, but let me talk to Mae. Maybe we can all go to the Executive Inn one evening in the next couple of weeks. Wednesday is prime rib night. Otherwise, I'll be at the market every day this week. Stop by sometime."

"Perfect. Hey, I almost forgot . . . did you know Daryl Stone has moved back to town? He was in here earlier with his wife and kids. Can you believe he has a wife and kids?"

"I heard he was coming back," Rosabelle said. "I bet his daddy's happy, him takin' a preachin' job at the Baptist church. That kind of prestige is right up Farmer Stone's alley."

"How'd he ever get the nickname Farmer Stone?" I asked. Having known Farmer Stone for most my life, I had never heard how he'd earned the name.

"Lord, folks around here've been calling him that since Jesus was in diapers. It's said that when he was a boy working his daddy's melon fields south of town, he'd come to a dead stop, whatever he was doing, and begin searching for old river stones. Apparently he had one hell of a collection. His daddy would tell anyone who'd listen that the only kind of farmin' his boy did was for stones. *Ain't nobody made a living selling stones*, he'd say. I guess since his last name was Stone, it all just kind of stuck. Farmer Stone did prove his daddy wrong, though. Ain't nobody around these parts made the kind of living Farmer Stone has. Of course, his trucking and shipping business has made him a pretty penny too. It's paid for everything Daryl and his older brother ever wanted, even though, Lord knows, he's a hard man. Set in his ways."

"See, that's where I thought they made their money. I always thought farming was sideline."

"It's hard to tell. Farmer Stone's daddy told everything he knew. Whereas Farmer Stone wouldn't say shit if he had a mouthful. I suspect Daryl's the same way."

"I don't know. Daryl used to talk. I remember he told me back in high school that his dad always hated the nickname. Daryl kind of implied that his dad and grandpa didn't get along. Anyway, I just wonder who Daryl thinks he's fooling coming back here. It sure isn't me. He said he expects to see *my* face in the pew next Sunday. I suppose Liberty University made him a straight, born-again Christian, and now he's going to do the same for me," I said.

"Honey, we all know that dog won't hunt."

"I am going at Christmas, though. Trace is real excited about Daryl taking on the youth choir. Says Daryl is making all kinds of changes, and rehearsals have never been better." Just then, I saw the Wabash Valley Baptist Church's ancient organist, Myrna Boil, shuffling her way across the dining room, her plate heaped high with fried chicken. Enough fried chicken for an entire football team.

"Myrna's got her plate full, and I mean that in every sense of the word," I told Rosabelle. "You should see her coming off the buffet line."

"You're terrible," Rosabelle said.

"She wobbles around town giving everybody orders like she's some sort of bacon-eating, Bible-thumping Baptist star or something. Anyway, I have to say I was shocked to see Daryl. I don't think I've seen him since high school, since after the grand jury investigation into Robbie's murder."

"Wasn't Daryl a part of that?" Rosabelle asked. "I remember someone coming to the orchard and saying Daryl had been called to testify, that he was one of the guys at the party when Robbie disappeared."

"Those were the rumors, but I don't think so. He and Robbie didn't really have anything to do with one another, unless it had something to do with Harrison's golf team. Daryl was always nice to him, kind of like I was. But Daryl being the jock and all, well, he had to keep some distance from Robbie."

"I don't know. I seem to remember some scuttlebutt about Daryl and Robbie at that party. I recall someone saying that's why Farmer Stone got Daryl the hell out of town. He called in a favor with some buddy of his, the golf coach at Liberty University," Rosabelle said. "I just can't shake the idea that Daryl is a lot like his mamma: self-serving and manipulative. Oh, the trials and tribulations she put upon her husband! Yep, when it comes to Daryl, I bet dollars to donuts that apple didn't fall far from the tree."

"I suppose so," I said. "But I don't remember Daryl and Robbie ever hanging out—at least not in public. Daryl wouldn't have risked it. Anyway, it sure is going to be interesting to see Daryl about town. I gotta tell you, he looks pretty damn good."

"Forbidden fruit always does, sugar."

I laughed. "You said *fruit*."

Rosabelle giggled.

"I should probably get back out on the floor." I said. "I'll pop by this week. Let me know about dinner."

"Okay, sugar. I'm glad you're back, and I can't wait to hear all about it."

"Only the PG stuff," I said.

We hung up, and I sat a moment thinking about what Rosabelle had said, about Daryl and *that* party. About Robbie. I began to wonder: *In high school, had Daryl ever shown up at Robbie's bedroom window like he had at mine? Had they fooled around too? Nah. I would've known about it.* I knew Daryl too well; he'd come back to Fort Sackville to prove something. He had reinvented himself as a man of God, and now, I suppose, he had to convince people.

GRAND JURY TO PROBE PALMER MURDER

By Foster Lawrence
Fort Sackville Sentinel staff writer

FORT SACKVILLE, Ind. — A grand jury will convene next week in an attempt to shed light on the death of Robbie Palmer.

Prosecutor Dallas Ellerman has been focusing his attention on the death of Palmer, which occurred at a party in Fort Sackville on the morning of May 3.

Fort Sackville Police interviewed party attendees, but no charges in Palmer's death have resulted.

A grand jury is an opportunity for the prosecutor to gather information. Grand jury investigations are considered private.

Ellerman said if all goes smoothly, the grand jury inquiry should take no more than a week.

Palmer's mother, Ruth Palmer, has pressed the Fort Sackville Police and the prosecutor to continue the investigation.

She believes there is more information to be uncovered and hopes the grand jury will provide more facts. "I feel deep in my heart they will find hidden information if everyone under oath is truthful," she said.

Chapter Three

December

The Thanksgiving holiday weekend came and went, and before I knew it December had arrived. With holiday business and private parties in the banquet room picking up, in addition to another one of Dad's "spells" and his time spent in the hospital, I'd not had the opportunity since returning from South Beach to meet Rosabelle and Mae for dinner. I barely had any phone conversations with Rosabelle, except for our Sunday one p.m. phone calls. I knew both she and Mae were up to their armpits in Christmas at the gift shop. Christmas was closing in fast—only a week away. Yet it was a warm Friday afternoon, unusual for the season. The sun was shining, and the air was alive and fresh like a spring day. I stood near the kitchen entrance behind the restaurant and looked upon the valley in which my hometown lay, savoring the final moments before Friday's supper rush.

Fort Sackville was first settled by French fur traders and became a spoil of war after American revolutionaries—during a surprise attack on the British—captured the town's namesake. Landlocked, the community lay in a flat flood plain bordered to the west by the Wabash River, the town and farms to the south safeguarded by a levee. The rest of the community to the north and east was isolated from the outside world by a crescent ridge of highlands from which one could look down—as I was—upon the valley of sycamores, grain silos, and shining white church steeples.

Farming and God were two industries by which family fortune might flourish or fail in Fort Sackville.

Its townsfolk had, for the most part since the American Revolution, succeeded in isolating themselves from wantonness, even from the occasional nonsense—whores, queers, and politicians—that washed downriver or traveled Highway 41 from larger cities. Robbie Palmer's murder twenty years ago was the exception. I had lived all of my life in Fort Sackville; most of the town ate in my family's restaurant. Daniels' Family Buffet was a benefactor of *the industry*, relying on its supply: farmers for food, God for customers—most especially the Sunday Christians and the Friday fried catfish Catholics.

Friday's supper rush was a big night and, like Sundays, we ran with a full staff. The teenage bussers typically arrived around four-thirty p.m. to eat dinner before clocking in for their five p.m. shift. While standing outside, feeling invigorated by each breath of the warm winter air and enjoying the remaining minutes of quiet control—soon to be controlled chaos—I saw the familiar black vintage Corvette whip around the corner of the restaurant parking lot, pull near me, and stop. It was Daryl. Trace was sitting in the passenger seat. *Why is Daryl bringing Trace to work?* I thought. As I stood there, certain my expression registered my curiosity, Trace opened his passenger side door, grabbed his backpack, and stepped out of the car. Then, without hesitation, Daryl whipped away as fast as he'd arrived, barely a smile to acknowledge my presence.

"Isn't that car cool?" Trace asked, approaching. "I've never ridden in a Corvette before."

"Yes, it is. And I have. That same one years ago. It was his dad's," I said.

"Oh, yeah. That's right. You and Pastor Daryl went to high school together. Were you guys friends?" Trace asked.

"You could say that." I paused a moment, my eyes focused on Trace, as if searching for hints of Daryl there. "I'm curious, if you don't mind my asking, why is Dar—I mean, *Pastor* Daryl bringing you to work?"

"My car's in the shop, and Mother and Father are attending the Walk to Emmaus committee meeting at church. I had choral practice at school, and since this will be my last holiday event at Harrison before I graduate, Pastor Daryl wanted to attend after-school rehearsals."

"Oh. When is the high school's holiday event?" I asked.

"Tomorrow. That's why I requested the night off. I am off work, right?" Trace asked anxiously.

"Oh, yes. Of course. I remember."

"Are you coming to Christmas service at church next week? Trace asked. "I really do hope you all attend. Our youth choir has been working really hard."

"So far it seems we're going. I swear, I don't know how you do it, Trace. High school and church choir? Work too? I'm surprised you can speak some days."

"My voice is my ticket out. Don't get me wrong, I love my hometown. I'm just ready for something more."

"As well you should be," I said. "Don't do anything to compromise your dreams, though. And speaking of, have you gotten word on your applications yet? Any auditions arranged?"

"No, nothing yet," Trace said, his face tight under the strain of waiting.

"Well, it's only December. My experience is that universities don't make decisions until the spring."

"Yeah, it's going to take forever. Well, I better get inside. I want to eat before I clock in."

"Yeah, you do. With this warm weather I bet we have a busy night. I'll see you inside," I said.

Trace flipped his backpack over his shoulder, grabbed ahold of the kitchen door's handle, and struggled a bit to open it. The door also served as the delivery and stock entrance; it was heavy-duty steel, thick and wide. As the door opened, I heard the whirl of the air curtain kick in, and then a thud as the door closed behind Trace. He was a good kid, kind, polite, and a bit naïve. The prospect of Trace forming a friendship with Daryl made me uncomfortable. A little over a month has passed since Daryl took the youth pastor's position at Wabash Valley Baptist, returning with his family to Fort Sackville. What were his intentions? Was he just being a concerned youth pastor? Trying to accommodate his congregants' needs? Offering a helping hand, perhaps? My gut said no. But I knew Trace's parents well enough, and if they had any misgivings, suspicions, or if they sensed ill intent toward their son, they'd be all over it.

I stood there behind the restaurant, dreading the night's rush and thinking about Daryl and his father's black Corvette.

At Harrison High School, Daryl Stone had been a year ahead of me. I watched him move through the halls. He was smooth like Tom Cruise in *Risky Business* with his penny loafers and black Ray-Ban sunglasses. Yet it wasn't until the following summer, during summer school PE, that I was granted access to his inner circle.

Harrison High curriculum required two semesters of physical education and offered an opportunity to take the class for credit during summer mornings. Most students took advantage of this, in order to participate in the various outdoor activities not offered during the school year. I took the summer option so I would not have to shower in the guys' locker room during school hours. I was fearful of being naked in a room full of boys. And, unlike my grade school body, my high school body had been developing, my hormones were raging, and erections were something over which I had no control. Getting a hard-on in my high school locker room would be devastating. That would get me labeled a *queer* for sure.

On that first day of summer PE before my tenth grade year I ate breakfast at Daniels' Diner, and then a few minutes before eight a.m. I rode my bike to the school's football field. After locking the frame of my Huffy ten-speed to the bike rack, I spotted everyone gathered around Daryl. When I approached, I heard him say, "Dad bought it for me in Indianapolis." Daryl was showing off the latest sports version Sony Walkman radio and cassette player with miniature headphones. "It plays both sides. You don't have to take the tape out to switch anymore." I had wanted a Sony Walkman forever.

A few PE classes later, Daryl invited me over to swim. We rode our bikes to his house after morning class. His family lived on their farm south of town, off Knox Road. Other than my Aunt Charlene and her husband, the Stones were the only family I knew that had a swimming pool. Daryl's older brother, James, a junior at Indiana University and home for the summer, drove a brand-new red Trans Am with T-tops and always seemed to have people around. Daryl's mom and dad were just as popular. Their house, designed by Mrs. Stone, had been custom-built for entertaining. Rumors circulated around the county that the Stones' money came from transporting drugs for which the trucking business served as a front. It was the only way they could have *that* kind of money, people said.

Parked in their four-car garage was a restored pink 1957 Thunderbird, which Daryl said belonged to his mother. Her father bought it for her to take to college—she was a Northwestern graduate. Daryl's parents had met there. Alongside the Thunderbird was Mr. Stone's restored black 1964 Corvette Stingray. A Cadillac Seville and Lincoln Town Car served as their everyday cars. I'd never seen one family with so many vehicles. Daryl and I spent the afternoon swimming and soaking in the sun.

"Hey, you hungry?" he asked.

"Yeah, I am."

"Let's go get Strombolis," he said.

"That sounds great."

Bowman's Pizza on Broadway had been in business as long as my family's restaurant. It was a staple in the community and a regular on many kitchen tables.

As Daryl and I stepped out of the pool and walked dripping toward the house, he turned to me then pointed, "Go ahead, shower over there. I'll grab us some towels." Affixed to the house near its expansive wooden deck, and somewhat secluded by two hemlocks, was an outdoor shower.

"Outside?" I asked.

"Yeah. It's no big deal. No one's going to see you."

I walked to the side of the house and turned on the water. Somehow I summoned up the courage to step out of my wet bathing suit and into the stream of water. It was warm. I felt as if I were getting away with something, like I shouldn't be showering naked outside. *This is the life*, I thought. Daryl soon appeared with towels.

"Looks like someone's got some shrinkage," he said, smirking. Thank God the pool water had been cold. My body didn't have time to react to the warm shower and Daryl's presence. "Here, grab a towel. Hold the car keys. We're taking the 'Vette!" he said.

I stepped out of the shower—leaving the water running—placed his keys on the deck railing, and began to towel off. Daryl peeled off his swimsuit and stepped in. His water-slicked black hair and body glistened in the sunlight. The tiny prism-like droplets streamed across his smooth, taut skin, descended the curves of his triceps, forearms, thighs, and calves, the tiny beads becoming trapped in the smattering of dark chest and pubic hair. Daryl was an athlete: track, cross-country, tennis, golf, and varsity basketball. I wished my body looked like his. Walking away, my towel wrapped round me, carrying my swimsuit, I took one last glance behind me at Daryl showering. I definitely wanted a body like his.

Once Daryl and I were dry and dressed, we walked around the house to the garage. "Are you sure we should do this?" I asked.

"Oh, come on. Get in. Do you always worry about stuff this much?" he asked, opening the driver's door.

The Corvette's hardtop hung from the garage rafters above us. I helped unlock the soft-top and fold it back, securing it behind the two seats. We hopped in. When Daryl started the engine, I could feel the car's power vibrate beneath my seat. The idling engine sounded restrained, first whining, then rumbling.

He backed out of the garage, then pointed the car toward the long paved driveway and punched the gas. The tires squealed; the sleek fiberglass body fishtailed before the tires took traction and rocketed us down the drive toward the Stones' front gate, pinning my back momentarily against the passenger seat.

The Stones' driveway led to Knox Road, a desolate two-lane stretch of blacktop, with farm fields of knee-high corn on one side and grazing cattle on the other.

"How fast do you think we can go?" Daryl asked, yelling above the sound of wind and Prince's "Darling Nikki" blasting from the aftermarket Bose speakers and cassette radio, cows and corn passing in a blur.

"I have no idea."

"The speedometer goes up to 160. I bet we can redline it."

"Go for it!" I said.

Soon the Corvette was racing down the road, its engine revved like a car in the Indianapolis 500.

"Guess how fast we're going?" he asked.

"No idea," I said, gripping the bottom of my seat with my right hand. Ahead of us lay the curved approach to Highway 41. "Think we should slow down?" I asked.

"Naw. Watch this. My brother does it all the time."

Approaching the curve, having no real knowledge of how fast we were going and allowing no regard for existing traffic, the car railed down the access road, shooting like a pinball across the two southbound lanes and into the northbound lanes, its speed sending the car into the highway's median, its tires kicking up gravel and dirt behind us. Once Daryl gained control and steered the car back onto the pavement, keeping it between the lines of the inner lane, I looked behind us. Fortunately, there were no other cars—just a brown dust cloud hanging in our wake.

"That's fucking awesome," I said, trying to keep my voice from shaking, and still white-knuckling my seat.

"It's like a roller-coaster turn, sort of. Like the Beast at Kings Island. My brother can take it faster in his car."

I was scared to death. But my fear was intricately mingled with the thrill of being in Daryl's presence, and this would be the experience against which I'd compare all my friendships and future loves.

Daryl had once seduced me. And standing there behind the restaurant, I wondered if he was doing the same with Trace. A silly thought, perhaps. I'd hoped Rosabelle's initial uncertainties regarding Daryl's return to Fort Sackville and his intentions, his manipulative ways and self-serving air inherited from his mamma, were incorrect, but after watching Daryl dropping off Trace and considering the ease with which a teenage boy could be drawn in by a confident, charismatic man in a vintage sports car—sports cars by design are meant to seduce—I began to reconsider her thoughts. But Trace was not yet a man. Trace had just turned seventeen. Maybe I was projecting my long-ago teenage entanglement with Daryl onto Trace. Certainly Daryl knew better than to mess with a teenage boy, right? I had to rid my mind of the thought. After all, I'd not been around Daryl in years. He was a lot of things; a pedophile I was certain he wasn't. Was I jealous? *That*, I thought, *is really twisted.* But no, I was not jealous. Daryl was good-looking, and as a teenager myself I had been attracted to him, but we had both been teenagers. He was a man now, and so was I. Perhaps I was suspect of his newfound man of God status, which contradicted his previous actions. I guess that's what born-again means: a delineation or separation of oneself from one's past transgressions. Was I concerned with Daryl's thoughts regarding our high school experience or his opinion of me today? I hadn't thought about him until he returned, until I'd seen him that Sunday. And certainly there were rumors of my own "confirmed bachelorhood" and Rio, my former "roommate," who now lived out of town. I was certain I had not escaped town chatter and whispers, eye rolls or comments. I could feel their eyes on my back when they passed me on the street. Even so, I never attempted to confront or confirm the chin-wags. For me, it was about conforming. Keeping talk at bay. If one conformed to Fort Sackville's ways, one did not create complications. Keeping *it* out of town, as Rosabelle had instructed me years ago, had served me well. Daryl, however, was not afraid of confrontation. He never had been. It was odd, though, his taking an interest in Trace. Daryl had said he had big plans for Trace that first Sunday we spoke.

Slipping out of my thoughts and into the warm December sunshine, I turned from my spot in the restaurant's parking lot overlooking Fort Sackville and walked toward the kitchen door. I, too, struggled to open it and then walked in, beneath the air curtain, and made my way through the kitchen's commotion to the front of the house. According to the time clock, it was almost five p.m., the bussers were all checked in, and the line of customers along the buffet was building. It was indeed going to be a busy evening. Soon I would be lost in the bustle of another Friday night supper rush. Yet for just a moment more, I couldn't help but wonder what Daryl was up to, why he'd really returned to Fort Sackville, and what the untold significance and implications were of his apparent and newly formed attachment to Trace. Somehow I had the feeling, as if hearing Rosabelle's voice in my ear, that "shit was gonna hit the fan."

Chapter Four

December

The Wednesday night before Christmas Sunday, I met Rosabelle and Mae for dinner at the Executive Inn. Even though a month had passed, it was the first opportunity we had to get together since that Sunday phone conversation when Rosabelle called to check in on me after my return from South Beach. The holidays were a busy time for Rosabelle's and for Daniels' Family Buffet.

The Executive Inn was a 1940s motor lodge and restaurant on the north side of town, a popular dining establishment with the upper crust of Fort Sackville society. Stepping through the front vestibule was like stepping back in time: the interior well maintained, its knotty pine paneling offered a rustic, Adirondack air, with pine-colored vinyl booths and chairs, wood tables, and a bar in which one might expect to see men in fedoras smoking cigars and drinking highballs along with men in flannel shirts smoking Camels and drinking Stroh's beer. Rosabelle often said the clientele was more crusty than upper-crust, but that she went there because the cocktails were strong and the food was good. When I arrived I found her and Mae sitting at the bar, waiting on our table.

"Who does someone have to blow to get a cocktail around here?" I whispered in Rosabelle's ear as I pulled out a barstool next to her.

"Sugar, you're in the wrong bar if you gotta ask that question," Rosabelle said, reaching around to give me a hug and kiss on the cheek.

"No shit," I said, smiling and winking at Mae. "They got a nice crowd tonight." I enjoyed going to other restaurants—not that Fort Sackville offered a large selection. I especially enjoyed restaurants that offered actual table service, as opposed to Daniels' get-it-yourself buffet. Rosabelle often said, "Honey, I don't type, I don't swim in dirty water, and I don't serve myself at restaurants. I want to be waited on when I go out."

The hostess arrived to seat us. The place was packed with locals—a crowd that was not Daniels' Family Buffet regulars. Looking around, I said, "It's funny how there's a whole group of people that eat out but whom I never see in our place. I guess they're like you, Rosabelle—they want service and a cocktail."

"What do you think about Daryl moving back to town?" Rosabelle asked me after we settled into our chairs at a table and ordered appetizers.

"It was a bit unsettling to see him in the restaurant. I had such a huge crush on him in high school, and our friendship ended so suddenly, disappeared with him right after graduation. And seeing him married with children . . ."

"Did you guys get a chance to talk?" Mae asked.

"Not really. It was all quite uncomfortable. At least on my end. He has that preacher's air about him. You know, that almost condescending demeanor. He always was a bit arrogant."

"A bit arrogant? A lot arrogant! He was an asshole as a teenager," Rosabelle said. "I can't imagine him as an adult. His mother was the same way. She thought her family money gave her permission to act like she was the Queen of Sheba."

"I was just blind to it, I guess. Anyway, he just seems to carry himself with that *God is on my side* kind of attitude. I can't stand that."

"It doesn't surprise me in the least. I've not seen any good come from anybody out of Liberty University. I wouldn't doubt that Condescension and Indignation are prerequisite courses," Mae said.

"Trace says Daryl has big plans for the youth choir, and it seems the whole congregation at Wabash Valley Baptist are excited to have him there. What happened between him and me in high school is in the past. I'm sure he doesn't even think about it," I said.

"Well, you be careful," Rosabelle said. "Don't let his charm suck you in. I don't trust him. Keep doing what you're doing, and for God's sake keep it out of town. You don't need Pastor Daryl stirring the pot at the restaurant . . . no pun intended."

"I'm not worried about Daryl. He and I both know what happened between us. He won't go there," I said. "Besides, like you always say, we'll just avoid each other like Baptists in a liquor store."

"Amen," Rosabelle said, and lifted her cocktail in the air before taking a sip.

INDIANA CIVIL LIBERTIES UNION
FILES SUIT IN PALMER MURDER

By Foster Lawrence
Fort Sackville Sentinel staff writer

FORT SACKVILLE, Ind. — The grand jury investigating the unexplained death of Robbie Palmer has been stalled until it determines if it or the county can be sued.

Palmer, 18, died at a party in Fort Sackville the morning of May 3.

The grand jury, after listening to witnesses, went into recess and released the following prepared statement:

"The grand jury is considering action that would bring to light the seriousness of attempts to obstruct their legal purposes. Although the grand jury is now recessed, it will reconvene at a later date to continue its deliberations on the Robbie Palmer case."

The grand jury issued the statement to prosecutor Dallas Ellerman, who declined to elaborate.

The ICLU is questioning the treatment of gay men appearing before the grand jury.

The ICLU alleges that "rumormongering" has surrounded the probe into the death of Robbie Palmer, who was last seen at a Fort Sackville party attended by several gay men.

Some of the men testifying before the grand jury say they have lost their jobs because of publicity surrounding the grand jury proceedings.

Other witnesses report they had rocks thrown at them outside the Fort Sackville courthouse and that an atmosphere of hysteria has developed, "promoting violence."

Prosecutor Dallas Ellerman has gone on record saying he was "investigating satanic, ritual homosexual practices particular to Fort Sackville."

The ICLU charges that the grand jury "witch hunt has tainted gays as murderous deviants, spurred antigay harassment, and damaged the lives of people questioned."

Robbie Palmer was last seen alive at a party rumored to be "an annual gathering of local homosexual men, at which drugs, alcohol, and sex were freely available."

One grand jury witness testimony, a detective with the Fort Sackville Police, said, "A young Harrison High School student innocently attended a party and found himself in the company of prominent local men whose homosexuality is not generally known. In order to protect reputations and positions, it was necessary to do away with the young man."

The ICLU suit charges that the antigay atmosphere in Fort Sackville was abetted by prosecutor Ellerman, who said that people at the party engaged in "deviant sexual conduct" that represented a "potential health threat to our community," and that "this kind of activity won't be tolerated in Fort Sackville."

The ICLU maintains that party attendees were comprised of Fort Sackville Community College theater arts students and their friends.

Chapter Five

December

Christmas weekend soon arrived, and life in Fort Sackville and at Daniels' Family Buffet fell into a cold, winter holiday rhythm. Folks went about their daily business of Christmas shopping, bundled and quick. Even the crisp chime of the courthouse clock seemed frigid and swift. Rosabelle always said, "Indiana weather can switch on a dime." And it did. This particular Friday was unusually cold for December, and the weather left little opportunity for shoppers to chat outside a Main Street store or for neighbor's to gather on front stoops. Like the season's gunmetal sky, Fort Sackville and its inhabitants remained consistent, including Old Man Atkinson.

Every day at ten-thirty a.m., a yellow cab brought Old Man Atkinson to Daniels' Family Buffet. Regulars watched through the Buffet's large plate glass window as he opened the taxi door and pulled his endomorphic frame from the backseat while the driver retrieved a folded walker from the trunk and slipped it over his forearm. Escorted through the double-door entrance, Old Man Atkinson gripped the cabbie's free arm tightly with one hand while carrying an empty water pitcher—the snap-lid kind found in hospitals—in his other.

Once inside, the cabbie unfolded the walker and placed it in front of Old Man Atkinson. After getting him positioned with the walking aid, the cabbie left and Old Man Atkinson watched him walk away, get in his cab, and circle out of the parking lot, back to Highway 41, his red taillights disappearing down the road. Once the cab was out of sight, Old Man Atkinson lifted his walker with both hands—its green tennis ball feet never touching the floor—and with his water pitcher secured atop one handle, he lurched defiantly down the pathway, carrying his walking aid toward the buffet, past the cashier's desk, to a table three rows beyond the salad bar—the same table every day. Unlike every other customer, he never stopped to pay before entering the dining room; he insisted his waitress take his money. Upon arriving, he sat his pitcher on the table, then placed the walker next to his chair and headed unencumbered to the racked dinner plates on the buffet. Our waitresses knew to fill the pitcher with water—not for dining, but to go. An hour and a half later his cabbie would return, and he would become crippled again.

On this day, as I passed his chair with my bus cart to clear a table nearby, in a rapid, revving voice, discharging his words like a pneumatic air wrench—the kind used in his tire store to remove lug nuts from truck wheels—he said, "Well, you decided to come back, did you, boy?"

"Excuse me?" I asked, turning to him.

"From down south. Decided to come back home. Where your bread is buttered," he said.

"Actually, I've been back for a while, Mr. Atkinson. It was just a vacation."

"Uh huh," he replied.

Old Man Atkinson—Ward Atkinson III, the great-great-grandson or uncle or something of a soldier who fought in the battle of Fort Sackville—was yet another longtime customer of the restaurant. He'd once been a part of the Coffee Club Clan, its membership comprised of local businessmen, farmers, and a car salesman from the dealership next door, their numbers varying based on weather or season. He sipped coffee with them every Saturday before he got pissed a couple of years back and quit the group. When Grandpa Collin was living, Ward Atkinson had been a fair-weather fishing buddy.

Old Man Atkinson owned and operated Atkinson Tire on Main Street, started by his father soon after the debut of Henry Ford's Model T. Before cars, it had been his grandfather's livery stable and blacksmith shop. The tire store made Old Man Atkinson's family a very nice living, and he had inherited his father's nineteenth-century redbrick and timber Banker's Tudor. It was the largest home west of Main Street, its structure and yard encompassing one city block. The Atkinson place was not an inviting home, and it lorded over the neighborhood like a raven at sunset, posed as if it were about to attack and swallow its prey. Children on their way to and from school walked several blocks out of their way to avoid passing the place. It was said Old Man Atkinson's wife had died a horrible choking death in the kitchen while eating breakfast one morning. They said he sat there eating and watched her die.

"You know, a fishing buddy of mine once had a grandson lived in Miami. Nothing but queers and Cubans down there. All of 'em got the AIDS."

Oh shit. Here we go, I thought. I kept bussing the table.

"Yep. They're all just fucking each other like them nigger-monkeys in Africa. You know that's where the AIDS came from, niggers fucking monkeys? Did you see that movie star lady down there? The one trying to save 'em all?" he asked. I felt my face heating up; his voice tore through the dining room before he sank his teeth into a fried pork chop, using his hands to rip the white meat from his mouth's grip.

"You mean Anita Bryant, the orange juice lady?" I asked.

"Hell no. She's been gone a long time. That crazy liberal bitch from California. The one that's married to the faggot husband. Sarandon something or other."

"Susan Sarandon? I don't think she's married."

"All the more proof she's a dyke. Said on the news she wants to bring all those Cubans with the AIDS to America. Give 'em free doctoring."

"Actually, I think it's the Haitians she wants to help. But that was a few years ago."

"Don't matter. Better off the saltwater niggers drown on the way over. We don't need their kind here."

I had no idea how to remove myself from the conversation. I could feel the anger-induced anxiety rising in my chest.

"I don't know, Mr. Atkinson, I didn't see anything like that while I was there." My hands shaking, I carefully and deliberately placed the salt and pepper shakers and sugar caddy back in the center of the table.

"Well, it's a good thing you're back, boy. That place ain't nothing but a goddamn modern-day Sodom and Gomorrah. You're lucky you got out alive. You need to keep your ass here and work for your father like you're supposed to," he said. *Honor thy father and mother*, that's what the Good Book says. Hear my words, boy." He held the pork chop in his right hand and again sank his teeth in, ripping yet another piece of white meat from the bone.

"Yeah. Well, I guess I'm lucky."

Continuing to chew his food, he said, "If it was up to me, I'd say let 'em all burn. They're going to anyway."

"Talk to you later, Mr. Atkinson," I said, and turned away. I returned my bus cart to the serving station and headed toward the office. Once inside, I locked the door behind me and sat at the desk, propped my elbows on the desktop, and rested my face in the palms of my hands. I tried rhythmic breathing. I wanted to tell the old man to fuck off. But he was a paying customer. My South Beach euphoria had dissipated weeks ago. Being back was tougher than I had imagined. All I could think was, *I should have said something.* I picked up the phone receiver and thought about calling Rio, but I dialed Dad instead. *Maybe*, I thought, *Dad wants to get out of the house for the evening. Maybe he'll cover my shift at the restaurant—if he's having one of his good days.*

Chapter Six

December

Dad was feeling better and he was ready to get out of the house, so he agreed to watch the restaurant on this Friday night before Christmas Sunday. I had called him after my encounter with Old Man Atkinson, not so much to tell Dad the story, but to get the old man's cynicism out of my system. Old Man Atkinson had rattled me. "I'd like to have the evening off, maybe head to Evansville and meet up with some friends," I said. "I know a lot of people will be out tonight, given it's Christmas weekend and all."

"We got a full staff tonight?" Dad asked.

"Yes. All but Trace. He found someone to work for him. He's got a holiday thing at church. I'll have everything ready to go for you," I said.

"I need to get out of this house anyway. I'm going stir crazy. Get the second shift going, and then you can leave. Tell them I'll be in around four-thirty p.m."

"Thanks, Dad," I said, my voice hollow.

"I'll open tomorrow too. You can come later in the afternoon. If you're going to Evansville, I know you'll be out late," Dad said.

"Damn, I caught you at the right time. Can I have a raise too?"

"Don't push it."

"Can't blame a guy for trying," I said with a giggle. I always knew what buttons to punch with Dad. Money was always a button with him.

"Enjoy yourself. Have fun. And for God's sake, don't drink and drive."

"I'll probably just stay the night somewhere. See you tomorrow."

"I love you."

"Love you too."

After I got the second-shift kitchen staff settled and the servers and bussers lined out for the night, I took off. It would be a busy night, but not a typical Friday rush. Christmas weekend business was always a little off since so many families were either traveling or gathering at home. In larger cities like Indianapolis—or even Evansville, for that matter—restaurants were packed, people went out. But in Fort Sackville, Christmas was still a celebration to be held at home.

After I puttered about my house for a bit and fixed myself an early dinner, I picked out my clothes for the evening. I was happy I had decided to be around some gay people. My life in Fort Sackville was riddled with heterosexuals, and at times it got the best of me. I didn't feel free to be myself. In Evansville, at Teana Faye's—the gay bar—I could be me. It was my Indiana version of Miami Beach. Plus, there was always the possibility I'd meet someone—a guy to dance with, ask on a date. There was possibility in Evansville. Fort Sackville was impossibility.

After showering and getting dressed, it was almost ten p.m. The nice thing about going out in Evansville was the time change—they were an hour behind Fort Sackville, so I could leave my house at ten p.m. and arrive at Teana Faye's at ten p.m.—just before the place got busy. Of course, the drive home wasn't as nice.

Looking and feeling even better, I jumped in my Infiniti G-35—my *snazzy sports-car*, as Rosabelle called it—and made my way through Fort Sackville to Highway 41 South. Highway 41 was my lifeblood. On more occasions than I could count, it had been my means to escape, my getaway north to Terre Haute, or south to Evansville. From those neighboring municipalities I could make my way to even bigger cities, like Indianapolis or Louisville. I tried to get out of Fort Sackville, away from my life there, every chance I got.

One particular Friday night fourteen years prior changed the trajectory of my life, a time when I was desperately seeking some sign of a gay community before I knew where one might exist. I met Chad Sowers.

I was sitting in the lounge at Chi Chi's, a Mexican restaurant near the Evansville shopping mall, during an afternoon off. A man in his midtwenties, about a year or two older than I, approached. He had spiky blond hair, sea green eyes, and a crooked smile that invited trouble. His Nordic looks and lean five-foot-eight frame were quite noticeable in the brightly colored bar. He greeted me with chips and salsa and flashed his smile when I ordered a Corona with lime. After he took my order I watched him walk away. I liked his walk.

I felt a tingle in the pit of my torso during those first moments after, a tingle similar to the ones I'd felt as a child during recess at LaSalle Elementary—laboring and pumping my legs, straining to fly higher and higher on the playground swings.

When he returned with the beer, he asked, "So, what's your name?"

"Grey."

"Chad. Are you from here?"

"No. Fort Sackville."

"Fort Sackville! Wow, small town. I've driven through it on my way to Indianapolis. Seems kind of redneck."

"It can be, I suppose. Evansville *is* the big city."

Chad grinned. "That's funny. I never thought of Evansville as a city."

I squeezed the lime into my Corona and took a sip.

"So, are you in school?" Chad asked. "I had friends that went to Fort Sackville Community College." He wrapped my spent lime in a cocktail napkin.

"No, my family owns a restaurant. I manage it."

"That's cool. What's it called?"

"Daniels' Family Buffet."

"Oh. Lots of meatloaf and mashed potatoes, I bet?

"You got it."

"Must be nice to have your own restaurant. I'd rather own one than work in one. I'd be out of here if tips weren't so good." Chad scanned the lounge.

"This seems to be a happening place," I said.

Two tables away, a lady who was sitting with her husband was trying to get Chad's attention, waving her thumb and forefinger, pressed together as if holding a pen, signaling she wanted her check.

"Listen, I've got to check my other tables. I'll put in another Corona for you."

"Thanks."

I sipped my beer as Chad dropped a check at the woman's table, then cleared cocktail glasses from another. The way he moved from table to table told the tale—he was a seasoned server. On his way to the bar, he sailed past the big-screen TV and switched the channel to *In Living Color*. The skit, with Damon Wayans and David Alan Grier, was a repeat in which their characters—parodies of movie critics—gave two snaps up for a film they were reviewing. Chad mimicked the zigzag motion of the effeminate characters with one hand while balancing his serving tray in the other. I giggled. When Chad reached the bar and dropped off the empty cocktail glasses, he turned and looked in my direction. Again, he flashed that smile. It seemed he somehow knew I was watching him. My face warmed when I realized he was flirting with me.

Thank God I have another beer coming.

Chad returned with the fresh beer and a ramekin of salsa. Retrieving my empty Corona and placing it on his serving tray, he pulled out a chair to sit down, placing his tray on my table.

"Do you think she wanted her check?" he said sarcastically. "Glad she's gone. She and her husband are regulars. Good tippers, but they run my ass off. They must think this is the River House or something. I hate to tell them, but this isn't fine dining. They never order food, just fill up on chips and salsa." He watched the couple disappear behind saloon-style doors.

"I guess I'm kind of doing the same," I said.

"No, you're cute. It's okay."

I smiled, not knowing how to accept the compliment but enjoying it just the same. I had never experienced a situation like this, open flirting from a guy. I had fantasized the scenario, but never until this moment had it happened. As a small boy—long before I knew about sex—I remember seeing a teenage grill cook in our restaurant who had a protruding Adam's apple. I thought it made the young man look tough; I knew then that when I got older, I wanted an Adam's apple like his. From that moment I felt different. My interests had never been like my cousins', and at the time I felt I couldn't ask my dad. Although he loved me and never laid a hand on me—unlike the welts and bruises he'd received from Grandpa Collin growing up—he was quick-tempered and easy to anger. On more than one occasion I found myself ducking a hammer or tool-turned-missile during home repairs or restaurant renovations. And I clearly remember the horrible death our plastic outdoor Santa suffered at his hands when it wouldn't light up one Christmas. Always self-aware, I worked hard at trying to do or be what others expected, so the schoolyard bully wouldn't beat me up like Dad had done to poor Santa.

But being in a supervisory position at the restaurant gave me some feeling of freedom and independence; I'd begun—subconsciously, perhaps—to seek avenues in which I could explore my feelings. Here I was in Evansville, being served by a cute guy obviously interested in me. I enjoyed the feeling and the attention.

What's wrong with that?

"So, are you staying in town tonight?" Chad asked.

"I hadn't planned to."

"I'm going out with friends after work. You should join us."

"Where are you going?"

"To a dance club. Come along. You'll like it."

"What time are you meeting?"

"Probably ten thirty or so. I'll need to swing by home to shower and change. Don't want to go out smelling like burritos."

"No. That wouldn't be good," I replied. "I don't know if I can sit here for five hours though. If I keep drinking, I'll be blasted before you get off work." I scrambled for an excuse to stay. I really wanted to. "I do have friends who live east of here. I suppose I could pop by their place and visit them."

"It's a plan," he replied. "Be back about ten, and we'll go from here."

"Sounds fun."

"Want another beer?"

"Just one, then I ought to go."

"Okay, one more. After that you're cut off—until later." Chad winked.

I smiled. There was no way I was going to visit my friends. They would wonder whom I was meeting and what I was doing. I would drive the hour home, clean up, then return to Evansville before ten p.m.

When I returned to Chi Chi's that first Friday night, after having driven the hour back to Fort Sackville, after showering and changing clothes, the anticipation was like stepping outdoors into the charged air of a spring thunderstorm riddled with lightening. It had been a long time since I'd felt excited about meeting someone and going out, and even then it was never like this. I'd dated girls in high school. Even as recently as six months ago I'd had one in my bed. It was never thrilling. I usually got drunk, and sex was about the mechanics—void of feeling and emotion, as if I were following the instructions of the mysterious narrator's baritone voice in the black-and-white health and safety films I'd watched in high school. Tonight, however, I felt what I supposed my straight guy-friends felt when they were meeting a girl.

Having arrived on time and surprised by how busy the lounge was, I found a seat at the bar and ordered a Corona. The earlier beers had worn off hours ago. Chad was not working the lounge, the bartender said—he had a section in the dining room and was about to get cut for the night. "I'll let him know you're here," he said.

Not long after, just as I finished my second beer, Chad came into the bar and sat on the stool beside me, his black apron rolled tight and bulging with the busy night's tips.

"I just cashed out. What a night! This place is crazy. The first semi-warm day so far, and the whole town decided to celebrate." He placed his apron on the bar and swiveled in his stool to face me. "Should we have a drink here, or do you want to have one at my house while I get ready?"

"We can have one at your place."

"I don't have Corona, only Bud Light. That okay with you?"

"Bud Light is fine."

Partially unrolling his apron, Chad pulled out a roll of ones, paid my tab, and then leaped down from the stool. I followed him out of the lounge, watching his walk.

"My friends are going to meet us there. They're not off yet," he said as we strolled out the front door of Chi Chi's, the sound of salsa music dancing into the clear night air.

"That's cool. It'll be nice to meet some new people."

I followed Chad's Honda closely in my convertible as we maneuvered beneath the orange sodium-vapor streetlights to his neighborhood on the northwest side of Evansville. I only knew certain parts of the city: the mall, Chi Chi's, the downtown area on the banks of the Ohio. He was definitely taking me into foreign territory.

We entered into the living room of the tri-level ranch house, and I sat on the sofa near the large picture window. "I'll get you that beer," he said, disappearing from the adjoining dining room into the kitchen. Returning, he handed me the ice-cold beer. "One for you and one for me." He popped his open. "Help yourself if you want another, they're in the fridge. I won't be long."

"Thanks."

I sipped my beer and watched Chad slip down the hall toward the bathroom; soon after, I heard him turn on the shower. I fantasized about joining him, but instead I chugged my beer and grabbed another from the refrigerator.

We decided to take my car. Chad directed us to a neighborhood tavern on Franklin Street, and after a few games of pool, which he won, and a couple of beers, we sat down in a booth and ordered another round.

"So are your friends meeting us here?" I asked.

"No. They're going to the Sho-Bar around midnight. Ever been?"

"Nope. This and Chi Chi's are pretty much it."

"It's a gay bar down the street. They have a drag show on Fridays starting at eleven thirty. I guess you've never been to one of those before."

"No. I haven't." I could feel a tinge of unease rising in my chest. "I mean, I have no problem going. I just didn't know there was a gay bar in Evansville."

"It's cool. You'll like it. I mean, it's mostly gay, but there are straight people too. Did you see *A League of Their Own*? You know they filmed most of it here, right? The baseball field and the play-off scenes? The little kid, Stillwell, he's from here. They had casting calls for extras and he got the part. Tom Hanks and Madonna rented houses out near McCutchanville. Anyway, some of the cast hung out there. I saw Penny Marshall and Rosie O'Donnell a couple times. Lori Petty and Madonna spray-painted their names on the wall. I got to meet Lori. She's pretty cool."

"Wow, I'd love to meet Madonna or Rosie. That's awesome. My dad told me when he was younger that Joan Crawford ate in my grandfather's diner. She was on a press tour; the train stopped in town. Our restaurant was across from the depot."

"*Tina! Bring me the ax!*" Chad said, parodying Faye Dunaway in *Mommie Dearest*. "Seriously, I promise you'll like it. The dance music is great, and the queens are a riot. I know a couple of them." Chad picked up his beer. "Here, a toast." I lifted mine, and we bumped the longneck bottles together with a clink.

"To your first gay bar."

"To my first gay bar."

Sipping my beer, I tried to mask my apprehension. My mind was racing. *What if someone from Fort Sackville is there?* After a couple more beers, Chad once again paid our tab, and we made our way to the gay bar.

Walking across the street from the poorly lit gravel lot to the Sho-

Bar, my anxiety began to rise. The building, a grubby white two-story shotgun clapboard with a lean-to on its right side, had clearly been neglected among the post–World War homes-turned-apartments and abandoned warehouses. The neighborhood seemed to have been forgotten decades ago. A freight train rumbled through the neighborhood, seemingly anxious to leave.

It never occurred to me that other people might be fearful of recognition. Of course, I hadn't completely made up my mind I was gay. I'd been living as I thought others expected for so long that I didn't know how to be myself. For years I'd been a skilled chameleon. It seemed tonight, though, my courage was breaking through. I felt like I was sitting in the last car of a roller coaster, waiting to crest and begin the descent. It seemed I'd always been following the steep incline of the cars ahead. But now *I* was peaking; *I* was at the precipice.

I followed Chad to the front door and silently commanded myself to stop being so worried, to continue enjoying the evening. I *could* walk into a gay bar. If someone I knew saw me, I would deal with it. I was having fun with Chad; I liked him. And Chad was having fun also. It seemed he liked me too.

As we sat in a booth to the left of the dance floor, under Madonna's fluorescent orange autograph, my attention was focused on the people in the bar. There were so many people my age and older. On Friday nights the Sho-Bar's cheap draft beer and shot specials attracted a large college crowd. Tonight was no exception. I simultaneously felt both a sense of fear and adventure—perhaps the same adrenaline rush a soldier might feel entrenched behind enemy lines, trying to comprehend his position.

Chad was concerned. "Are you okay?" he asked.

"Yeah, I'm fine. I'm just trying to take it all in."

"You seem nervous. We can leave if you want."

"No. It's all right. I'm all right. I just didn't expect so many people."

"Friday nights are busy. Plus it's the weather," Chad said. "Everybody's ready to get out and have some fun."

"God knows I'm ready to have some fun," I said.

"So you think you'll come back here, then?" Chad asked.

"Absolutely. I have to admit, I didn't realize there were so many gay people. I only know a few at home. They're not open about it. Not like this," I said.

"Probably not," Chad replied hollowly. "I've met some people from Fort Sackville here. Not many though. Of course, not *everybody* here is gay."

Now, tonight, driving south on Highway 41 I entered the city limits of Evansville. Local folks often referred to it at Stoplight City. I had made the trip so many times over the years I knew how to catch the lights and exactly what speed to maintain in order to make all the greens before the downtown exit to Teana Faye's. My thoughts about Chad made the drive fly by. More than a decade had passed since that first night in my first gay bar. It seemed a whole life had been lived. Yet I still found it thrilling to drive into Evansville and spend my time with *my* community.

I arrived in downtown Evansville to all kinds of car and foot traffic. Some sort of holiday festival was taking place. Teana Faye's was located on Riverside Drive, near the old Atkinson Hotel, on the banks of the Ohio River. *Atkinson,* I thought. *I can't get away from that goddamned name.* I wondered if this Atkinson was some relation to Old Man Atkinson in Fort Sackville. He'd blow a carotid artery if he knew of my past overnight escapades at the Atkinson Hotel. It was often where I landed after a night of partying across the street at the gay bar. It was most likely where I'd end up tonight. I usually just left my car in Teana Faye's lot and walked across to the hotel.

Teana Faye's lot was packed. It was going to be a fun night. I suspected the place would be busy, but I had no idea the festival was taking place. That would draw a large crowd, and Teana Faye's would be the place to be afterward. Well, for those that were gay or gay-friendly, at least.

* * *

Teana Faye's was the gay bar that opened after Sho-Bar mysteriously burned to the ground. Prior to it being a gay bar, it had been the Kingfish Restaurant, a building originally designed to resemble a dual–paddle wheel riverboat—the kind found cruising the Mississippi in Mark Twain novels. Patrons walked the gangway near the starboard paddle wheel to enter its hostess area, which served as the bar's ID checkpoint. There, a cover charge was collected for advertised events: special-guest drag performances, Christmas shows, and AIDS benefits. Its stern was the bar; its bow, formerly the restaurant's dining room, was the dance lounge. From the steamboat's empty pilothouse above the black-and-white checkered dance floor hung a mirrored disco ball and vibrantly colored spotlights that illuminated the drag stage and its glittering silver lamé curtain.

As I entered the bar, I spotted Rio sitting in a booth beside the dance floor. *How is that possible? What is he doing here? Why didn't he tell me he was coming to Indiana?* I assumed he was visiting his mother for Christmas. Rio's mother and father were married but lived separate lives: his corporate lawyer father in Miami, and his mother the only heir to her family's wealth, farm, and grain mill located on the Ohio River in Mt. Vernon, Indiana, just thirty minutes west of Evansville. It was after Rio graduated law school that he decided to spend a year in southern Indiana learning the business end of his mother's farm and grain mill. That was the year we met and began dating. Ours was a whirlwind romance, a year filled with zeal and passion. When Rio decided to follow in his father's footsteps and practice corporate law, he asked me to move with him to Miami Beach, but I refused. I felt I couldn't leave *my* family's business. We tried to model our relationship after his parents—a long-distance love affair—but after a couple of years it cooled into an annual or sometimes semi-annual South Florida rendezvous, with permission to date other men in the interim.

After paying my cover charge at what was once the hostess desk, I had the choice to go right, onto the dance floor and toward Rio, or I could go left into the bar and get a cocktail. I chose left and a cocktail.

I stepped up to the bar and ordered my vodka and club soda, and just as the bartender placed the drink in front of me, I felt a nudge against my shoulder. It was Rio.

"Did you think I didn't see you walk in?" he asked.

He smiled. I took a deep breath.

"It's so good to see you, Rio." I reached out to hug him. His body felt tight and toned. Pulling from our embrace and looking at his face, his bedroom eyes were shining and his temples wrinkled when he smiled. His coal-black hair had slight gray streaks just above his ears. *That salt-and-pepper hair*, I thought. That skinny, nerdy-cute guy with glasses I'd met in this same bar ten years ago had grown up. He was even sexier in Indiana.

"It's good to see you too," he said.

"I sure wasn't expecting to see you here. I even thought about calling you earlier today but figured you were busy. I never would have guessed you were coming here for Christmas. Why didn't you say something?" I said.

"Well, truth be told, I wanted to surprise you. I called the restaurant this evening to make sure you were working, and your dad answered the phone. I was going to drive up, surprise you, and have dinner. But your dad said you were heading here. So I thought I'd surprise you here!"

The bartender placed Rio's drink in front of him.

"Here, I got this," I said, and pulled a twenty from my wallet.

"Why thank you, sir," Rio said. "So come on, come sit at my table. I can tell by all the activity downtown this place is going to be hopping. Well, for Evansville. They're having a show tonight. I don't want to lose my table."

I picked up my cocktail and followed him. I had to admit, seeing him was an unexpected Christmas surprise. I began to feel those familiar stirrings in my stomach—butterflies, some might call them. Rio still had a way of making me all gaga on the inside.

Sitting across from him in a booth next to the dance floor was nice; conversation with Rio was always effortless.

"Doug's here tonight," he said.

"I thought I saw his picture on the holiday poster," I said. Doug was my first friend at Teana Faye's, after Chad and Sho-Bar. Unlike Chad or Rio, Doug and I were never lovers. We were drinking buddies. Doug was also a drag queen.

"Did you know he was a drag queen when you first met him?" Rio asked.

"Yes. He was in drag. Or *she* was in drag, I should say. His father's boat was the inspiration for her name: Tekela Bree," I said.

"That's right. And Melissa was with him. That's how you met her?"

I began to sense that maybe Rio was just as nervous as I was, that he was trying to get the conversation going by talking about a past both he and I had spoken about many times over the years.

"No. I met her a couple of weeks after Doug. We struck up a conversation when she found out I was from Fort Sackville. She'd just enrolled in Fort Sackville Community College's law enforcement program. She wanted to know about the commute from Evansville to campus. I told her it sucked. Especially when the time changed. She asked if I thought she should move there. I said, *Hell no!* The commute would suck less."

"That's right. It's all coming back to me now," Rio said.

"Well, okaaay, Celine Dion," I said, referencing her song.

"All right, smart-ass," Rio said. We had both finished our drinks rather quickly. "You want another?"

"Are you trying to get me drunk?" I asked. "It's kind of early for that, don't you think?"

"That's the plan. I'll get this round," Rio said. "And remember, I know you. I know exactly what it takes to get you drunk. And other things," he added.

"Oh, okay. So we're flirting," I said.

"No, not flirting. Just happy to see a good friend."

"An old boyfriend, you mean."

"That too. I'm going to get us another round." Rio slipped from the booth and walked across the dance floor to the bar. In Rio's wake

Tekela appeared, seemingly from out of nowhere, wearing her signature white leather jumpsuit with matching thigh-high stiletto boots.

"Girl! It didn't take you long to swoop in on him," she said.

I laughed. "What do you mean?" I asked.

"That boy is your ex. His Puerto Rican shit will get you in trouble," Tekela said with a wink.

"Rio is not Puerto Rican; he's half Cuban and half German. And I fell into trouble with him a long time ago. Don't you have a show to do?" I asked with a mischievous grin.

"Those queens backstage are working my last nerve. I had to come out and get some air and a fresh cocktail, or else one of those bitches was going to get cut."

Rio returned with our drinks.

"Well, if it isn't Miss Tekela Bree," Rio said, hugging Tekela while giving her air kisses on each cheek.

"Your momma brought you up right—never kiss a queen with her face on," Tekela said.

"You know she did," Rio said. He slipped in next to me on my side of the booth. "Sit down. Let me buy you a drink."

"No. Thank you, darling. This leather don't stretch that well; I need to stand. Besides, I got my drink coming. I've got to get back there and get ready for my number, whip up my wig. It's like my grand-momma used to say: *The higher the hair, the closer to Jesus.*"

"Oh, so we're going to church tonight?" Rio asked.

"Darling, there'll be some testifying and testimony before the night is over. Got my sights set on that little piece of chicken sitting right over there." Tekela pointed to a barely legal frat boy wearing a University of Evansville sweatshirt. "Says his name is Klein. As if. I asked him if he wore Calvin Klein underwear. He said yes. I told him before tonight was over I would de-Klein him."

"Where do you come up with this shit?" I asked. Looking at Rio, I continued, "I'll never forget going with Doug . . ."

"*Tekela!*" Doug interjected.

"Going with *Tekela* to a drag pageant in Paducah one summer weekend years ago. Before I met you. He wrapped those young guys around his finger. They were falling all over him," I said. "*She* called them *chicken*."

"Finger-licking good! What about you?" Tekela said, pointing to me, then looking at Rio. "This bitch got us thrown out of our motel room for skinny-dipping with the sheriff's son."

"The sheriff's son?" Rio asked, looking at me with a raised eyebrow.

"I didn't know he was the sheriff's son until he told the manager. It's probably the only reason we didn't get the police called on us."

"So you got some chicken too?" Rio asked.

"No. *I* was the chicken," I said.

"Please, Mary, that boy looked like he was in high school."

"He was twenty-one."

"Barely," she said.

"Look, my family makes a fortune selling chicken. I know all about it," I said.

"Technically, it's fried chicken," Rio said.

"It's still all chicken," I said.

"Oh lord! Here we go again. You two are gonna be down each other's throats before the night is over."

"If all goes well," Rio said.

"You two always did fight in all the best places," Tekela said.

"Oh darling, it'll be more like wrestling," Rio said.

"Oh, good lord," I said, rolling my eyes.

"I gots to go," Tekela said. "It's getting deep, and the night is still young. I can't get this bullshit all up in my stilettos. You girls enjoy yourselves." Tekela sashayed away from our table toward the bar, snatched her drink, then with a wink disappeared behind the silver stage curtain.

"She's a riot," Rio said.

"He's not even drunk yet," I said.

"You mean *she's* not even drunk yet. You never told me about Paducah. Sounds like you two had quite a time."

"Actually, that's when I met Melissa. The three of us went together. That's the night she told me I should meet you," I said.

"Oh, okay. That's right. But you never did tell the rest of the story," Rio said.

"I didn't?" I asked in an impish tone.

"No, you didn't."

"I can't imagine how it slipped my mind all these years," I said.

"Yeah. Remind me again how you found me?" Rio asked.

"What's with the trip down memory lane?"

"I just want to hear it again, from you." Rio took a sip of his cocktail.

"You're up to something, Mr. Iglesias," I said.

"No. Really. I swear I'm not. It's just nice to see you. This all reminds me of that holiday, that first Christmas we spent together coming here. Running around. I loved that time in my life. And I love to hear you tell the stories."

"You just like to hear me talk about you," I said.

"Well, that too," Rio said, smiling.

"Melissa told me to look for this really cute, thin, dark-haired guy with glasses. She said you usually hung out here on the nights you weren't working. She said she'd be here. That she'd make sure I got the right guy."

"Oh! So you don't even know if you had the right guy?" Rio asked.

"I thought maybe it was you," I said, trying to pull off my best monotone voice and straight face.

Rio's forehead furrowed and his eyes tightened.

"I'm teasing! Yes, I knew it was you. It's so easy to get a rise out of you." I laughed. "I'd seen you before, from a distance."

"Well, who's to say I hadn't seen you first?" he said.

"So maybe I'm the one who was set up?" I asked.

"I'll never tell," Rio said. "Anyway, what about Paducah and the sheriff's son?"

"Not much to tell. The reason we all went is because Doug had entered some drag pageant at that bar DV8. I drove us over. The funny thing is we went in the restaurant's Ford Explorer; it had a nameplate on the front that said *Daniels' Family Buffet*. You know Fort Sackville so you can appreciate the fact that there we were, the three of us, speeding down the Western Kentucky Parkway into the oppressive August night loaded with duct tape, wigs, stilettos, beaded gowns, and feathered headdresses all piled in the back of the SUV. Did you know that cock feathers are Tekela's favorite? She has this huge headdress made entirely of cock feathers. It's all she talks about. The back of the SUV looked like we'd trapped a gay rooster."

"I've seen her wear it before," Rio said.

"Of course. Well, Melissa started talking about you while Doug was getting ready in the front seat."

"Wait. He dressed in the SUV?"

"Oh yeah. He had his tackle box with him, which he balanced on his lap. As he opened it, it stair-stepped into one of those four-tiered kind. *This is where* she *sleeps*, he said. I was mesmerized. Instead of fishing lures and hooks, each rack was its own cosmetic counter. *This is my Tekela to-go box*, he said. Before then I'd only seen *her* stacked on a table in the dressing room here. Melissa and I watched as he began his transformation using the visor mirror. Two hours later, Tekela emerged."

"Your parents would have been proud," Rio said.

"Oh yeah. Like they knew. Anyway, Doug ended up losing the drag pageant. Said one of the fat queens competing had blown one of the judges before we got there. Then I got us kicked out of the motel. On the way home we made plans to meet up at Teana Faye's. That's pretty much it. That's how I ended up meeting you that night."

"But you still aren't for sure if I was the guy Melissa was talking about."

"Oh, I'm sure. I've spent several years with him. On and off." In that moment the bar patrons who were dancing cleared the floor and gathered along its edge as the center of the darkened dance floor was lit by a rose-colored spotlight.

"All right! The drag show's starting," Rio said, his voice competing with the sound of the crowd's revelry and applause. "This is great! I haven't seen Tekela perform in years. Probably since the last time you and I were here together."

The song began, the people parted at one end, and Tekela, a rather imposing drag queen in her six-inch stilettos, stepped through the crowd onto the dance floor and into the light.

"Holy shit!" I said. I knew the song well. She was doing "Proud Mary." The song always reminded me of the jukebox in Daniels' Diner and those childhood nights I spent there with my family.

Most evenings as a kid I ate supper with my parents at Daniels' Diner. Afterward they'd sit, drink coffee, and talk to Grandma Dixie and Grandpa Collin. We were always the last to leave. There was nothing to do but play the jukebox or help Janitor Earl mop the floor. He smelled like bleach water, and he looked like his mop.

At the jukebox, slipping my dime into its coin slot and then making my selection—first a letter, then a number—I watched the forty-fives circle to my choice. Watching through the framed glass window was my favorite part. The Ferris wheel of records paused just before the mechanical arm picked mine out and placed it on the turntable. When the needle hit the record there was a scratching sound, then music. I knew A5 by heart:

"You know, every now and then I think you might like to hear something from us nice and easy. There's just one thing, you see, we never ever do nothin' nice and easy. We always do it nice and rough. But we're gonna take the beginning of this song and do it easy. But then we're gonna do the finish rough. This is the way we do Proud Mary. And we rollin', rollin', rollin' on the river. Listen to the story now."

As I sang with Ike and Tina Turner, Mom sat at the table and smiled. Dad was too busy talking to Grandma and Grandpa. They didn't even notice. I had seen Tina on TV once. She wore a dress made of orange fringe. Before "Proud Mary" I'd only seen fringe on the outer edges of Grandma Dixie's bathroom rugs. When Tina danced, the fiery tassels of her dress leapt from her body and twirled about. I imagined, dancing there in front of the jukebox, that I was wearing that very fringe. When the song finished, the needle stuck. Its scratching repeated, over, over, over. I wanted to continue spinning, my fringe twirling, but Grandpa Collin got up, walked toward me, and unplugged the jukebox. Its lights faded with the scratching sound.

I just stood there, embarrassed by his scowl. Frightened. Grandpa Collin had a way of staring down at someone, his contempt boring into their being, his wrath a weight upon their spirit. I knew—no, I *sensed*, he didn't like me. I was the exact opposite of his Depression-era street kid experience. In my mind, he was saying, "Goddamn, I'm glad you're not *my* son." And I knew then it would be a long time before the jukebox was plugged in again.

"Grey. Hey, Grey! Are you okay?" Rio asked. "What do you think?" His voice returned my attention to the drag show.

"Oh, yeah. Isn't she great? I guess I sort of zoned out there a moment," I said. "I was thinking about the jukebox."

"You still have it, right?" Rio asked.

"Of course I do. I'll never part with it. Are you kidding? Dad gave it to me after Grandpa Collin closed Daniels' Diner and opened Daniels' Family Buffet. Grandpa Collin probably rolls over in his grave every time I play and dance to 'Proud Mary'," I said with a smile, and then took a celebratory sip of my cocktail.

"You are twisted in your own loveable way," Rio said.

Rio and I spent the night drinking and dancing and catching up. It was nice spending the Christmas holiday with him again. I was reminded of why I had fallen in love with him so long ago. After the last drag show, it was well past two a.m., and Rio and I decided to head out and over to the Tennessean, a local twenty-four-hour diner for some breakfast. A little something to settle our stomachs from the many cocktails we'd drunk.

As we headed out the front door, Rio put his arm around my shoulder. It felt nice. Familiar. I looked at him and smiled. We headed down the gangway and toward the parking lot. The Tennessean was on the next block, behind the Atkinson Hotel.

"You know, I have a room there," Rio said, pointing toward the hotel with his head. "You're welcome to stay the night."

"Uh huh. It's all making sense now. First you surprise me, then you get me drunk, and now you're going to try and get into my pants," I said.

"Darling, it doesn't take much effort to get into your pants. If that was my goal, it would have happened by now," Rio said, grinning.

"Oh, so I'm easy, eh?"

"The easiest," he said.

I smacked him on the ass. He looked at me and smiled and pulled me closer. Just as I thought he was about to kiss me, I heard my name being called. "Grey! Hey, Grey!" I looked around and spotted Trace Thompson standing next to my car.

"Who the hell is that?" Rio asked.

"An employee of ours. Trace Thompson. How the fuck did he find me?"

"I was going to ask the same thing. What is he, twelve years old?"

"Close. He's seventeen." I said.

Together we walked toward Trace and my car. My mind was swirling with scenarios of why Trace was standing next to my car and what it could be about.

When we approached I introduced them.

"What are you doing here?" I asked.

"I just knew this was your car. I saw it from my hotel window," Trace said. He seemed excited to see me.

"You're staying at the Atkinson?" I asked. "I have to say, I can't believe you're here. And that you are staying at the Atkinson." The Atkinson Hotel was a renovated historic hotel, once used by the army for quarters during World War II training. It had a rich history, but also a sordid one. Since Teana Faye's opened, the hotel offered convenient opportunity for tricks and one-night stands.

"Yeah. We're all there. Tonight was the Riverfront Festival of

Lights. We performed. The youth choir," Trace said, searching for some kind of acknowledgement.

"Oh, yes. That's right. That's why you had the night off. I guess I didn't make the connection. I thought it was something in Fort Sackville, at Wabash Valley Baptist," I said.

"No. Pastor Daryl got us into this. It's an interdenominational thing," Trace said.

"So Daryl is across the street too? In the hotel?" I asked. I giggled a bit and winked at Rio. Rio had a general knowledge of Daryl, and the fact that he'd moved back to Fort Sackville to serve as youth pastor at Wabash Valley Baptist Church.

"Yeah. He's the one that brought us down here. How else would we get here?" Trace asked, somewhat bewildered.

"Well, of course," I said. "So, I'm curious. Why are you waiting at my car?" I asked.

"Um, can we talk about this on the way to the diner?" Rio asked. "It's fucking freezing out here. Trace, you want to join us for some breakfast?"

"Sure. I don't see why not. Everybody's asleep. No one's gonna know I'm gone."

I wasn't sure how I felt about Trace joining Rio and me, but I agreed.

"Okay then. Let's go," Rio said, and led the way. The three of us walked toward the Tennessean while Trace recounted the highlights of the Riverfront Festival. I knew Daryl would snap if he found out Trace had been waiting for me in the parking lot of a gay bar. Yet part of me liked the thought of Daryl snapping.

Chapter Seven

December

The Tennessean was a greasy spoon diner that had been in business at least as long as my family's restaurant, and it reminded me in many ways of Daniels' Diner. We were seated in a booth near the end of the lunch counter, next to a window overlooking the sidewalk and 4th Street.

Looking at Trace sitting across the table from Rio and me, I said, "Obviously Pastor Daryl has no idea you're AWOL."

"No. He doesn't. Please don't say anything," Trace said.

"Trust me, Trace, I keep my distance from Pastor Daryl."

"What is it with you two?" Trace asked, pulling a menu from the stainless steel menu holder attached to the end of the table just under the window.

Rio kept quiet, but I could see the gleam in his eyes. I knew what he was thinking: *I can't wait to hear how in the hell you're going to answer this one, Daniels.*

"Let's just say Pastor Daryl and I have a history," I said.

"Uh-huh, a history. C'mon, Grey, you can do better than that," Rio said. He smiled and nudged my shoulder with his.

"You are loving this, aren't you?" I said, giving Rio a playful yet stern look.

"This moment has made my trip home *totally* worth it," Rio replied.

The waitress appeared at our table. I could tell she'd made her career at the Tennessean. She was old and seasoned. "Watcha boys gonna have?" she asked, chomping her gum like a cow chewing cud.

"I'll take the number two, eggs over medium with wheat toast, and a tall glass of water. Lots of ice, please," Rio said.

Our waitress rolled her eyes.

"I'll take the same," I said.

"How 'bout you, sug?" the waitress asked Trace, not missing a beat with her chewing gum.

"I'll take the pecan pancakes and a large iced tea," Trace said.

"It's colder than a well digger's ass outside, and you boys are drinking iced drinks. I'll never figure out this younger generation," the waitress said, and walked off as quickly as she had appeared.

The three of us just looked at one another and broke into laughter.

"Well, Trace . . ." I paused a moment. "Pastor Daryl—I mean Daryl, I can't really call him Pastor—we were best friends in high school, and it kind of became more than that."

"What do you mean?" Trace asked, utterly baffled.

"Oh, this is good! He's going to make you work," said Rio.

"You know. We . . . we fooled around," I said.

"I think it was more than just fooling around," Rio said. "At least the version of the story I got suggested it was a whole lot steamier."

Trace's face turned red. He looked down at his silverware, placed haphazardly on the white dinner napkin. He was silent.

"Does my being gay bother you, Trace?" I asked.

He didn't answer. I held my gaze, waiting for a response. Trace looked up.

"It's really no big deal," I said. "I mean, it was a long time ago. I'm sure Daryl never thinks about it, and God knows he'd never say anything. You did know I was gay, right?" I asked.

"To be honest, Mother and Father did say something about it. That it was a rumor. That they didn't know if it was true or not," Trace admitted.

"Oh, it's true, girl," Rio said, grinning.

"Trace, Rio is my ex-boyfriend. We met several years ago. He's in town visiting his family. We ran into one another tonight at the bar."

"Do you live here?" Trace asked.

"No. I live in Miami Beach," Rio said.

"Yeah, fending off the SoBe muscle queens," I said, returning the earlier shoulder nudge Rio had given me.

"What does that mean?" Trace asked.

"Oh, nothing. Grey is just being snarky. He can't stand his competition," Rio said.

The waitress returned with our drinks.

"Competition. Right," I said.

"So why did you two break up?" Trace asked.

Rio and I looked at one another and smiled. "That would take the rest of the weekend to explain," I said. "Suffice it to say we're better friends than lovers."

"I don't know if that's true," Rio said. "We made pretty good lovers too. Grey has some issues to work through."

"Are we really going to go there?" I asked.

"Now don't get all huffy. I'm just being honest." Rio turned his attention to Trace. "Grey finds it tough to be totally out in Fort Sackville. He's only halfway out of the closet. I tried to pull him out totally, but he wouldn't budge."

"Well, if *your* classmate had been murdered for being gay, you'd be a bit apprehensive too," I said.

"Murdered? Who was murdered?" Trace asked.

"Robbie Palmer, a high school classmate of Daryl's and mine. In fact, Daryl and Robbie were in the same graduating class and on the golf team together," I said.

"Wait. Pastor Daryl had a classmate that was murdered?" Trace asked.

"Yes. He was also my classmate."

"Sorry. I didn't mean anything. I just can't believe Pastor Daryl has never said anything about it," Trace said.

"Why would he? I mean, it was a long time ago, and Daryl's only been back in Fort Sackville a couple of months."

"I'm just surprised. Pastor Daryl and I talk quite a bit," Trace said. "About high school. He's always asking me how things are going. Who my friends are. Stuff like that. He's told me some stories of when he was in high school. I'm just surprised something as big as having a classmate murdered, someone he played golf with, hasn't come up."

"It was quite a scandal. The murder was never solved. There was even a rumor that Daryl was at the party where Robbie was allegedly murdered, the one he disappeared from."

"Holy cow," Trace said. "Is it true? Was Pastor Daryl there? How was the guy murdered?"

The waitress brought our plates and set them in front of us, each one with a forceful thud.

"It's all rumor and speculation. Nothing was ever solved. Robbie apparently went there to meet a guy he was dating from Fort Sackville Community College. Some people said Daryl went there to pick Robbie up and take him home. Supposedly Robbie was drunk and had called Daryl. I can't imagine it though. Other than being on the golf team, they never really hung out," I said.

"Wasn't it a sex party or something like that?" Rio asked. "I thought you told me there were some really important people there."

"That was the rumor. Certain doctors, a TV news anchor, the president of Fort Sackville University—all sorts of city fathers and men in powerful positions. I remember the newspaper reporting that the party was *homosexual in nature*," I said. "That set the local pulpits into a fire-and-brimstone frenzy."

"Wow. I never heard any of this," Trace said.

"I'm not surprised. Folks in Fort Sackville worked really hard to sweep it all under the rug. They didn't want to talk about it. I even heard that threats were made to people who tried to push it," I said. "Ask Pastor Daryl about it. See what he says."

"Now you're just setting the poor kid up," Rio said.

"No, I'm not. There's Daryl right there. He just walked in the door," I said, and nodded toward the entrance.

"What! Oh, shit!" Trace said, and turned to face the front door.

"Just be calm, Trace. It's no big deal." Trace turned back, his face suddenly pale and afraid. Daryl approached our booth.

"Trace. What are you doing here?" Daryl asked.

"Hey, Daryl," I said. "Fancy meeting you here."

"Hello, Grey. Trace, did you hear me? What are you doing here?" Daryl again asked.

"Daryl, this is Rio Iglesias, a friend of mine from Miami Beach. He's staying at the Atkinson," I said.

"Nice to meet you." Daryl's tone was curt, and he barely glanced at Rio.

"I saw Trace in the lobby and invited him to join us for a late-night breakfast. I wanted to hear all about the festival," I said, smiling. Trace began to straighten up. He turned to face Daryl.

"Is that true, Trace?" Daryl asked.

"What do you mean, *is that true*?" I asked. My eyes focused on Daryl's.

"I mean exactly what I asked," Daryl said.

"Yes. We were talking in the lobby, and they asked if I wanted to join them," Trace said.

"I told him it would be okay. Jesus, Daryl, I'm his boss. What the hell do you think is going to happen to him?"

"Well, I'm the one responsible. He and the others are in my care, and I don't like the fact that when I went to his room he wasn't there," Daryl said. Indignation peppered his voice.

"It's three a.m. Why are you going to his room at three a.m.?" Rio asked.

"I don't see how this is any of your business, Mr. Iglesias," Daryl shot out.

"Please, call me Rio. I'm just curious. Why in the world would you be going to his room at three a.m.?" Rio was playfully exercising his courtroom counselor courtesy.

"*This* is the reason. Finding Trace here without a chaperone," Daryl said.

"I'd hardly say Trace is without a chaperone, Daryl," I said. "It's just breakfast. Lighten up."

"Trace, get up. We have to go." Daryl reached into his back

pocket, pulled out his wallet, and threw a twenty-dollar bill on the table. "That should be enough to cover his meal and the tip." Trace was embarrassed and said nothing. He slid out from the booth and stood beside Daryl.

"Mr. Iglesias." Daryl nodded. "Grey. Enjoy the rest of your breakfast. I'll be sure to tell Mr. and Mrs. Thompson you took care of Trace during his absence."

"You do that, Daryl. Trace, I'm glad you joined us," I said.

"Yeah, it was nice meeting you, Trace. You too, *Pastor* Daryl," Rio said.

Daryl turned and walked away. Trace kept pace behind him, looking as if he were on a death march.

"He's trying to fuck him," Rio muttered.

"What?"

"He wants to fuck him. Daryl is. He wants to get into that kid's pants," Rio said.

"How do you know that?" I asked. It wasn't a question so much as a disturbing confirmation of what I'd hoped I had been imagining.

"Why in the hell else would he be going to the kid's room in the middle of the night? Mark my words, that dude is up to something," Rio said.

"Holy shit," I said under my breath. I paused to let Rio's words settle. "Well . . . I suppose that middle-of-the-night thing is kind of his MO."

"Yeah, but you two were in high school, almost the same age. Daryl is old enough to be that kid's father. That's just sick," Rio said.

Rio and I watched through the diner's windows as Daryl rested his arm on Trace's shoulders and walked with him down the sidewalk toward the Atkinson Hotel.

"I think you might be right," I said.

"Darling, you should know by now I'm always right," Rio said.

And although I knew we had done nothing wrong, I felt a twist of shame in my gut, as if we were the ones who had crept down the hall and knocked on Trace's door in the middle of the night.

Chapter Eight

In 1995 Greg Louganis appeared on *Oprah* to speak of his recent HIV diagnosis and his new book *Breaking the Surface,* and I began to think seriously about my own HIV status. Fort Sackville had a community college, but no bookstore except the Christian Bible Book Store on Main Street. During one of my trips to Evansville to meet Rio during his visit from Miami Beach, I went to the Barnes & Noble near the mall to buy Greg Louganis's book, and stopped at the sports store next door to buy rollerblades—I imagined myself developing muscular legs like Rio's, and thought I could do so by rollerblading.

Breaking the Surface was a wake-up call. I'd watched Greg Louganis diving and found him and his polished smile quite handsome. But it never occurred to me that he might be gay. How could someone so athletic and healthy be HIV positive? I recalled watching him hit his head on the edge of the diving board. The blood. His story convinced me that I needed to be tested. But how? Where would I get an HIV test? HIV and AIDS were a big-city issue.

The morning I finished reading Greg's book was my day off. It was a beautiful and warm early spring day. I decided to rollerblade downtown and have lunch, then rollerblade back. Nearing Main Street, I passed Doc Vonderbreck's office. Doc was my general practitioner and had been since I could remember. He wasn't a man to worry over what people thought—he didn't play Fort Sackville's game of whispered words to avoid awkward or uncomfortable conversations. He liked young, good-looking nurses with big boobs and his office was full of them, and he didn't care what people said. He was the best doctor in town, and nobody was taking him down. My instinct told me to talk to him.

His office was housed in an ornate one-story Victorian. A hundred years before, perhaps, it had been nicknamed the Wedding Cake because of its intricate gingerbread architecture. I rolled to a stop and hesitated on the sidewalk in front of its black wrought-iron fence, then found myself entering the yard through the gate. A moment later, I was navigating the steep front porch steps between two flowering pear trees and rolling myself through the front door.

The foyer served as a reception area, with its right parlor a patient waiting room. A long hall with a wood floor and a twelve-foot ceiling dissected the shotgun house. Doors on each side served as portals to examination rooms. The receptionist greeted me, stared at my rollerblades, then asked if I had an appointment.

"I just need to speak with Doc for a moment," I replied, my voice shaky.

Doc Vonderbreck appeared at the far end of the hall in his blue jeans and cowboy boots. Tufts of his curly gray hair slipped out from under his cowboy hat. "Grey, what in the hell are you doing?" he asked.

"I came to see you."

"C'mon back."

The nurse smiled and motioned for me to go. I rollerbladed down the hall and followed Doc into an empty examination room.

"Well, that's the first time I've had a patient roll in, toes down. They're usually rolling out, toes up," he said.

"Because *you've* killed them," I said with a smile.

"You can't win them all," Doc said. "What can I do for you?"

"I have a favor to ask. I don't know how to ask it, so I'm just going to say it. How can I get an HIV test?"

"We can do one here."

"Thing is, I don't want anyone to know."

Doc's expression did not falter; he nodded slowly in understanding.

"I mean, my health insurance. I don't want anything on record."

"How about we just take some blood and figure it out?" he said.

"Can I pay you in cash?" I asked.

"You can buy commercial containers of extra virgin olive oil, right?" Doc asked. I was mystified.

"Like, vegetable oil the restaurant uses? It comes in five-gallon jugs."

"Yes. But I need extra virgin olive oil. I use it on my horse saddles."

All of my life, Doc had raised horses on his farm a few miles south of town.

"Sure. I can buy it through Sysco or Valley Wholesale."

"I tell you what. Order twenty-five gallons—that's five, right? Order five containers and bring them to the office. That'll be your payment."

That familiar anxious feeling began creeping into the pit of my stomach. I was nervous, and Doc saw I was trying to hide my shaking hands.

"Grey, are you scared you might be HIV positive?"

"This is going to sound crazy—I'm not as scared of being positive as I am of people finding out if I am positive. I don't know what would happen then."

Doc snorted. "These folk around here are idiots. Fuck everybody."

"But if I'm positive and people find out, I don't know what will happen to the restaurant. You saw what this town did to Robbie Palmer's family."

Doc leaned against the examination table upon which I was sitting and crossed his legs, one shin resting on the other. His boots looked like anvils weighing him down. He leaned in and faced me eye to eye. "There's a whole lot you don't know about Robbie Palmer's murder. I was the coroner. I testified in front of the grand jury. Robbie's family was poor, and from the wrong side of the tracks. Neither he nor his mother stood a chance. Your family has history in this town. Daniels' has been around for fifty years, and trust me, those Christians aren't going to give up their fried chicken. You're going to be okay."

My anxiousness began to dissipate.

"Do you test the blood here?" I asked.

"No. We send it to Mercy. But don't worry. I'll send it under my ex-wife's name."

I couldn't help but smile, remembering talk about the divorce battle between Doc and his ex-wife and the young nurse that had started it all. How the gossip had reached a legendary pitch in the community. Doc was giving *me* advice on how to handle Fort Sackville when a report of his divorce court proceedings was featured on the local evening news broadcast from Terre Haute. Details emerged that his wife had left him not only because of his philandering, but because after she confronted him about it, he shot three of her pet pygmy goats—after which Doc purchased a billboard on Fairground Avenue, a few blocks from the restaurant, to advertise a $10,000 offer to any local citizen willing to run against his ex-wife's new husband, a popular long-serving judge, in his bid for reelection.

"That's perfect. Thank you," I said.

But I didn't share his optimism. I knew if I were HIV positive and people found out, the restaurant was fucked. Customers of Daniels' Family Buffet would never eat in a restaurant owned by a man whose son had AIDS.

Two weeks later my test came back negative.

I've often wondered about the day the lab received a blood sample from Doc's ex-wife.

GRAND JURY RESUMES INVESTIGATION INTO PALMER MURDER CASE

By Foster Lawrence
Fort Sackville Sentinel staff writer

FORT SACKVILLE, Ind. — A grand jury investigation into the unsolved murder of Robbie Palmer is back in session.

The grand jury reconvened this week after issuing a prepared statement earlier in the month suggesting attempts had been made to hinder its investigation.

Prosecutor Dallas Ellerman declined to elaborate, but jurors were concerned about being sued if they returned indictments.

"The problem is still there," Ellerman said, "but the problem may be abating in the eyes of the jury."

Ellerman said a grand jury has legal protection from civil lawsuits. "Yes, they do. So do prosecutors, so do judges. The immunity of the grand jury should be complete, and everybody should understand that.

"You don't go threatening them while they are in session."

It is unclear if the grand jury was threatened.

Chapter Nine

December

Daniels' Family Buffet was closed on Christmas Day. It had been a busy week of holiday parties, and I was looking forward to spending quiet time at my parents' house—just Mom, Dad, my younger brother Cameron, and me. Rio was spending the day with his family, and Cameron was home from the University of Southern Indiana. It was the first Christmas holiday my family had spent in Fort Sackville in some time. For several years we vacationed on Marco Island, closing the restaurant the week of Christmas through New Year's and then driving on December 25 to avoid traffic. This year, because Dad's health had at times been touch and go, Mom pulled out all the stops. She had the house decorated, cooked dinner, and arranged for us to attend Christmas service at Wabash Valley Baptist Church.

Ours was not a regular church-going family; we hadn't been regulars since my brother was little. The restaurant consumed our lives. But Mom had grown up in the church; she often recalled going to First Baptist during her youth in Hartwell, Indiana. Aflame in her memory were the rainbow-colored stained glass windows. The sacred panes reminded her of *A Christmas Story*, with its Christmas tree decorated in colors that would *blaze like a Baptist window*. Mom wanted to kick off our family Christmas by attending Wabash Valley Baptist Church to hear its youth choir and show support for Trace. So after a busy Christmas Eve at the restaurant and a restless night's sleep—I was still recovering from my Friday night at Teana Fay's and the Tennessean—that morning I showered, tidied up my house, then walked down the lane to my parents' house.

Mom had breakfast on the table: a family favorite of biscuits and gravy, baked ham, and fried potatoes. We ate, then loaded ourselves into their Cadillac STS. Dad sat in the front seat with the portable oxygen tank he was forced to use since his lung surgery last summer. Mom and Cameron were in the back. I drove, arriving just in time for eleven a.m. service.

The parking lot was packed. "See, there are other Christmas Christians," I said.

"I hope they don't drag this goddamn thing on for two hours," Dad said. "It's the only other day I get to relax at home and not worry about that goddamn restaurant. Which reminds me, Grey, after this we need to swing by and check the coolers." My dad worried our walk-in coolers and freezers would suddenly shut down, resulting in a substantial loss of product. He worried about a lot of things.

Wabash Valley Baptist Church was a striking antebellum three-story redbrick structure. Wide steps led from the street to the five white columns that supported the gabled roof. Behind the massive pillars, three white double doors gave entrance. The multiple two-story windows on each side of the building depicted Biblical scenes in a kaleidoscope of colors. Inside, beneath the white domed cupola, which allowed dusty sunlight to filter down, oak pews were filled with parishioners in the theater-style sanctuary. I'd always preferred to sit in the balcony. I liked watching the people below.

For Christmas service we sat on the main level near the middle. The sanctuary was almost completely full; we took the remaining seats. Many of the faces among us were Daniels' Family Buffet regulars.

Beyond the main level pews was the raised pulpit. Reverend Damien's podium stood center stage. Behind it were risers with chairs for Daryl's youth choir. To the right of the pulpit was the organ, to its left the large baptismal font. Because of its size, as a little kid I thought the baptismal font was an old indoor swimming pool—smaller than the one in the basement of the YMCA downtown, but large enough to swim underwater.

Poinsettias, held in plant pots wrapped in green foil, alternated in color like red-and-white footlights along the stage. Near the baptismal pool was a mammoth Christmas tree constructed of red poinsettias with a silver star placed on top.

As we settled in our seats Myrna Boil, the organist, began to play the choir's entrance queue: "Adeste Fideles." They filed onstage from the wings, taking their places and standing in front of their chairs. All of them wore white robes with the exception of Trace; he stood in the center of the choir wearing red. Trace shone like the Harvest Moon Theater's marquee on a snowy midnight Main Street. The chorus united in a medley of traditional Christmas hymns.

Mom's face was beaming.

Following the medley of Christmas songs was Trace's solo, "Angels from the Realms of Glory." His blond hair and blue eyes were pallid against his red robe. He hit each note of the Baptist hymn soft and sharp, like the angel hair with which Mom used to line her Nativity scene at home. He was a Christmas star, born for Broadway. His singing reminded me of the afternoon I happened upon choir practice at Westminster Abbey in London. I walked into the Abbey and heard a soloist I could not see, his voice at first floating above me, between thick stone walls and over tombs of Anglo ancestors centuries old, before it wrapped around me in Poets' Corner. At once my skin felt as if it were on alert; the hairs on my arms and neck stood at attention. I was in the presence of God. Trace's solo took me there again.

Trace's performance was met with a rousing ovation from the parishioners. Mom, Dad, Cameron, and I stood with the crowd, applauding and cheering. It was the first time I'd heard Trace sing solo. I knew then it would be his star one day shining bright in the eastern sky.

After the choir, Reverend Damien walked onto the stage and took his place at the podium. With a side-glance toward the choral members, clasping his hands together against his chest, he said, "Thank you, choir. Thank you for sharing your angelic voices, your gift from God, with us on this blessed day." Then he turned to face the sanctuary. "How about that, ladies and gentlemen? Praise Jesus!"

"Praise Jesus," the parishioners responded.

Turning his attention to the organist, he said, "Mrs. Boil, you've given glory to God with your commitment to these fine young men and women."

Again, the parishioners erupted in applause. Reverend Damien returned his attention to the packed house.

"Pastor Daryl, you and Mrs. Boil should be proud. You've done a wonderful job with our youth. Come on up here, Pastor Daryl. Give him a hand, ladies and gentlemen!"

In the front pew, on our side of the sanctuary, Daryl Stone rose, turned, then waved to the parishioners as he made his way up the steps to join Reverend Damien. I could see the back of his wife's and his two sons' heads, their hair slicked back in their Christmas best. The parishioners went crazy. Pastor Daryl was a Wabash Valley Baptist Church rock star.

"Thank you, Reverend Damien. It's always a pleasure to guide our youth into the light of Christ," Daryl said.

"What news do you have for us today?" asked Reverend Damien. He had been battling throat cancer for a couple of years; his voice was often raspy and dry. He had often offered up the stage and the Sunday service to the youth pastor before Daryl.

"I have good news of great joy! Christ is born! Hallelujah!"

Reverend Damien and the parishioners shouted, "Hallelujah!"

After he hugged Daryl, Reverend Damien retreated to his chair near the pulpit's right proscenium. The youth choir sat in the riser seats. I whispered to Mom, "Had I been asked in high school, I would've never guessed Daryl would become a preacher."

During his Christmas sermon, Daryl captivated churchgoers. I thought about how he once had captivated me. He was charming; his smile was warm and bright. I thought about how I could still see that former athletic, reckless teenager peering out from inside this now grown man of God.

Daryl stood before the podium and looked out upon the parishioners. He held their gaze in silence. Not a person stirred. The moment seemed to last well over a minute. He then opened his Bible and read:

> *"Luke 2:8-20—And there were shepherds living out in the fields nearby, keeping watch over their flocks at night. An angel of the Lord appeared to them, and the glory of the Lord shone around them, and they were terrified. But the angel said to them, 'Do not be afraid. I bring you good news that will cause great joy for all the people. Today in the town of David a Savior has been born to you; He is the Messiah, the Lord. This will be a sign to you: you will find a baby wrapped in cloths and lying in a manger.'*
>
> *"Suddenly a great company of the heavenly host appeared with the angel, praising God and saying, 'Glory to God in the highest Heaven, and on earth peace to those on whom His favor rests.'*
>
> *"When the angels had left them and gone into Heaven, the shepherd said to one another, 'Let's go to Bethlehem and see this thing that has happened, which the Lord has told us about.'*
>
> *"So they hurried off and found Mary and Joseph, and the baby, who was lying in the manger. When they had seen him, they spread the word concerning what had been told them about this child, and all who heard it were amazed at what the shepherds said to them. But Mary treasured up all these things and pondered them in her heart. The shepherds returned, glorifying and praising God for all the things they had heard and seen, which were just as they had been told."*

Pastor Daryl closed his Bible and stood again in silence at the podium. Again he held his gaze upon the parishioners. "Glory be to God, Jesus Christ is born this day!" Daryl shouted. The parishioners erupted in thunderous applause. It was staggering—as if it were a rock concert or political rally. Standing, celebratory shouts of "hallelujah," "praise

Jesus," "glory be to God," and "amen" rattled the rafters of the Wabash Valley Baptist Church.

Moving away from his podium and walking back and forth, using the full breadth and width of the stage, Daryl continued. "It was an angelic proclamation *for all the people,* and the shepherded knew this proclamation was true when they saw a child in a manger. The child, this baby, Jesus Christ was their concrete evidence. Irrefutable. Falsifiable. Jesus Christ cannot be proven false. He is testable! He lives!"

Daryl stood for a moment, just above Myrna Boil sitting obediently at the organ, her round full neck straining to see him, her eyes locked on him. "Just like this youth choir, these individual lights of our Lord and Savior, they came together this day in unity, their voices as one. Just like these young men and women shepherded, they glorified and praised God for all things they had seen and heard. Praise be to God!"

Once again the Wabash Valley Baptist parishioners exploded in rapturous applause.

"I know it's been at least a year since we've been to church, but I don't remember services being this loud, this provoking," I said to Mom, sitting beside me.

"It does seem Daryl has brought a new perspective and way of doing things," Mom said. I looked at my dad and at Cameron sitting in the pew with us. They each had the expression of someone watching something disturbing on television—perhaps a medical show on which a melon-sized tumor was being surgically removed, and they weren't quite sure why they were sitting in their pleasant home watching it on TV.

Daryl, moving across the stage once again, continued. "The birth of Jesus Christ is no mere birth, no arrival of just another life—as extraordinary as such an event is. The story of Christ's birth is not told so *new* parents can identify. No! The *event* of Christ's birth is God's word coming to pass. Christ *is* the baby whose birth is announced to shepherds."

Daryl paused in front of the youth choir, beside Trace.

"I am the shepherd. I am a Baptist. I am a Christian. I am the body of our Lord and Savior," Daryl said, focusing first on Trace and then on the parishioners. "I am the way to Christ."

I leaned close to Mom's ear and whispered, "Is it me, or did this all just take a weird turn?"

Mom turned to look at me. "I don't know that I am comfortable with this." Dad overheard Mom and me. He leaned in and said, "This is the last goddamn time we sit in the middle of the sanctuary." I giggled. There was no way for us to get out; we were ensconced by awestruck Baptists.

Daryl turned his focus back to Trace and the youth choir. "You are my flock. You are my charge. You will be tempted to stray, lost lambs. Others will tempt you to wander beyond our flock, beyond the love of Christ. Do not be deceived. These people are wolves in sheep's clothing. These people are doing the bidding of the Great Deceiver. These people are the charge of Satan."

Trace and the youth choir were stoic, stone-faced, entranced by the charismatic ebb and flow of Daryl's voice.

Then Daryl stood toward the opposite end of the stage—farthest from Myrna and her organ, near the Christmas tree—and asked, "How do shepherds spend their time? Do shepherds look to women outside the bonds of holy matrimony to spend their time? Do shepherds look to alcohol, drugs, marijuana, cocaine, and other substances to alter their state of mind to spend their time? Do shepherds look to cards and casinos, the bright lights, bells, and whistles of Las Vegas or Atlantic City to spend their time?"

Daryl moved center stage and stood in front of the podium, his eyes locked on me. "Do shepherds look for gay bars and teenage boys in greasy spoon diners to spend their time? I know one shepherd that did, a few years ago in Laramie, Wyoming. He wandered from the flock. Look what happened to him."

Daryl turned his gaze from me and moved back across the stage toward Myrna Boil.

"I have the answer," Daryl said. "Christ has the answer. The answer is *no*! No to all of the above. Shepherds spend their time with Christ. Shepherds spend time with their flock. Shepherds tend only to those things that give glory to God!"

Daryl ended his tirade with the word *God* as his vocal punch, and the parishioners went crazy. Folks all around the sanctuary, on the main level and in the balcony, rose to their feet and danced in the aisles. Many waved their arms and hands in the air. The thunder of their revelry shook the floor beneath us. Mom, Dad, Cameron, and I stared at one another in stunned silence. This Christmas service was Wabash Valley Baptist Church on steroids. Reverend Damien had been the head pastor for as long as I could remember, and he never whipped parishioners up into the kind of fury, this kind of fire and brimstone frenzy, that Pastor Daryl did this day.

As the excitement waned, Pastor Daryl returned to the podium and said, "Only through Jesus Christ and by tending our flock can I—as a shepherd, as a Baptist, as a Christian, and as a messenger of God—only this way can I, and you, ever hope to live in the glory of God." He lifted his Bible into the air above him and said, "Give me an amen!"

Celebratory shouts of "amen," "hallelujah," "praise Jesus," and "glory be to God" again rattled the rafters of the church. With a final *hallelujah* the sermon was finished, and from the pulpit Daryl closed his Bible and asked parishioners to bow their heads in prayer. Sitting there with my family on that Christmas Day I found my mind racing, my anxiety skyrocketing, and my anger building. I'd said nothing to anyone about Trace waiting for me in the parking lot of Teana Faye's, or Rio inviting him to breakfast with us at the Tennessean. Or the fact that Daryl had come looking for him in the middle of the night. It was clear, crystal clear, that Daryl was using the pulpit to revel in his sick sense of admonishment.

"Amen," Pastor Daryl said.

"Amen," replied the parishioners.

After the prayer Daryl walked off the stage, down the steps, and returned to his seat. Rebecca, his wife, kissed him on the cheek.

Daryl always needed, wanted, and received adoration. He got it from his parents, from sports, from girls in high school, and from me. His parishioners loved him, it was obvious. He was easy to love. But I saw the gaping cracks in his Father, Son, and Holy Ghost façade. Nonetheless, as I listened to the congregation's thunderous applause, it became quite apparent that I—my family and I—were the only ones.

I looked toward the youth choir led by Trace as they began to file off the stage. The service was over. I said a silent prayer for him. And for me.

SEALED INDICTMENT RETURNED BY GRAND JURY INVESTIGATION IN PALMER MURDER

By Foster Lawrence
Fort Sackville Sentinel staff writer

FORT SACKVILLE, Ind. — A sealed indictment was returned by the grand jury investigating the Robbie Palmer murder.

Prosecutor Dallas Ellerman would not comment specifically on who was indicted or how many charges were filed.

He said those matters would become public after an arrest.

Robbie Palmer, 18, of Fort Sackville, apparently died early May 3 at a party in Fort Sackville. Although Ellerman has said he is treating the investigation as if it were a homicide, no cause of death has been determined. Two autopsies were performed after Palmer's body was discovered in a ditch on Highway 41 South near Knox Road.

An announcement of the indictment caused a flurry of activity inside and outside the courthouse.

Ellerman would not say whether the charges were felonies or misdemeanors, or who the persons charged were. However, at the beginning of the grand jury investigation, Ellerman identified Riley Salters, 21, of Greenfield, Ind., a Fort Sackville Community College law enforcement student and alleged lover of Palmer's, as a "target witness" of the grand jury probe.

He said a target witness is someone who is the subject of the investigation and has some rights not accorded other grand jury witnesses. For example, a target witness has the right to be represented by a lawyer if he testifies.

However, Salters had not been questioned in the first two days of the investigation, and Ellerman would not say whether he has been subpoenaed.

This is not the first time Salters' name has surfaced in the investigation.

Ellerman suggested early in the case that Salters could be charged with illegally moving a dead body, and moving a body without notifying a coroner.

While the grand jury in Fort Sackville was deliberating, Salters' attorney said he planned to enter an innocent plea on those charges "should they come up."

In the days after Palmer's body was discovered, Salters told Indiana State Police investigators that he panicked after he saw that Palmer had "passed out" and was "lifeless" the morning of the party and left the house immediately.

Chapter Ten

February

The Friday before Lent, I was sitting in the restaurant's office totaling time cards when Trace walked in. It had been a busy night—Trace was the only employee left, and he had taken his time closing the dishroom.

"I just punched out. You want my card?" Trace asked.

"Yeah, I'll take it," I said, and added his to the stack.

"You mind if I hang out a minute?" he asked.

"Sure, go ahead. Sit down. But it's Friday night. Don't you have plans?" I asked.

"No, no plans. Just going home after this."

I could sense Trace had something on his mind.

"Everything okay, Trace? Did you hear from any of the universities?"

"Yeah, I'm okay. And no, I haven't heard a word yet. I probably won't hear anything until spring."

I stopped totaling hours and turned to look at him.

"Are you sure you're okay? You look a little worried. Did your parents discover you applied to programs out east? What's going on?"

"No. They're still in the dark. Thankfully. They're kind of in the dark about a lot of things . . . Can I ask you a question? It's sort of personal."

"Absolutely."

"You promise you won't get upset? You won't fire me?" he asked.

"Fire you? Why would I fire you? You're the best busser I've got."

I was pretty sure I knew where the conversation was going. I feigned ignorance.

"Shoot," I said.

"Well, you know, since you told me you were gay, I've been doing a lot of thinking." He paused. "How did you know? I mean for sure."

It was the first time anyone in Fort Sackville had flat-out asked me about my experience. I tried to summon within me my South Beach courage. I longed to be honest. I had never discussed my sexual orientation outside the confines of my family and a few close friends—never with employees, and certainly not with customers. I wanted my response to seem self-assured and comfortable. I laughed.

"It's just . . . it's just I've heard some talk recently," Trace said.

"Really? That's not surprising," I said. Common sense told me there had to be some sort of town gossip; I'd always expected it. In traditional terms I was sure folks didn't think of me as a local eligible bachelor, although at times I did have grandmothers who ate in the restaurant show me wallet photos of their granddaughters in an attempt to fix me up. "Fort Sackville's not a town that minds its own business," I said.

"Have you ever had any problems? I mean, has anyone ever said anything to you? Tried to hurt you?"

"No. Not really. But you have to understand, I don't really talk about it. I figure it's no one else's business," I said.

"I'm sorry. Never mind then," Trace said, his voice deflated.

"No. No. It's okay. What do you want to know?" I asked.

He shifted in his seat. "What did your parents say when you told them?"

"That I was gay? Well, it was kind of fucked up. I was forced to tell them."

The moment I came out to my parents was etched into my soul. Like remembering where I was when Princess Diana was killed, or when the Towers collapsed. To me, the experience was monumental and terrifying. I took a deep breath.

"It was Thursday, August 27, 1992."

Twenty minutes had passed since I'd called my parents' house and asked to speak with them. At nearly eleven p.m. on a Thursday night, they knew something was wrong.

That particular night I walked out my front door, down the lane, across their lawn, and entered Mom and Dad's house through their garage. Once inside I slipped quietly upstairs, past my little brother Cameron's room—careful to not wake him with my footsteps on the wood floor—and into my parents' bedroom at the end of the hall.

I found myself standing at the foot of their bed, my chest as heavy as the oppressive August air outside.

How would I tell them?

My parents' master suite made me feel as if I were standing on the stage of a darkened movie palace, its grandeur barely discernible in the half-light, and lacking a visible exit. My mother's Waterford crystal chandelier hung above me, ensconced in the coffered ceiling. It captured the solitary light in the room flickering from the television. I watched it hold the beams prisoner, dissecting colors inside the handcrafted teardrop pendants. The only sound, low and coming from behind me, was David Letterman's interview with Tom Hanks about his new movie *A League of Their Own*. Sitting up in bed, my parents were alarmed, waiting for me to speak. All I could do was think about the earlier phone call from Chad Sowers, and how my future would be tethered to this night. The moment I confessed, nothing would ever be the same. I was stepping through a gate that would forever close behind me.

Their gazes were fixed upon me like two unwavering spotlights, yet their expressions were strangely blank. I'd seen the look before—their faces became an impenetrable fortress when they felt uncomfortable or irritated, stoic expressions that could not be breached. The urgency in my voice over the phone earlier had tipped them off; this news would change everything.

"I need to tell you something," I said.

The silence was awkward, acidic, like the sourness seeping up from my stomach; I could taste it in the back of my throat. I felt like throwing up.

"I met a guy. He's pretty angry with me—he's threatening to call you and tell you I'm gay."

Those weren't the words I wanted to say. The silence amplified. Beads of sweat formed on my upper lip and along my hairline. The back of my neck became wet and clammy.

"What I mean is, I met a guy last spring. We hung out. He's the reason I went to Florida last month. I lied to you about my vacation. I didn't go to Orlando; I flew to Tampa to meet him. He'd moved there from Evansville a couple of months after we met."

Mom's and Dad's faces were hard as a brick facade. I couldn't breathe.

"The vacation didn't end well. He's pissed off. He says I owe him money for a parking ticket he got picking me up at the airport. He told me I need to send him money to pay for it or he's going to call you and tell you everything."

"Do you owe him the money?" Dad asked.

"No. I rented a car. He just parked there to meet me in the terminal. I had nothing to do with it."

My parents' eyes remained fixed.

"Why does he think you're responsible?" Dad asked.

"I don't know why. Something about his license being suspended. Says the ticket has to be paid or else there'll be a warrant out for his arrest. I really didn't ask for the specifics."

My mother sat silent, motionless.

"How did you meet this guy?" Dad asked reasonably.

"At Chi Chi's in Evansville. He was a server there. I hung out in the lounge one night and we ended up drinking together. He invited me to go with him and some of his friends to a gay bar there. I went."

My legs were rooted to the floor, stiff as tree trunks. I wondered if my face looked like Mom's and Dad's; mine felt like fear was written all over it. Was it showing?

My dad let out a long sigh. "Well, you're not sending him the money."

"I didn't plan on it. But I wanted to get to you guys before he did."

That didn't sound right.

"What I mean to say is, I wanted to be the one to tell you," I said.

"So, is this true? You think you're gay?" Dad asked.

"Yes. It is."

He looked at my mother. She wouldn't look at him and kept staring at me. There was a blankness in her eyes.

"I suppose it doesn't surprise me," she said.

"What do you mean?" I asked.

"I always kind of knew."

The fear overwhelmed me. I didn't want to discuss this with them any further.

"Look, it's not like we have to hang a banner in the restaurant tomorrow announcing it to everyone. Let's just keep it to ourselves. I don't want Cameron to know," I said. "We'll just talk about it later."

"I agree," Dad said.

"Good night," I said, turning to leave.

"Grey? Don't give that guy money," Mom said.

"I'm not. I'm not talking to him again."

"We'll see you in the morning," Dad said calmly, reassuringly.

I hurried out of their bedroom, into the hall, down the stairs, and out the garage door to their drive. How would I show up for work tomorrow and face them? Before reaching the road, viscous bile erupted from my stomach, knocking me to my knees in their yard. Once I stopped throwing up, my stomach cramped from the convulsions, and I could feel the front of my shirt soaked in the green syrupy mess. I took it off, walked to my house, and stuffed it deep down into the trash can near my garage. Shirtless, I walked inside my house and locked the front door behind me.

"Oh my God," Trace said, sitting on the edge of his chair. I noticed he had pushed the phone and black wire desk tray filled with the restaurant's invoices aside and rested his crossed arms upon the desktop. "Really? That's how it happened?"

"Really. That's how it happened," I said.

Trace was silent. He reminded me of a child enraptured by a story of mystery or suspense. His blond hair was feathery like duck fluff, his eyes wide and blue. He looked so innocent, so naïve. I could almost see his thoughts spinning about in his head.

For a moment it seemed Trace had slipped out of our conversation; he'd gone somewhere deep into the recesses of his mind. Then he came back.

"So that bar in Evansville, the one I saw you and Rio leaving, is that a gay bar?" he asked.

"Yes. Didn't we talk about it that night at the Tennessean?"

"No. You just told me you were gay. You didn't say anything about that place being a gay bar. I kind of assumed it might be," Trace said. "I wasn't sure."

Trace was captivated. I could see I wasn't going to finish the employees' time cards. I didn't mind. It felt nice to tell someone about my experiences.

"So what happened with Chad?" Trace asked.

"It's a long story. You need to go out and meet your friends, drink beer, road-trip, get into trouble. Do what other seventeen-year-olds are doing. Don't waste a perfectly good Friday night here with me."

"Tell me," Trace said.

I took a deep breath and let out a long sigh.

"Chad moved to Tampa, and I went down to visit him. Two nights later we ended up arguing in a gay bar there. It turned out Chad had a boyfriend. Apparently, he was going to try to juggle the two of us. Thought maybe the other would never find out. It was a mess. I ended up renting a hotel room on the beach and spending the rest of my vacation by myself. I came back home on schedule, no one the wiser. I tried to lose touch with Chad, but that didn't happen."

"So he really did try to blackmail you?" Trace asked.

"Yes, he did."

"Did you ever send him the money?"

"Hell no! Like I said, I told my parents everything. I got to them before he did. Mom did cry for a few days. It took a while for everything to get back to normal. But eventually it did. If you asked Mom and Dad today, they'd tell you they'd rather be around gay people than straight people. Gays are more fun, they say. They've met a few of my friends from Evansville; they just don't say much about having met my friends to people they don't know well, employees or customers. They know Rio."

"My family would never be that cool," Trace said with a sad smile. Then his expression became vacant. I sensed he was trying to stem his pain. His eyes began to water. I knew the look. I knew his fear. I'd once been where he was.

"Trace, are you okay?" I asked.

He shook his head no. A recalcitrant tear slipped down his cheek. He covered his face with his hands and started sobbing.

I reached across the corner of the desk and placed my hands on his wrists. "Trace. Trace. Shhh. It's okay. Everything's going to be okay," I said.

"No. No, it's not. I don't want to be this. I don't want to be this way," he said, his words choking in the back of his throat. I moved from my chair, kneeled beside him, and put my arms around him. He placed his head on my shoulder. I could feel his tears soaking my shirt. "I keep praying for God to take it away. Or to take me away."

I remembered my own prayers to God and that Friday afternoon, the day after I came out to my parents, going to the empty sanctuary at Wabash Valley Baptist Church and sitting in a balcony pew crying, asking God to help me.

"It's okay. Don't say that. You're okay. I'm here. I've got you," I said to Trace.

Trace continued sobbing. He was frightened. *Why did I have to bring up Chad? I could kick my ass.* Using Chad as my example for coming out with a young man struggling to accept his orientation was stupid. I had only added to Trace's fear.

I pulled back. I raised his chin with my thumb and looked into his eyes. "Trace, not all gay guys are like Chad. It's like everything else—

there are wonderful people, and there are assholes. You met Rio. Rio is a good guy. There are good gay guys out there," I said.

"That's not it," he said. "I don't know how I can ever tell my parents. They're not like yours. And Pastor Daryl? He will totally freak."

Pastor Daryl.

"Listen. You don't have to do anything. The only thing you have to do right now is breathe. Just breathe." I paused a moment, then nodded a silent *okay*? "And you don't worry about Pastor Daryl. He's got his own issues."

I gave Trace a handful of the napkins stacked on the corner of the desk.

"Look. I understand. I swear I do. And I'll do whatever I can to help. But you have to know something. You're okay. There's *nothing* wrong with you. You're intelligent, good-looking, talented . . . so fucking talented, and a hell of a worker. You're going to be successful. There's no doubt about it. You can be everything you are, everything you want to be, *and* be gay. It's part and parcel."

"How'd you get through it?" Trace asked.

"It takes time. And I had a good friend. I had Rosabelle. And you have me. Okay? You understand what I'm saying?"

"I feel so fucked up. Like I'm going to burn in hell," he said, again covering his face with his hands.

"Trace, you're not going to burn in hell. Your orientation, who you choose to love, has nothing to do with heaven or hell. Look at me." I gently pulled his hands away from his face, again turning his chin toward me to look him in the eyes. "How you treat yourself, how you treat others, that's what determines whether we're good or bad. I've seen you. I see the way you interact with people. I've heard about your involvement at church. You're a compassionate guy. Right now, you need to show *yourself* some compassion. Okay?"

"Please don't tell anyone. Please."

"Trace, I'm not going to say a word. I promise. But I don't want you struggling with this alone."

I grabbed a pen and a napkin.

"Here's my home number. I know you have my cell. You call me anytime. Day or night. Ask me anything. You're not alone. No matter what happens, you remember that. You're not alone."

I thought about Daryl. Pastor Daryl Stone. What would he think if Trace announced to the world that he was gay? Daryl was hell-bent on keeping his secrets and was desperate that those around him keep theirs as well, most especially if he sensed their secrets were the same as his. Trace was right to be concerned—his family was involved in the Wabash Valley Baptist Church, the same church that had conducted a character assassination on Robbie Palmer after his murder and all but branded his mother and sisters with a scarlet *H* for being the family of a homosexual. Trace's parents adored Pastor Daryl—everyone at Wabash Valley Baptist Church did. It was the largest and most influential church in Fort Sackville. I was concerned for Trace. Daryl, it seemed, had forgotten his middle-of-the-night visits to my basement bedroom back in high school. Apparently Daryl was good at denial. After all, when Daryl first introduced me to his wife that November Sunday at Daniels', he'd told her he and I were just *classmates*.

Chapter Eleven

March

I tried hard to avoid restaurant customers like Myrna Boil, the organist from Wabash Valley Baptist Church, when I was out in public, away from Daniels' Family Buffet. However, one could never avoid Myrna Boil for long. She found me during my afternoon break from the restaurant at Walmart in my quick quest to do some household shopping. I was still concerned about Trace's confession to me a few weeks earlier and his current state of mind. I wanted him to take his time and allow himself to be accepting of himself before he looked to his immediate family and his Wabash Valley Church family for acceptance. I knew the church would be a difficult sell—especially with congregants like Myrna Boil.

Myrna Boil looked as if she had eaten one too many of her own homemade lemon pies, her lips constantly puckered as if something much too tart were in her mouth. Even her hair looked beat, whipped like egg whites into meringue, its glossy peaks perched impeccably upon her head. Her makeup, polyester trousers, everything about her appearance was fifties-housewife impeccable—a place for everything and everything in its place. Somehow her doughy legs, despite their lumbering gate, managed to carry her religiously to Daniels' Family Buffet and prior to that, for decades, to Daniels' Diner. She wasn't just the organist at Wabash Valley Baptist Church; she was its self-appointed matriarch. To me, growing up in the restaurant, it seemed she'd always been old, an immortal. There were others of her ilk. They too had silver-blue hair. Whenever there was a tragedy, she and her allies always brought baked goods in dishes marked with masking tape, their black signatures penned upon the manila adhesive pasted to the bottom to ensure their containers, after grief, found their way back home. I was certain *she* was their ringleader.

One could always see Myrna coming: she crept along Highway 41 behind the wheel of her enormous blue Cadillac, backing up traffic, and in the restaurant she bullied her way down the buffet line. This day at Walmart, while I was stocking up on essentials, she spotted me just as I spotted her. She turned her motorized shopping cart—Rio called them girth movers—toward me as if it were a ballistic missile and I were its target.

She ran over my foot.

"Grey! I must have a word with you about your Swiss steak. It's baked to death. Cremated!"

It was because of customers like Myrna Boil that I rarely went out in Fort Sackville.

"Myrna, it's not. Last Sunday alone we served twelve full steam-table pans, each one four inches deep, loaded with steak. Do you realize how much Swiss steak that is? If it'd been cremated, there would have been other complaints. You're the only unhappy customer."

"I disagree. I'm certain there were other complaints. You're just not telling me the truth."

"Yes, Myrna, you're absolutely right. I'm lying to you. Now if you don't mind, I'd like to finish my shopping."

This was not a new game for Myrna. She was a pro. I was blocked, squeezed against the Charmin by her cart.

"You know, there are others."

"Other what?"

"Other restaurants! I can take my money elsewhere."

"Perhaps, then, you should."

"Your problem, young man, is you don't go to church, and when you do, you must not pay attention. The Bible says you are supposed to respect your elders. Perhaps you need to read your Bible again. I suspect you need to reread your Bible for other things as well."

I gave her my best frozen face, my Midwestern stare—the same look my parents had mastered so well and worn the night I came out to them. Now I understood that, like my parents, I too had perfected the stoic look as a coping mechanism for people like Myrna Boil.

Sensing my disinterest in her complaint, with an audible *harrumph*, she fired up her cart, backed up beeping, and took off at a snail's pace toward the bakery.

I abandoned my shopping, left Walmart, my foot throbbing, with memories flooding my brain of why I didn't shop there or show my face in the community outside of the restaurant.

As soon as I returned to the restaurant, I had a phone call waiting in the office. After my conversation, I sat for a moment behind my dad's massive oak desk. It had a history; everything around me had history. The desk had been purchased at an auction when the Gimbel Bond on 2nd and Main Street, the forerunner to New York's flagship store, went out of business in the 1980s. The desk had been a fixture in the store's Fort Sackville office for forty years, and had been one in ours for over twenty. On it, a bill for catfish fillets lay atop a stack of invoices from Friday's deliveries. Friday was fish day at Daniel's Family Buffet, as it had been at Daniels' Diner.

Friday's lunch hour at Daniels' Diner had been a fisher of Catholics. It was the second-busiest lunch of the week, and its swivel counter stools were filled with men in hats. A fleet of fedoras docked at the restaurant's speckled Formica counter; the fifty-seat dining room filled to capacity with businessmen, priests, and ladies who lunched. The Diner's popular Friday lunch menu often forced Grandpa Collin to lock the front door at the height of rush. For any number of customers leaving, only as many were allowed to enter. Diners would line the front sidewalk along Fairground Avenue, between parked cars and the two-story brick flatiron building, sometimes angling around the corner onto 8th Street. The smell of home cooking enticed travelers from the train depot across the street as well.

On Fridays they did not wait long. Tables turned.

Waitresses in their white starched uniforms, lapel name tags, and black aprons darted between tables, behind the counter, through the kitchen's swinging doors like albino worker ants, carrying green-band Buffalo china, glassware, hot cups of coffee, or the day's plate special: fried catfish fillets with all the fixin's and creamy coleslaw in monkey bowls.

One of those fedora-wearing men sitting at the counter was a new salesman for the Ohio Valley Uniform Supply Company located in Evansville, Indiana. Years later, when recounting the events of this particular Friday, Grandpa Collin nicknamed him Red because he'd never seen a man's face turn so bright a color. He looked to be in his thirties, about the same age as my grandfather. Perhaps he'd recently begun working for the company and was responsible for their Southwestern Indiana territory. During the first few months he must have done his research; he'd known that Mean's Clean Towel Service, a local company, had been supplying the Diner since my Grandpa Collin bought the restaurant four years earlier.

This particular Friday, in 1955, Red must have timed his stop in Fort Sackville precisely at noon to have lunch at Daniels' Diner. The day-shift cook had called in sick, and Grandpa Collin found himself in the kitchen working the grill. At the height of the lunch rush, he spotted his waitresses gathered around the fedora-wearing man sitting at the end of the counter. Not one for pretense, my grandfather yelled from the kitchen, "Get your asses back to work!" The waitresses quickly returned to business. Only moments later, when Collin again looked up from the grill, the waitresses were once more gathered around the man, his cigarette smoke wafting above their huddled heads, circling his hat.

This time, Collin stormed toward the group. One of the waitresses saw him approaching. She signaled the others. Attention was once again hastily returned to the Friday lunch crowd. Red, seeing Grandpa Collin for the first time, stood. He offered a handshake, introduced himself, and tried to speak about the uniform business. Clean towels too. "You've got a great place here, Mr. Daniels. I'd really like the opportunity to be your supplier."

"Mister, we're covered up. You got to leave my girls alone."

"Absolutely. I was just showing them some of our latest styles. Where do you currently get your uniforms? I assume Mean's is your towel supplier?"

"I don't have time to talk. Neither do the waitresses. Looks like you've finished your lunch. One of the girls will bring you a cup of coffee shortly."

Grandpa Collin returned to the kitchen.

In Fort Sackville, it was common knowledge that my grandfather hated two things: salesmen, and salesmen that took another paying customer's seat.

But Red? He didn't give up so easily.

Grandpa Collin had a reputation. He'd grown up during the Depression, suffered abuse, known hunger. He was a Navy man who could fight. Grandpa Collin did not like fools. If tramps riding the rails or vagrants wandering from town to town appeared at the restaurant's back kitchen door, they got a meal. Grandpa Collin understood their kind. But salesmen? Forget it.

Red sealed his fate when Grandpa Collin, for the third time, looked up from the grill to find the waitresses gathered around him once again. Red had his uniform sales book open and the waitresses' attention captured.

Grandpa Collin slammed his steak weight on the grill; the dining room fell silent. When he again sailed through the kitchen doors, removing, then throwing his grease-stained apron to the floor, and approached Red from the service side of the counter, utensils paused in midair.

"Get your ass out!" Grandpa Collin said.

Red stood.

Customers heard: "Goddamn it!" "Son of a bitch!" "Then I'll throw your ass out!"

From the opposite side of the lunch counter, Grandpa Collin grabbed Red by his collar and pulled him closer. Everyone was staring at the fedora-wearing man, now leaning over the end of the counter.

"His face was redder than a drunken Irishman. That son of a bitch. Had *me* seein' red. Which was more than he could see," Grandpa Collin had said once when recounting the story. "That's when I punched him."

Gasps echoed through the silent lunchroom.

Grandpa Collin had knocked Red's glass eye out of its socket. It rolled among those counter Catholics, pinballing between their plates loaded with Friday's lunch special.

When Collin picked up his apron and headed back to the kitchen, one of the waitresses handed Red not a guest check but his glass eye. He never came around again.

Grandpa Collin said that, as the bustle of the restaurant began to build once more, after Red made his way out the front door with his uniform sales book under his arm, past diners looking through the front windows, a voice from one of those counter men in hats cried out, "Eye for an eye, Collin? You're a good Baptist!"

Mryna Boil encouraged the same kind of loathing in me that the supply company salesmen had for Grandpa Collin. Naturally, I could not hit her. I was nothing like Grandpa Collin; I never resorted to violence, except perhaps the passion-fueled prizefights Rio and I engaged in when we were lovers. But that was different. He and I were younger then, and it was perhaps because we loved each other so fervently that we were unable to understand each other, or ourselves. Grandpa Collin's anger seemed to manifest from a hate stowed deep within his gut. It was, after all, an abdominal aneurysm that killed him not long after he retired from the restaurant and sold it to Dad and Mom. I wasn't about to go down the road he'd traveled. I wasn't going to let customers like Myrna Boil or Old Man Atkinson or even Pastor Daryl get the best of me. I needed to reinforce my defenses, build the walls around me higher and thicker. I could not let them get in. I could not let them get the best of me. I was not going to go down like Grandpa Collin, or allow myself to have health issues like Dad, because of this goddamn restaurant. But I also knew if I reinforced the fortress walls around myself I was doing the very thing that Rio said would one day destroy me.

FATAL FIRE AT "HOMOSEXUAL PARTY" HOUSE

By Foster Lawrence
Fort Sackville Sentinel staff writer

FORT SACKVILLE, Ind. — A 21-year-old Fort Sackville Community College student died Sunday morning in a fire that gutted the same house where 18-year-old Robbie Palmer died of unexplained causes last May.

County coroner Vonderbreck said, although the deaths were not connected, investigators do suspect foul play.

"I have no reason to believe the deaths are connected," Vonderbreck said. "It's just a weird coincidence."

Authorities are not releasing the name of the student pending notification of family members.

The student's charred body was found in a locked upstairs bedroom, the same bedroom reported to have been the last place Robbie Palmer was seen alive.

Fort Sackville firefighters were called to the home at 25 E. 1st Street at 3:44 a.m. Sunday. The wood-framed home was completely engulfed in flames. It is suspected that the Fort Sackville Community College student was overcome by smoke and unable to escape.

Arson is suspected.

The house was the site of a party in which 18-year-old Robbie Palmer died. Two autopsies failed to determine the cause of Palmer's death. A Greenfield, Ind., man, 21-year-old

Riley Salters, was arrested earlier this month for obstructing justice for "secreting" a dead body.

Salters told police he fell asleep at the party and panicked when he awoke and found Palmer dead. Investigators allege that Salters drove Palmer's body to a drainage ditch where he dumped it.

Vonderbreck said the Fort Sackville Community College student who currently rented the house and died in the blaze did not live at the residence last May, and Vonderbreck does not think the student was in attendance at the party in which Palmer was last seen alive.

Chapter Twelve

April

Easter Sunday arrived, and with it, spring weather. Folks were out and about: grocery shopping, going to church, and eating at Daniels' Family Buffet. Trace remained quiet and I gave him space. I made sure that if I talked to him about my trips to Miami Beach—I was itching to go back—I painted a positive picture of the acceptance and freedom I had found there. I wanted to hear him sing again, and he had been talking about his excitement at being given another solo by Pastor Daryl on Easter Sunday, a song Trace had picked out himself, an old southern Baptist hymn and his favorite: "Just As I Am." I sensed—hoped, perhaps—that Trace was beginning to accept who he was. He hadn't said much of anything since that Friday night confession, so I wanted to be in the sanctuary at Wabash Valley Baptist Church to support him, if only via eye contact. Mom, Dad, and Cameron decided to go also. I sensed they had a suspicion Trace was struggling with his orientation, and I was sure they wanted to show their support.

Sitting next to Mom in the pew at Wabash Valley Baptist Church, I notice Daryl's dad across the aisle in front of us. "His father sure is pleased," I said, pointing toward the aging Mr. Stone. He was smiling, his posture erect and his chest puffed out with pride.

"I sort of feel sorry for Walt since his wife left him. It seems Daryl returning to Fort Sackville has been his dad's saving grace," Mom said.

Daryl retrieved his Bible from the podium, its pages tagged with colorful Post-it notes.

"*Jesus said to her, I am the resurrection and the life. Whoever believes in me, though he die, yet shall he live, and everyone who lives and believes in me shall never die. Do you believe this?* John 11:25-26. Praise Jesus!"

Celebratory shouts and affirmations rose from the sanctuary.

"John 8:12 says, *I am the light of the world. Whoever follows me will never walk in darkness but will have the light of life.*" Daryl paused for effect as his eyes traveled among the parishioners. "Are you in darkness? Have you seen the light? Do you know Jesus?" He motioned toward the youth choir with his Bible, then returned his focus to the parishioners. "Look at our choir. Look at the light in their faces. I see our savior Jesus Christ in each of them. His light shines through."

Trace sat with the choir, smiling, anticipating his solo. All eyes, including Daryl's, were on him.

"John 1:10 says, *He was in the world, and the world was made through him, yet the world did not know him.*"

Daryl paused.

"Are you in darkness? Have you seen the light? Do you know Jesus?"

Building momentum, Daryl walked toward the baptismal side of the stage carrying his open Bible. "Look at our world. Technology. The Internet. Listen to the music. Look at the TV. Just the other night my sons wanted to watch that show, *Will and Grace*!"

Again he paused.

"Galatians 5 tells us: *Now the works of the flesh are evident: sexual immorality . . . things like these. I warn you, as I warned you before, that those who do such things will not inherit the kingdom of God.* Praise Jesus!"

"Praise Jesus," shouted the parishioners.

Daryl walked to the right side of the stage, then stood just above Myrna Boil, who sat attentively at her organ. He beat his Bible in the air above him for emphasis. "Homosexuals on television. For *my* sons to see. For *your* sons to see. An abomination celebrated. What has man created? Is the light of Jesus reflected in this? Does *our* world not yet know Him?"

He paused. "John 1:11: *He came to his own, and his own people did not receive him.*"

Daryl pointed his Bible toward the parishioners, toward my family and me, and continued. "Are you in darkness? Have you seen the light? Do you know Jesus?"

Returning center stage, Daryl placed his Bible upon the podium, everyone's attention harnessed. The ebb and flow of his evangelical voice drew parishioners as water draws those who thirst.

"Like many of you, I know someone that's made the lifestyle choice to be a homosexual. This person has disobeyed God's Word. Today, standing here in this sacred house, as we gather to celebrate our Savior's resurrection, to celebrate Him, He that shed His blood for us, to this person I say: *You* are in darkness! *See* the light! *Know* Jesus!"

My face hardened. Mom placed her left hand upon my knee. Her diamond wedding ring shimmered in the cupola's dusty sunlight.

Daryl continued, "Today I give you good news of great joy: the true light, which enlightens *everyone*, shed His blood for us. He saved us from our sins. Praise Jesus! Christ is risen!"

Once more parishioners rose in rousing ovation to Daryl's declaration. Mom, Dad, Cameron, and I sat there for a moment, hesitant, unsure whether or not to follow those in the pews around us. Concerned, we rose slowly, staring at one another; separately, in a stunned stupor, we surveyed the sanctuary.

Daryl proudly stood at the pulpit, accepting the crowd's unrestrained adulation, his smile wide, teeth white; his posture erect, not unlike his father's, as he triumphantly raised his Bible in the air. The youth choir stood behind him, fervently applauding. Reverend Damien danced a jig in front of his chair. Trace stood motionless, like me, his face expressionless. Only his eyes moved left to right, looking around. Daryl's sermon frightened him and cemented my suspicions. Daryl had whipped the church into such a frenzy, he appeared to have forgotten Trace's solo. Now time was up, the service was over. I sensed Daryl had done it on purpose; he had chosen to silence Trace for whatever reason. Maybe Trace had said something?

After minutes of applause, admiring parishioners began to file from the pews and down the aisle—some toward the exit, others toward the pulpit. Trace and the choir left the stage as they had entered.

Making our way through the throngs, my family and I headed to the parking lot. I broke through the crowd early, my attention focused entirely on getting to the car. Mom and Cameron kept up with me. Dad lagged behind, wrestling his portable oxygen tank. Arriving at the car, I positioned myself beside the driver's door, resting my arms on the car's roof, the key remote in my hand. We waited on Dad, Cameron by my side, Mom standing opposite Cam and me beside the rear passenger door.

"What the hell was that about?" I asked.

"It wasn't about you," Mom replied.

"Bullshit! It was exactly about me. The whole sermon was directed toward me. The only reason I came to this house of horrors was to support Trace. Daryl didn't even let Trace sing."

"I'm sorry. I just thought we could have a nice Easter Sunday as a family."

"Well, it sure as hell wasn't a Judy Garland movie in there."

"Those people were totally kissing his ass," Cameron said.

"What?" I asked.

"Daryl. He was getting ego-fucked by everyone in there. It was epic," Cameron said.

When Dad arrived, I clicked the remote. The car beeped, its lights flashing twice. Dad opened the front passenger door. Mom, Cameron, and I opened ours.

"Cameron, enough. Grey, you too," Mom said. "Let's just get in the car. We need to get to the restaurant. We'll forget we even came."

I shouted, "Forget? It was a public lynching! That place is loaded with people—"

Dad interrupted me. "Get in the goddamn car! I'm ready to go home." He wrestled his portable oxygen tank onto the front floorboard. "Grey, stop at the Quik Stop on the way to the restaurant. I'm buying cigarettes."

"CJ, you are not smoking," Mom said.

"The hell I'm not. Happy Easter Sunday to me!"

"Praise Jesus!" Cameron muttered.

Everyone except Mom got in the car. Three doors slammed in succession. Sitting behind the wheel, I looked over my shoulder to see if she was in. Her expression revealed exhaustion. For the first time in my life, her face looked old.

"Are you coming?" I asked.

Quietly, she slipped herself into the backseat and closed the door.

The drive to my parents' house was silent. I could not believe what Daryl had said in church or what he'd done to Trace. I couldn't help but think that Trace's selection of "Just As I Am" made Daryl uncomfortable. Daryl was smart; I knew he could sense that Trace was gay. After all, in high school, Daryl was the one that showed up at *my* basement bedroom window.

From the moment Daryl first invited me to swim at his house that summer of high school PE, we'd become best friends. We spent most of our time together. But the end of his senior year was quickly approaching, and graduation was around the corner. I still had another year of high school remaining, and I wasn't looking forward to his leaving for college. The first weekend in May ushered in the beginning of Senior Week, celebrated by a host of impromptu underage parties around the county—mostly keggers in cornfields outside city limits, beyond the watchful eyes of the Fort Sackville Police. It was a tradition that Harrison High seniors were let out of school two weeks before the underclassmen. Their class of '86 graduation was the third weekend in May.

At two a.m. on that Saturday morning of Senior Week, Daryl appeared at my basement bedroom window, tapping on the glass pane. I'd moved my bedroom from the second floor of my parents' house to our half-finished basement in order to gain some independence, creating the Midwestern equivalent of a one-room apartment. The windows along the foundation were large enough to open, thus enabling my friends and me to enter and exit without my parents' knowledge. On several late-night occasions, the window served as a portal for pizza delivery.

Daryl knew I was home, which on a Friday night was unusual. He'd been on a date with Shanni; I'd been asleep. I got out of bed, walked to the window, and opened it, feeling the cool spring air on my bare chest.

"What are you doing?" I asked.

"I figured you'd be up. What are *you* doing?"

I could smell whiskey on his breath.

"I was sleeping. I didn't feel like going out tonight. Where is Shanni?"

Daryl climbed down through the window. I shut it behind him.

"She's at home. We went out for a little bit, hit a couple of parties—they were lame. Then we went back to her place to watch a movie. Her parents weren't home. We drank almost a fifth of Jack Daniel's."

"No shit. I can smell it."

"She can be such a bitch."

I turned on the lamp next to the sofa. We sat down.

"What happened this time?"

Daryl and Shanni had been dating for less than two years and were notorious for passionate romance and equally passionate quarrels. Shanni was in my junior class; she and Daryl were "the couple" and I was the third wheel. "She's all pissed off because I don't want to stay in town and go to Fort Sackville Community College for one year until she graduates. She has this idea that we're going to go to Indiana University together. I keep telling her I'm going wherever the athletic scholarships are; I just have to decide which one I want. She got all bitchy and told me to get out."

"So you came here?"

"I figured I could crash here, then go home in the morning. I didn't want to drive through town with all the cops out."

"Sure. No problem. Dad said they'd be out in full force this weekend."

"You got anything to drink?"

"No. All the liquor is in the kitchen cabinet upstairs. Mom and Dad are asleep. Cameron's been having trouble sleeping through the night. He may hear us; I wouldn't want to wake him. Probably shouldn't chance it."

"Dude, I still can't believe you have a little brother. Your parents are having more sex than you."

"Whatever."

"It's true. When's the last time you got laid?"

"I don't know. A while ago, I guess."

"Was it Marci? Did you guys do it in the backseat of one of her daddy's Oldsmobiles?" Marci Eisenhut's father owned the Chevrolet and Oldsmobile dealership in town and was one of the Coffee Club Clan guys at the restaurant.

"Maybe," I said.

"You haven't gotten any since, have you?"

"That was it. First time, last time."

"Did she go down on you?"

"You're drunk. You need to go to bed."

"All right. All right. Don't you get all pissy too. I'm just messing with ya." He playfully punched me in the shoulder. I got up from the sofa, switched off the lamp, and went back to bed.

"What? You're just going to leave me here?"

"Go to sleep, Daryl."

Moments later, I heard his belt buckle clink as it hit the basement's tile floor. Then I felt him crawl into bed opposite me.

"I'm not sleeping on that sofa," he said. "It sucks."

"Whatever. Just go to sleep."

A few minutes following there was silence. I could tell Daryl was asleep by his deep breathing; he had passed out. I fell asleep too.

Just before sunrise, I awoke to find Daryl spooning me, his torso pressed against my back, his right arm under mine, with his hand inside my cutoff sweats stroking my semi-erect dick. He'd taken off his underwear during the night, possibly after his belt hit the floor before he got into bed. At first I silently panicked, but then decided to go with it. My heart racing, I reached behind me and felt he was hard too. He inched himself under the covers and pulled my shorts to my ankles. I kicked them off. Soon I felt his warm mouth, his lips press against the base of my hard-on. I didn't last long. Just as silently he resurfaced behind me. I followed his lead and reciprocated. I kept my eyes closed. I remembered his body in the outdoor shower that first summer. My hands felt the warmth of his thighs, their tight sinewy muscles contracting as I pressed against them with the palms of my hands. I heard Daryl moan. He didn't last long either.

Our encounter was odd; it played out in that strange space between sleep and wakefulness—or at least it was orchestrated to appear as such. Regardless, that morning was electrifying for me, far better than what I'd experienced with Marci in the backseat of one of her old man's Oldsmobiles. The encounter with her was unnatural; I felt misplaced, awkward, in the wrong body. With Daryl it felt right. My instinct guided me.

Having fallen back asleep, Daryl and I did not wake until almost noon. I felt him get out of bed, then heard him grab his clothes and dress.

"Grey," he whispered from across the room, "you want to shut the window behind me?"

"Just go upstairs, out the backdoor. Mom probably took Cam to the restaurant to eat lunch with Dad."

"Naw. I'll just go out the window."

"Hold on a second." I had to find my shorts under the covers near my feet, and as I got out of bed Daryl turned his back to me as I put them on.

"What are you doing tonight?" he asked.

"No plans. I don't have to work this weekend."

I walked over to where he was standing near the window.

"I'll call you later tonight. Let's hang out."

"Okay."

Daryl opened the window and climbed out. I shut and locked it behind him. I smiled. It wasn't full-on sex, but it was close enough. I wondered what he was thinking as I watched him walk down the drive, a bit disheveled, toward his car; he was driving his brother's Trans Am. *Will he just ignore what happened? Should I?*

Later that evening I called his house, but Mrs. Stone said he wasn't home—he was on a date with Shanni. I stayed home that Saturday night and went to bed early, hoping that maybe there'd be another two a.m. knock at my bedroom window. There never was.

The night Daryl showed up drunk at my bedroom window was the same night Robbie Palmer disappeared. Apparently Robbie had gone to a party near Fort Sackville Community College with his boyfriend. It was the last night anyone saw him alive. Following Robbie's disappearance, his boyfriend was questioned, then released. Others at the party were also questioned. No substantial information was discovered. The partygoers' silence seemed pervasive. They feared being outed by authorities or the newspaper. As the week passed, talk among Harrison's student body, especially in accounting class, became wild. Gossip flew. Robbie's decomposing, disfigured body was found two weeks later in a drainage ditch on the outskirts of town along Highway 41 South, not far from Daryl's house. His body had been ravaged by rodents and wild animals.

During Harrison High School's 1986 graduation ceremony, Robbie's black gown was carefully draped over his empty chair, with cap and tassel placed in his seat and a single red rose on top. He had been buried earlier the same day.

After the ceremony, Fort Sackville swallowed whole the rumors concerning Robbie's murder. The community's appetite was insatiable, and the local newspaper had a field day. In one report, the paper printed the off-campus party was "homosexual in nature." In another, a journalist conducted an interview with Robbie's mother Ruth. In it, a private conversation between Robbie and his mother was revealed—a conversation in which Robbie told Ruth he was gay. Local pastors dusted off their "evils of homosexuality" sermons. According to their logic, Robbie died because he chose the wrong path.

On the Sunday following Robbie's funeral, Reverend Damien gave the following sermon: "According to Romans, God's message is clear. Beware: men turning from the natural uses of women will result in death." Robbie's mother Ruth sat in the middle pew, unable to leave without disturbing the entire row. She never attended another service. Several of our restaurant's customers repeated, embellished, and propagated the story. Ruth and Robbie's sisters stopped eating at my family's restaurant in an effort to avoid the community as much as possible. Later that same year, in October and November, our cooks saved the used pie pans as usual, but Ruth never knocked on the kitchen door to collect them. The garbage bag the cooks kept for the used pie tins, overflowing in the corner of the kitchen, was eventually tossed into the restaurant's dumpster. Passing behind the restaurant one evening, trying not to draw attention to myself, I pulled the bag from the trash and put it in the trunk of my car. The next night I took it to Ruth's house. I knocked on her door but no one answered. I left the bag on the front porch near her rusted glider. No one ever said a word.

When I heard about Robbie's murder, I knew then that Daryl and I would never be together. We couldn't. Although he'd told me his golf scholarship made it necessary for him to leave for Liberty University just after graduation, I was certain Robbie's murder was the real reason. He was just as frightened as I was.

Robbie's murder taught me Fort Sackville's game early on and how to play by its rules. The unspoken commandments were that one can be gay but must not *act* gay; there is no talking about it, for acknowledgment is akin to acceptance; if ever brought up in conversation, the word *gay* must be whispered, as when one says *cancer* or *alcoholic*.

After stopping by the Quik Stop to get Dad cigarettes and then dropping Mom, Dad, and Cameron off at their house, I made my way through the church traffic to the restaurant. Upon entering the dining room, I could see the place was beginning to fill up with the after-church crowd. Employees from the back to the front of the house were in full Sunday dinner rush swing, with one exception: Trace. Trace did not show for his shift after church. He didn't show up for his shift the next day either. No one called. At his house, no one answered the phone, and no one answered the door. Trace had disappeared without a word. He had graduated midterm from Harrison High and was working at the restaurant to save money for the fall semester at whatever East Coast university would facilitate his Broadway dream. Since he wasn't in school, his friends had no idea what had happened to him. I feared the worst. It wasn't until a week after Easter Sunday that his father called and left a message with our cashier, telling us Trace would not be returning to Daniels' Family Buffet. His parents had sent him away.

I understood then with a terrible surge of dread what had happened: Trace had come out to them.

Chapter Thirteen

May

One month after Easter Sunday, I received my first letter from Trace.

Dear Grey,

Please don't let anyone see or read this letter! I'm not supposed to have contact with the secular world. I could get into a lot of trouble. One of my "brothers in Christ" here helped me mail this by sneaking it into a neighbor's mailbox. I'll explain it all to you later. I don't know what to do.

I'm sure you've heard by now that Pastor Daryl found a place to help me become straight. My mother and father brought me here a week ago. It's called Victory House on Dogwood Hill, and it's in Fergus Falls, MN. It's run by one of Pastor Daryl's Liberty University classmates. I'm sitting at a desk in my room, looking out the window at some river named Otter Tail. I can't believe I'm here. I can't believe they did this to me.

I stopped reading and sat in silence at the desk in my home office, eyes closed, my face resting in the palm of my hand. What had they done to Trace? Victory House? Dogwood Hill? What the hell was Dogwood Hill? In my mind I imagined dogwood trees atop Mount Golgotha, the hill upon which Christ was crucified, which reminded me of my Grandma Dixie and the dogwood tree in the backyard.

As a child, after Sunday school and church service at Wabash Valley Baptist, my mother and I would go to the Diner to eat Sunday dinner with Dad. One Sunday, the school lesson was about the dogwood tree. My class had been given a mimeograph copy of the tree to color in while we listened to the teacher—Mrs. Eisenhut, Marci's mom—teach the day's lesson. The paper tree captivated me; it looked like the one in Grandma's backyard, the one in which I would climb as high as I could and then sit in its top branches, reclining and balancing myself on a limb in order to watch its leaves glow a golden green in the summer sunlight above me. The tree was very old. It was as if I could feel its age in the wood. I wanted to color my paper tree to look just like Grandma Dixie's, with its flowers in the spring: heart-shaped white blossoms with faint pinkish-red marks at their tips and a green bud center. I was so intent on getting the color just right, struggling to use just enough of the pink and red crayon, that I totally missed the lesson. When we arrived at Daniels' Diner for Sunday dinner, since Dad was already busy with customers, Mom and I sat with Grandma Dixie at the front table while she manned the cash register. I showed her my dogwood tree.

"Grey, this is lovely. It looks just like the one at my house. Did you do the coloring?"

"Yes."

"Well, aren't you the artist. Why, you're going to be the next *Mo-net*." To this day I giggle when I think of her saying *Mo-net*, like fishing net. She was also fond of red wine. "I can't wait to go home and put up my feet with a glass of *caber-net*," she'd often say. Ours was a diner family, not a family that dined.

"Who's *Mo-net*?" I asked.

"Never mind," she said. "Just a famous painter I saw in a book once. So tell me the story of your tree. What did Mrs. Eisenhut tell you about the dogwood?"

"I don't remember."

"Well," Grandma said, "the dogwood is a very important tree. It's the one they used to make the cross that Jesus was crucified on. See the blossoms here? Each spring they remind us of His love, that He shed his blood for us. See how you put the red marks on the tips of the white petals? On the real tree, just like you've done here, those are symbolic of his being nailed to the cross." She pointed to the green center. "This is His crown of thorns. After they crucified Jesus, God said the dogwood tree would never grow large again. That's why they're so small—small enough for you to climb."

"Does God hate the dogwood tree?" I asked. I loved Grandma Dixie's tree. I couldn't imagine anyone hating a tree, especially one with such pretty springtime flowers and leaves that glowed.

"No, of course not. God doesn't hate anything. He made all of it. Everything belongs to him. He loves it all. He loves us all. God just wanted, I suppose, to give us a reminder of what His son did. That He wiped away our sins. That we always have the chance to be reborn. Just like the rainbow reminds us that God will never flood the earth again. God will never hurt us."

And yet Pastor Daryl, along with Mr. and Mrs. Thompson and Victory House, were trying to wipe away Trace's sin. They felt themselves God's representatives, empowered by Him to "fix" Trace.

After you and I talked, I wanted to wait for the right time to talk to Mother and Father. Then Pastor Daryl gave his sermon on Easter Sunday, and I felt like he was calling me out in front of the entire church. That night it was just Mother, Father, and I—we were having leftovers from my aunt and uncle's Easter dinner—and without thinking (Grey, I was so scared), I said, "Will you pass the mashed potatoes? Oh, by the way, I'm gay." You could have heard a pin drop. My father just sat there holding the bowl of potatoes midair, his face frozen. And then something did drop: my mother's fork and knife on her plate—the clanking sound startled all of us. She looked so shocked and fearful at the same time. I tried to explain to them that I'd always felt this way, but they wouldn't listen. I tried to tell them about you and your experience, but they said you were just trying to recruit me into your lifestyle. Now I'm here.

I don't know what to do.

I stopped reading. Had I sealed Trace's fate by telling him to be honest with himself? In telling him my story, had I given him the impression that his parents, like mine, would love him unconditionally? What had I done?

> *They called Pastor Daryl, and he came right over. He said he had been expecting me to pull something like this. He said he figured that I'd been talking to you. He reminded me of God's word, that homosexuality is an abomination in God's eyes. Then we prayed. He told Mother and Father that he knew exactly how to fix my problem, and he called Mike, the guy that runs this clinic. Pastor Daryl helped my parents pack my things, and we left the next morning before sunrise and arrived here way after eight p.m. that night. On the drive up, Pastor Daryl talked the whole time about how he had worked with places like Victory Hill in Lynchburg, Virginia, at the University there, as part of Liberty's internship outreach program. And how they'd been successful in bringing those poor unfortunate souls suffering from my same sickness to the light. That God's love had transformed their suffering into joy. They had been saved through Jesus and born anew in Him. Pastor Daryl said there is a reason they call it "pray the gay away." He went on and on and on for the entire drive.*

Pray the gay away? Did Daryl really believe that praying could change Trace's sexual orientation, *my* orientation? I knew Daryl was steadfast in his faith. But still, it was hard to erase the high school memory of my dick in his mouth. He was a smart guy. A 4.0 student all through high school. I had envied his intelligence back then. How could he have abandoned biology? Logic? Had Robbie's murder fucked him up that much? I did understand his veiled attack against me in church Easter Sunday; we had a history he obviously wanted to forget. I knew Daryl too well. He wasn't attacking Trace that day. He was sending a clear message to me: Pastor Daryl the new born-again man of God. But what had Trace done, other than trust him?

> *This place is a three-story brick house that was once painted white but seems to have washed out and faded over the years. The red color of the brick is seeping through. The front porch is white, wooden, and wide, very ornate with ferns and white wicker furniture and ceiling fans. There are gas lamps on each side of the front door. It looks like something a grandmother would live in. A long narrow sidewalk leads to the front steps.*

I wondered if Victory House was a modern-day, brick-and-mortar version of a psychiatric unit using shock therapy or lobotomizing patients—both procedures once used to "cure" homosexuality. Was Victory House operating under the same misguided principles in trying to "fix" Trace? What license or medical training was behind this treatment? Or was Victory House merely operating by biblical principles and interpretation?

> *Mike, the director of the program, met us on the front porch. When I walked up the steps behind Pastor Daryl, he introduced my parents and then me. Mike shook my hand and then offered to take my backpack. There were two men waiting in the foyer that stepped out and took my two pieces of luggage. I was only allowed to bring two bags, plus my backpack with some personal belongings or mementoes that were important to me. Pastor Daryl said they encourage the brothers in Christ—that's what I am now—to bring pieces of home with them. It's to make me feel more comfortable, he said.*

I wondered what Trace had chosen to take with him.

Mike took us into the front parlor and we sat down. Another guy came in and offered up some iced tea. Mike said he tried to bring a bit of the south to Minnesota—that Victory House always has iced tea on hand. After the drinks arrived, Mike asked me to recount my story for him. My parents just sat there with no expression. A couple of times my mother hung her head, and it looked like she was trying to hide tears. Mike said my story was not unusual. He said men like you lead many young men like me astray—guys trying to take advantage of youth and purity. That people like you see a light in boys like me and are drawn to it, but in perversion. That you want it and mistake the light for sex. What guys like you are really seeing in guys like me is Christ's love shining through and His attraction. But the light is meant to call one to Christ. It's not meant for self-gratification and defilement of the body temple.

We sat in the parlor for about an hour, and then the two guys that took my luggage came back and took me to my room. I said goodbye to Mother and Father and Pastor Daryl. Mike said he needed to talk to them in private but that I'd get to see them at breakfast in the morning before they left. He kept my backpack.

When I got to the room, my things were not there. There was a pair of pajamas, bottoms and a top like I used to wear in grade school, folded neatly on my bed. There was also a towel and a washcloth. The guys said my things would be delivered to my room tomorrow and that for the time being I could use the towels and sleep in the pajamas they'd provided. When they left, I walked over to lock the bedroom door, but there was no lock on it. I decided to just go to bed. I slept in my clothes.

I did get up during the night to go pee and found a guy stationed in the hall near the bathroom door. He smiled but said nothing. It was like he was a guard or something. I found out later there are night-shift guards posted on the second- and third-floor halls. They monitor bedroom and bathroom activity at night. Some of the guys here call them the Penis Police. I quickly figured out why there are no locks on the bedroom doors: they're allowed to do random room checks any time, day or night. I can, thank goodness, at least lock the bathroom door.

The next morning, I went down to the breakfast room and saw there were half dozen or so other men of all ages sitting and eating. These were my "brothers." And when I entered, Mother, Father, Pastor Daryl, and Mike were at a table together and motioned for me to join them. Mike asked how I'd slept. I told him okay. Mother asked if I'd slept in my clothes, that it looked like I had. I told her yes. For the most part breakfast was quiet. Pastor Daryl said grace, we ate, and afterward Father said that he and Mother needed to get on the road if they wanted to make it home at a decent hour. Father said they had a nice meeting with Mike last night and for me not to worry, that I was in good hands. Most importantly, that I was in God's hands, and that He was working through Mike and the good people at Victory House. We said goodbye, and I watched them pull out of the drive. Father waved. Mother wouldn't look at me. I could tell she was crying. Pastor Daryl was smiling.

I have so much more I want to tell you, but I need to go. I have a pretty tight schedule here with Bible study, behavior modification class, group therapy, private therapy, chores, and development of my discipline and my restoration plan. Please don't tell anyone I sent you this letter. I don't want to stay here any longer than I have to. I get my first evaluation on the fortieth day. The whole thing is supposed to take six months. I hope to be home soon after.

Sincerely,
Trace

I sat there, motionless, trying not to vomit, the sour acid rising in my throat. What had I done?

I spun around in my chair and threw up in the paper shredder receptacle next to my desk. The pungent smell of bile gagged me, and I threw up again.

What had I done? What had Daryl done? Daryl went to Liberty University to escape his own demons, but how could he do this to Trace?

DEAD TEEN'S GAY LOVER ARRESTED ON GRAND JURY INDICTMENT

By Foster Lawrence
Fort Sackville Sentinel staff writer

FORT SACKVILLE, Ind. — A Fort Sackville Community College law enforcement student was arrested on a grand jury indictment issued in connection with the mysterious death of a Fort Sackville, Ind., teenager last May.

Riley Salters, 21, of Greenfield, Ind., was arrested at his parents' home and charged with obstructing justice in the death of 18-year-old Robbie Palmer, said Fort Sackville prosecutor Dallas Ellerman. Ellerman said the charge stems from "secreting a dead body."

Salters told police he and Palmer were sitting on a stoop while attending a party in Fort Sackville when Salters fell asleep. He said he awoke to find Palmer dead, then panicked and left the party. Salters denies charges that he took the body to a drainage ditch located on Highway 41 South near the Knox Road exit. He does not know how Palmer died.

Salters will appear in court next week to face two misdemeanor charges for illegally moving a dead body and moving a dead body without notifying the coroner.

His defense attorney Eli Montgomery entered innocent pleas on the charges. A trial date has not been set.

Two autopsies were performed on Palmer's body when it

was found on May 17 last year but failed to determine the cause of death.

Rumors regarding the alleged murder of Palmer and those attending the party have spurred antigay harassment, including an anonymous citywide mailer campaign citing biblical text and "God's punishment against homosexuals," as well as scathing editorials in the Fort Sackville Sentinel.

Ellerman maintains that he will continue to treat the investigation as if it were a homicide but feels confident that Salters' arrest is a "major step in solving the Palmer case."

Chapter Fourteen

June

After Trace's letter, I felt the need to talk to Rio. Over Christmas, he'd invited me for a summer visit, and now thoughts of him began to resurface.

During my drive to Miami Beach from Fort Sackville, the anticipation of spending time with Rio began to build. I was looking forward to seeing him again.

When I arrived, I parked my car in his parking garage guest spot. Rio met me at my driver's door and he gave me a hug.

"Do you have luggage?" Rio asked.

"My backpack," I said, retrieving it from the passenger seat. "And a suitcase in the trunk." I popped my Infiniti G-35's trunk. Rio reached in and retrieved my suitcase.

"I'm so glad you're here. You're going to stay more than a week, aren't you?" he asked.

"I thought we'd just play it by ear," I said.

"It's no big deal. Really," Rio said. "I want you to stay. It sounds as if things are heating up in Fort Sackville."

"It's crazy. I don't understand what Daryl's beef is," I said.

"I told you what it is—he wants to fuck that boy."

I still couldn't wrap my mind around the possibility of Daryl being a pedophile. He couldn't be. "Daryl is gay, yes, but not a gay guy that goes after kids," I said. "He's a lot of things, but not that." We walked toward the elevator door in the parking garage.

"Well, with Daryl it appears there isn't much difference between a kid being seventeen years old or eighteen years old. Legal or illegal, it seems to me the good pastor has some residual issues remaining from high school."

"Don't we all?" I said as the elevator doors opened and we stepped in.

"Suppression and denial of oneself is a dangerous cocktail, Grey. And speaking of cocktail"—Rio's eyes lit up and he flashed his crooked grin—"I got a new bottle of Grey Goose La Poire vodka. I'm thinking we need some peartinis!" He slapped my ass and gave me a wink.

"You know, sometimes you can be really gay," I said. The elevator doors closed, and we began our ascent to his penthouse.

When the elevators doors opened, I saw the new piece of furniture. It was a midcentury mahogany-and-glass display cabinet near the dining room, loaded with Rio's martini glasses that he'd collected during his travels.

"You finally found a display cabinet," I said, stopping to admire it.

"And it lights up," Rio said, stopping to flip the wall switch.

"Oh, look at all these choices for my peartini!" I said, mocking Rio's earlier enthusiasm.

"Oh no, girl! Those are for show. You break stuff, so you get the cheap martini glasses from the kitchen," Rio said as he rolled my suitcase toward his bedroom. From his room he called to me, "I put clean towels and washcloths in the bath—I figured you would want to shower after your drive."

"Yeah, I'm going to. It's been a long day."

With my backpack in tow, I headed to the bathroom. During my shower, I heard Rio rattling around the condo. All I could think about was how I was at Rio's in Miami Beach and how he was happy, and that I would eventually have to return to my life in Fort Sackville. My life was indeed fucked up.

Sometime in the middle of the night, I arose from Rio's bed and went into his living room to sit and stare out across his terrace at the Miami skyline in the distance. I was having a hard time falling asleep and didn't want to wake him. Soon after I settled myself on his sofa, I heard his soft bare footsteps coming down the hall from his bedroom.

Walking into his shadowed living room, he asked, "Are you awake?"

"Yes."

"Do you want something to help you sleep?"

"No. I'm okay," I said.

"Are you sure?"

"Yes."

"Why aren't *you* asleep?" I asked.

"*You're* keeping *me* awake,"

"I am?"

"I'm worried about you," Rio said. "Are you sure you're all right?"

"I guess being here is stirring up the past," I said. "I was thinking about how I treated you, how we treated one another when we were together."

"That's over and done with. You and I both know we were young, dumb, and full of . . ."

"Yeah, yeah," I said, interrupting him.

Pausing for a moment, I watched as Rio sat in the chair opposite me wearing only his short blue cotton boxers, his face no longer veiled in shadow. From the window behind me the tropical moonlight fell softly upon his skin, washing his trimmed black-haired chest in an amber angelic glow.

"Do you remember our first date?" I asked.

"Now look who's fishing for a story," he said, grinning. I knew he was referring to our conversations over Christmas at Teana Faye's. "Of course I remember."

A week after I first met Rio at Teana Faye's, and following several long-distance late-night phone calls, I invited him to Fort Sackville. He drove up for our dinner date at the China Palace on 2nd Street near the college. The Chinese restaurant had a fairly substantial carryout business but rarely any customers in its dining room. Students from Fort Sackville Community College were employed as waitstaff—the restaurant was within walking distance of their dorms—so I knew, considering locals rarely mingled with the mostly out-of-town student body, that no one would recognize me there having dinner with a stranger.

Sitting among the Fingerhut-inspired Chinese decor—paper lanterns, gilded dragons, and bonsai trees painted on the walls—Rio looked a bit out of place in his paisley, coffee-colored long-sleeve shirt and dark denim jeans. It wasn't the bold paisley of my grandmother's sofa or drapes but soft, tear-shaped, cream-in-coffee whirls. During the meal it did occur to me, after a couple glasses of wine, that his paisley began to look like cartoon versions of spermatozoa spinning wildly about his chest.

I laughed.

Spermatozoa. How did I know that word? From health and safety class in high school? In my mind, I saw a sepia-toned 8 mm movie of Captain Spermatozoa and his band of thin-tailed tadpoles racing upstream like salmon, jumping over one another in their frenzied attempt to be first.

If Rio and I have sex tonight, their journey would be fruitless, I thought.

"What are you thinking?" Rio asked. "You have a curious smirk."

"Oh. Sorry. I'm just really enjoying this evening," I said.

"Don't be sorry." He smiled. "So am I."

I returned my focus to Rio. In an attempt to take my thoughts away from tadpoles, I imagined him without his shirt. *What is that saying? Something about the carpet matching the drapes?* I felt my face flush with heat.

He was handsome sitting there. Placed. Feet firmly rooted. Owning his spot in the world—my world. I wondered what he was thinking. *Is he looking at me the way I'm looking at him? Is he wondering if he'll be staying the night? Is he thinking about sex? God, I hope he's not picturing me without my clothes on.*

There was a calm ease about us through dinner—silent recesses between stories, a comfortable quiet. The conversation wasn't forced; it slipped effortlessly between our pauses.

After dinner, I drove Rio around Fort Sackville. He'd never been to my hometown. Unlike me, his life had been lived both in rural Indiana along the Ohio River and in Miami. When he was younger, he'd ridden dirt bikes along gravel roads, among cornfields, and in the river bottoms, as well as gone surfing, scuba diving, and deep-sea fishing. He'd gone to high school in Miami and graduated from the University of Miami School of Law.

We returned to my house. I offered him a beer. He complimented the shadowed lighting in my living room and the overstuffed sofa on which we were sitting; its milky cotton fabric went well with his paisley shirt. After becoming the restaurant's general manager, I set about creating my own beach-inspired bungalow in colors of a tropical sunset, inspired by my love of all things Florida. Rio's tan skin fit in to a tee.

"So, what do you want to do now?" I asked.

He moved closer to me. We kissed.

"If I don't watch myself, I may do something," he said. "Like kiss you again."

"Then don't watch yourself."

And it was then I lost my awareness of everything with the exception of what Rio was wearing—or rather, what he began not wearing—and the smell of his cologne. I could feel the presence of him; he filled the moment. I snatched from my mind the prospect of saving myself from him. *This is nice. This isn't the backseat of an Oldsmobile or a secret black basement. This is my living room.*

His hand pressed warm against my back as he rested me softly on the sofa. Lying there unclothed, my hands caressed his naked torso, our bodies dissimilar, his contours fully molded. I felt inadequate, embarrassed by my physical appearance; Rio did not seem to agree. There was a channeled energy between us. With his chest mounting in deep breaths, he weighed himself upon me, his skin touching mine. Ours became a physical understanding.

Nearly naked, with the exception of his Ralph Lauren ankle socks, we worked nearer and nearer and became accustomed to each other's rhythm. He felt safe and slippery, full of curious fuel. My world had become white-hot, clear, followed by sweet heavy breath.

"I think you are beautiful," he said, his words steaming my ear.

"You do?"

"Yes." Hesitating, he lifted his head from my shoulder. His hazel eyes set sight on my blue ones. "Can I ask you a question?"

"Yes."

"Do you believe in love?"

"I've never felt it myself." I said. "I don't know." This feeling was intense, different from what I'd first felt for Daryl back in high school.

"I've always believed."

He kissed me, then returned his head to my shoulder.

Looking at Rio sitting there in the shadows of his South Beach living room so many years later, I contemplated why things had ended between us the way they did.

"Instead of fighting with each other, why didn't we fight *for* one another?" I asked.

"I think in our own way that's what we were doing," Rio said. "There was just a lot of white noise, a lot of distractions."

"It's so confusing." I paused a moment and then scooted up on the sofa, propping myself on the pillow that just a second before had cradled my head. "I never told you that after we broke up and you moved away I thought about killing myself," I said.

Something about telling secrets in the dark made it easier.

"What?" Rio asked.

It was a late December night after work, and I was sitting in my brand-new Ford Expedition with the garage door closed, the windows of the SUV down, and the engine running. I don't know how long I sat there. Death, I thought, would be a relief from my false life; reparation for not getting my college education; the sentence for being stuck in the family business; for not having the spirit to be honest; for feeling trapped.

I closed my eyes.

In that moment, Ashley—my four-year-old Doberman, a gift from Rio, one I kept after our breakup—began scratching, clawing at the side door of the garage. Her whimpers became howls and pierced something inside me.

I remembered what Rosabelle had said.

I shut the motor off. Opened the door. Walked out of the garage, then sat on the sidewalk outside. Ashley sprang upon me, nudging my cheeks with her nose and sniffing about, assessing my condition.

Rosabelle once told me a story about a time in her life when she felt overwhelmed, during her last relationship with a guy named Eugene. "That crazy son-of-a-bitch Buick salesman," she called him. "Everything had become too much."

She took pills.

I don't know the details of that night, but she was rushed to Mercy Memorial's emergency room, which resulted in a few days' recovery with evaluation in the fifth-floor psychiatric ward. She was then released, no follow-up care needed. It was a moment. An emotional hiccup. Nevertheless, some people kept saying, "You know, she spent time on the fifth floor."

"I wanted to bury my head in the sand," she said. "I hid at home for almost a week. I unplugged the phone, locked myself away."

"Did you know people were talking about you?" I asked.

"Yes. Of course. They talk about others. Why not me?"

"Weren't you pissed?"

"Hell yes! But then my friend Frank showed up Friday night and started knocking on my door. Relentless. He wouldn't give up. I had to let him in. He told me to shower, find my best dress, my boldest jewelry, to make myself up like no tomorrow. *We're going out for dinner and then barhopping,* he said."

"Did you go?" I asked.

"He talked me into it after a couple of cocktails. Driving to the Executive Inn, he told me I was going to walk in smiling with my head held high. I was to stroll through the dining room waving hello while stopping at every table along my way. I had to make sure everyone saw me. Make sure they knew I was there."

Rosabelle said Frank wanted her to take ownership—confront the community, the rumors; destroy their power. Nothing could be proven. "Do it," he said, "with sincerity. Don't ask them how they're doing. Tell them what a wonderful evening *you're* having. Show no weakness." Rosabelle had been masticated by Fort Sackville. That night she made them choke on it.

"You need to do the same," she'd said to me.

Rio held his gaze with mine. It was intense. I felt his compassion, his concern, his kind heart. "We'd been fighting," I told Rio. "Every time we saw one another it was an attack. I was over the restaurant, over Fort Sackville. I was over it all." I said. "But I couldn't leave. Even after you asked me to leave with you and move here."

"You never said anything," Rio said. "Why didn't you tell me?"

"We could barely be in the same room together. How was I supposed to?"

"Do people in Fort Sackville know? Do your parents know?" Rio asked.

"No. No. I never said anything to anyone. You're the only one that knows. I just don't think I can ever be my authentic self in Fort Sackville. God knows I've tried to play the game."

"You've never tried to be your authentic self there," Rio said quietly, without accusation.

"I'm afraid to."

"Grey, you've got to face it sooner or later."

I had been struggling with whether or not to come out to customers and restaurant employees for years. Robbie Palmer was murdered because he was gay. Trace had been shipped off because he came out. Daniels' Family Buffet was steeped in the scandal of it. Accusations and associations were being hurled my way. What would the community and restaurant customers do to me? What repercussions would I face if I were to be honest with others and myself? Living one's truth in a large city seemed simpler than in a small town. Would Rio feel the same way if he were living in Mount Vernon, his mother's hometown? He'd been absent from my daily life for too many years. To whom was I supposed to turn for guidance? Who was going to tell me things were going to be okay? It didn't feel like they were. What I really wanted was for Rio to carry me to the bedroom, for us to continue talking while holding one another, like we once did: our arms holding each other tight, my head on his shoulder, feeling and listening to him say in a warm whisper, "It's all right, baby."

I missed that feeling.

Chapter Fifteen

July

I spent ten days with Rio in Miami Beach and then returned to life in Fort Sackville and Daniels' Family Buffet. In mid July I received my next letter from Trace. The summer had begun heating up, along with the gossip surrounding Trace's absence and my involvement in it. Mr. and Mrs. Thompson were still eating in the restaurant but refused to acknowledge me. Sometimes they dined with Pastor Daryl and his family.

Mr. and Mrs. Thompson, along with Pastor Daryl and his family, came to the restaurant for Sunday dinner the weekend before the Fourth of July Fort Sackville Founders and Follies Celebration, that festive time when everyone in town, it seems, dons their American Revolution getups: the men in brown costume with tricorn hats carrying reproduction muskets, and women in bonnets and calico prairie dresses playing mother and nursemaid to the revolutionaries. Spectators gather on the original site of the fort near the Wabash River to watch participants reenact its capture from the British, complete with powder horns and cannon fire. Every year, at night, after the battle's been won and the fort captured, fireworks are set off from the Illinois side of the river.

This Sunday, I was standing at the restaurant's buffet as the Thompsons moved down the line. I watched as Mr. Thompson picked through the steam table pan of fried chicken; I knew he was looking for a leg.

"If you're wanting a leg, Mr. Thompson, we've got a fresh pan of chicken coming out in just a moment," I said. He did not reply and kept his back turned to me.

"If you let the waitress know what you want, as soon as it's ready she'll bring it to your table," I continued. It was clear I was being ignored. Even those few customers nearest the Thompsons heard me and acknowledged my offer with a smile and nod. Pastor Daryl and his family were a few steps ahead of the Thompsons. They too refused to recognize my presence. That Sunday we had fewer diners than the Sunday before. Business was slowing.

And my father's illness was advancing. Although sales were down, we chalked it up to the recent spike in gasoline prices, caused by our nation at war in Afghanistan and Iraq. Everything had increased, including food costs. But I knew it was more than the national economy. Once, it was expected, understood, that customers on Sunday would wait upwards of an hour before being seated. Now there was barely a line. It was as if the loss in revenue was reflected in the restaurant's empty Formica tabletops. Fewer and fewer customers were filling the chairs, which meant Mom and I had to move some staff to part-time and let some staff go.

Mom and I tried to keep the town chatter at bay by assuring our employees and remaining customers that the world had indeed gone crazy but that things would straighten out. They always did. The restaurant had weathered national and local economic downturns before. We held an employee meeting to instruct everyone on what to say and how to address town gossip, which was beginning to reach a fever pitch. Our employees were aware. We told them that in order to maintain business as usual, we *all* needed to avoid involvement; we *all* recognized the restaurant as our lifeblood, and we couldn't do or say anything to jeopardize it—we could not piss off the Sunday Christians. Grandpa Collin always said Monday through Saturday paid the bills but Sunday was profit.

Without fail, Sundays were our busiest day of the week. Mom and I worried. We had seventy employees, two-thirds of whom were full time. Many had worked for our family for twenty-plus years. We had payroll, bills, taxes, a mortgage, utilities, and peoples' livelihoods to consider and protect. We had listened to the vitriolic gossipmongers and local pulpits after Robbie Palmer's murder back in the '80s. We had witnessed their power. We could not allow our business to be affected by this current scandal involving Trace Thompson. I wrestled with guilt. By reaching out to Trace that Friday night after closing, without realizing it, I had set in motion both his potential destruction and the destruction of my family's business. My dad was aware something was taking place.

I wanted to be an openly gay man. I wished I could have the life in Fort Sackville that I'd experienced in Miami Beach. The kind Rio said I never tried to have. I told myself I had the ability to make my own happiness. It was all about perspective, how I chose to see my life. I wanted to believe that I could lead an authentic life in Fort Sackville, Indiana. After all, it wasn't as if I were marching down Main Street in a gold lamé Speedo with a gay pride flag screaming, "I'm queer, I'm here, get used to it!" I was being respectful of others and of the restaurant—most especially the restaurant. There was a history to consider greater than my happiness. Dad accepted the explanation regarding the slipping sales. "That fucking George 'Dubya' Bush killed the economy," he'd say. But I sensed that Mom felt as I did—that something local was at work, and Pastor Daryl's smile was behind it. That summer, she and I watched the restaurant's customer count decline.

When I opened Trace's second letter, all of this was swirling about in my mind like the muddy whirlpools in the Wabash River:

Dear Grey,

Hello. I hope this letter manages to get to you. The way things are now, I have no idea if you even got my first letter. I hope you did. If you are getting my letters, please do not share them with anyone. Don't let anybody see them or know I'm writing you. I could get into so much trouble if they ever find out I'm mailing letters.

I don't know where to begin. I kind of lose track of the days, but I know it's been at least a month, maybe six or seven weeks since I sent you my first letter. I finally got my things. After I arrived I told you they took my bags and backpack. They searched through everything and disposed of the items that were considered gay. No Calvin Klein underwear—especially boxer briefs. No tank tops, no tight-fitting pants or shirts, no sandals or flip-flops. They took me to buy new underwear and clothes to hold me until we all went shopping later. There can be no jewelry—a watch is the only exception for single men, and a wedding ring for married men. If a man wants to wear a necklace, it must be a cross, so that's the only thing they let me keep: my gold crown of thorns cross necklace Pastor Daryl and the congregation gave me after the Riverfront Festival of Lights soloist competition I won in Evansville last Christmas. There can be no secular music, only Christian, so they confiscated my Celine Dion CDs and my CD player.

The counselors here keep us really busy. I've met all the guys—there are eight total. The ninth guy, Jeff, left about a week ago. It was his second time here. He was in the attic room. My room is on the second floor. There are four rooms and a shared bath on the second floor and the same on the third floor. All the rooms are single occupancy to help us avoid temptation. The house is really old but has been well taken care of. This neighborhood is some kind of historic district. But you'd never know we are here. There's no sign or anything in the front yard saying, "Hey, there are gay guys in this house." What neighbors I've met seem friendly enough. Most of the guys in here know the postman's schedule and sneak letters out. Jeff is the one that taught me how to do it. He was a nice guy. I'm going to miss him. They put his name on the chalkboard in our group therapy room. They call it the Resurrection Room because it's where we are born again into our heterosexuality. They asked me to add Jeff's name to the list of guys' names on the chalkboard that have either quit the program or are considered "backsliders"—ones who have fallen back into homosexuality. During our group therapy meetings there is always one empty chair that symbolizes these guys. Tonight I am in charge of leading the prayer for Jeff, in hopes that he returns to Christ and Victory House. I kind of hope he does come back. He reminds me of you.

Things can get pretty intense in the Resurrection Room. It kind of freaks me out, especially when the conversation is about those that refuse to change and then we are asked to pray that the Lord let them die so they can no longer spread evil. They pray that in death these lost souls on the chalkboard will find peace that passes all understanding in the next life. I usually just bow my head and force my mind to go blank. I can't pray for anybody to die.

I was assigned a prayer partner the second week I was here. His name is Keenan. He is a black guy from Chicago's South Side that got really involved in the crystal meth scene there. He is probably about your age. He said he used to "sell himself" on the "down low" to mostly married men. I can't say I don't like him, but his stories freak me out. He's done some really wild stuff. And I kind of feel like he's hitting on me sometimes. Keenan says that homosexuals are just confined straight people who have been deceived into thinking they're gay. He says meth only exacerbated his feelings toward men, but once he was cleansed of his addiction he began to see the life that God has been calling him to live. He says, "Healing is a process, a walk with Christ." He said he used to stay up for days at a time, his life controlled by meth. Now Christ controls his life. He said being gay is only an identity, like being a meth addict, or living in a particular state, or being a certain kind of athlete. "Michael Jordan once identified himself as a basketball player," Keenan said. "It was his identity. But when Michael retired, he no longer was a basketball player." Keenan is no longer a meth addict and is no longer gay. He says we can change our identity. To be honest I'm really confused. Mike, the director of the clinic, says that Keenan is the perfect example of what God's love can do. That we can all walk in Christ's light and have our prayers answered just like Keenan. Keenan sometimes is one of the Penis Police. It kind of freaks me out that he may come into my room one night.

Three times a week the guys and me have to participate in behavior modification. It is usually in groups of four. They teach us how men are supposed to sit and cross their legs. I have to practice placing my right ankle on my knee—that is the only way. We go shopping for men's clothes at JCPenney and Sears. We are not allowed to shop in a mall and by all means must avoid Abercrombie & Fitch! They've even taken us to batting practice and bowling. I hate baseball. I can swing a bat and catch a ball. I played on the Fort Sackville YMCA team all through grade school and middle school. I'd rather sing. Director Mike says I can sing, that Christian music is the opportunity for me to do so. When I told him I wanted to star on Broadway one day, he said I could. That one day God would answer my prayers and Broadway would see a Christian musical. But until God is ready for that to happen, and only if Broadway recognizes God's plan, will I be able to sing there. Until then, I must trust in Him and let Him lead me.

We don't really get to watch television or movies. Computers are completely off limits. Last night they showed us an old black-and-white TV show called CBS Reports. The episode was called "The Homosexual." Director Mike said the show had aired in the late '60s and over forty million people watched it—that Mike Wallace was a consummate reporter, always did his research and was ready to present the facts, and that this episode stood the test of time. We discussed it in the Resurrection Room afterward. Some of the guys made really valid points about the information in the show. I'm beginning to think there is something seriously wrong with me. Maybe it's good I'm here. These guys and Director Mike might be able to help me. I'm just so confused, and you're the only guy I've ever talked to about my feelings. You didn't judge me. You know what it's like. Am I crazy?

I need to go. I have Bible study in an hour, and I haven't finished my reading. We are discussing Leviticus 18. Pastor Daryl has discussed this before in our youth group. I kind of know it, but I need to do a refresher just in case.

Again, please don't let anyone see this letter or the other one. There is something inside me that needs to send you these and tell you what is happening. Don't freak out. I'm not in love with you or anything like that. But you made me feel good about myself, and when I write to you I feel good about myself.

I hope everyone at the restaurant is well. I miss everybody so much. I wish you could tell them I said hello. But don't.

Sincerely,
Trace

P.S. I failed my forty-day evaluation. It looks like I'm going to be here the entire six months. Jeff told me before he left that everyone fails it.

I wanted to rescue Trace. I wanted to tell him he was not crazy, he was beautiful. I wanted to tell him he could follow his dream to Broadway. Yes, he was seventeen. Yes, his parents were currently in control, but he would be eighteen one day soon and free from their choking grip, free to make his own decisions, free to take charge of his life. My mind ached, trying to figure out a logical way to help him without making things worse. He'd trusted me, and now he was paying the price. But it seemed he still trusted me. Why else would he risk sending me letters? I wanted to tell him his parents ate in the restaurant and ignored me. I also wanted to tell him that Daryl and I had run into each other the weekend of the annual Fort Sackville Founders Day and Follies celebration.

Chapter Sixteen

July

Each year, the Daughters of the American Revolution set up their tent on Revolutionaries Row—also known as 1st Street—bordering the historic site of the old fort along the Wabash River. Local organizations like theirs, churches, and eighteenth-century-inspired vendors peddled their wares and fed the Fourth of July Fort Sackville Founders Day and Follies history buffs. For as long as I can remember, the restaurant has donated a dozen or so homemade cobblers to the DAR as part of their weekend raffle to raise funds for the organization. Most folks quietly joked that the raffle money was really used to pay the water bill for the DAR fountain, located in the center of southern Indiana's only roundabout on south Main Street.

I was walking back to the restaurant's delivery SUV after dropping off the cobblers when I ran into Pastor Daryl. He tried to ignore me, but I decided I would not give him that opportunity. I called out to him. He pretended not to hear. I quickened my pace.

"Daryl! I know you can hear me," I said.

"I have nothing to speak to you about," Daryl replied.

I stepped in front of him, blocking his path. "Yes. I think you do."

"Grey, you and I have fundamentally different values and lives now. You've made it perfectly clear. Your life's path is that of the Great Deceiver." Daryl tried to get past me. I stepped in front of him again.

"Great Deceiver? Are you fucking kidding me? The only deceiver here is you. You're deceiving your family, your wife, your kids, your congregation, and your community. I get it—you're not gay. Or you're trying to suppress your sexuality based on some mythological Moses who handed down edicts 3,500 years ago! Perhaps what happened between us—sucking each other's dicks, you remember that, don't you?—was just two teenagers fooling around. But it meant more to me. You ignored me afterward. And then Robbie was found murdered two weeks later. You left town. You never spoke to me again. Do you have any idea how that made me feel? The message you sent with your silence? My world crashed down around me. It was heavy stuff for a kid to deal with by himself. You were my best friend. I trusted you. It seemed afterward that you only cared about getting off—with whomever. Whenever. Me? Shanni? God only knows."

"That is not true, Grey. I was confused. I too was scared. I knew it was wrong. I was ashamed."

"Then why didn't you talk to me about it? I was scared also," I said.

Daryl paused. "I don't want to talk about this. It's the past. Leave it in the past, Grey."

"No. I won't. I want to talk about this."

Daryl tried once again to sidestep me. I grabbed hold of his right arm. "You're not walking away from me this time, Daryl."

"You're making a scene, Grey. Let go of my arm. You're embarrassing yourself."

"No! You're scared that I am going to embarrass *you*. Call you out in front of your precious Wabash Valley Baptist Church congregation. Let them know you're a queer just like me. Like Robbie Palmer. That I'm going to call you out like you did to me during Easter Sunday service, in front of my family, in front of my hometown."

"Grey, listen very closely to me." Daryl's tone was stern and hushed. "You are going to let go of my arm, and I am going to walk away. We will never speak about this or to each other ever again. Do you understand?"

"Fuck you, Daryl. You don't have the power any longer. You're not the hot guy in high school anymore. You're pathetic. Living vicariously through Trace; using him to work through *your* issues; trying to 'save his soul,' when really you're trying to save your own. No, Daryl!

You're the Great Deceiver. You've been the Great Deceiver since high school." I paused to catch my breath. "Did you fuck him, Daryl? Did you?"

His face turned suddenly white, his eyes wide with confusion. "What are you talking about?"

"Trace. Did you fuck him? Are you a pedophile? Was sending him away atonement for *your* sins? Trying to cleanse yourself?"

"Grey, you need help. Counseling. I'll not stand here and listen to this a moment longer." Daryl attempted to release himself from my grasp. I held firm and stood my ground.

"I see through you. No one else may, but I do. You left Fort Sackville confused and scared. You thought finding God would cure you. There is no cure for being gay, Daryl. You're even deceiving yourself." I let go of his arm. Daryl tried to compose himself. I could tell I had shaken him.

"Why are *you* so concerned with Trace?" Daryl asked. "What are your intentions with a teenage boy?"

"I see myself in him. I see you in him. He's scared, and I feel his fear. He's struggling with his identity, his sexual orientation, all the same things I struggled with at his age. The same things you struggled with at his age."

"*I* am not gay. We may have had one unfortunate encounter. As I recall, I was really drunk. You took advantage of my state."

"Oh my God! Only one—is that what you tell yourself? You were the one that initiated it! *You* came to *my* house."

"Grey, I'll not discuss this with you. I will, however, express my concerns regarding your inappropriate relationship with Trace Thompson. His family made it very clear to me that they want him keeping his distance from you. They don't like the idea of Trace working for a homosexual, let alone having conversations with one."

"Well then, how do you get away with it?" I asked. "And for the record, Trace sought me out. Probably because he sensed he could talk to me and not be judged."

"The Bible clearly states that homosexuality is an abomination in the eyes of God," Daryl said.

"Yes, and it also states that those given to gluttony should take a knife to their throat. Are we going to read that one literally too? If so, you better tell Myrna Boil to start to slicing!"

"You really have gone over the edge, haven't you?" Daryl said coldly.

"Daryl, you and I both grew up in the church. We can bandy word for word, scripture for scripture, all afternoon long. I understand that we have fundamentally different perspectives regarding the Word. But you're killing Trace. You're killing countless local gay teens with your words. Don't you feel any compassion at all?"

"It's my job to bring the unwashed to His light. God called me. He tested me and then He called me. I failed the test with you. But I was saved by His grace. It's my job to save others who might fall prey to homosexuality. You were trying to convert Trace to *your* lifestyle."

"*My* lifestyle? What kind of crap is that? And you think *I'm* the one that's gone over the edge? You're something else, Daryl. If anything happens to Trace, you will be the unwashed one. You'll have his blood on your hands."

Daryl began to walk away.

Standing there alone, a good distance from Daryl, I called out to him again. "You know what else the Bible says? *The soul of Jonathan was knit with the soul of David, and Jonathan loved him as his own soul.*" Daryl kept walking toward the festival. "I loved you once, Daryl! And I know you loved me too!"

Daryl stopped. He then turned to face me from across the parking lot. Motionless, he tried to maintain his pious composure, but I'd struck at the very core of his being. I paused only for a moment to register his look of contempt.

"You have no idea what you're doing to Trace," I said.

I turned and walked away. I got into the SUV and drove off, watching Daryl in my rearview mirror. He stood there alone in the parking lot amidst the sound of cannon fire and the acrid smell of gunpowder. I almost felt sorry for him.

PALMER MURDER TRIAL GRANTED CHANGE OF VENUE

By Foster Lawrence
Fort Sackville Sentinel staff writer

FORT SACKVILLE, Ind. — Riley Salters will not be tried in Fort Sackville, but lawyers, court employees, and law officers will be allowed to make public statements about the case following the rejection of a motion for a "gag order" by defense attorney Eli Montgomery.

A Fort Sackville Superior Court judge granted the change of venue. Salters will be tried an hour south of Fort Sackville, in Evansville, Vanderburgh County, Ind.

Riley Salters, 22, was indicted by a Fort Sackville grand jury on charges of obstruction of justice. He was indicted for allegedly moving the body of Robbie Palmer, 18, from a home on 25 E. 1st Street to a drainage ditch on Highway 41 South during the early morning of May 3. Salters and about a dozen other alleged homosexual men attended a party on 1st Street, where Palmer allegedly died.

Palmer's death has remained a mystery. A cause of death has not been determined, and no other charges have been filed. Salters faces two misdemeanor charges of moving a dead body and failure to notify the coroner of a dead body. Salters maintains his innocence. He told investigators he awoke to find Palmer dead, panicked, and left the party.

A Vanderburgh County Superior Court judge rejected defense attorney Eli Montgomery's request for a protective order and said both attorneys will abide by state supreme court guidelines on what attorneys are allowed to say.

During last week's hearing, Montgomery said the publicity surrounding the Palmer murder would make it "virtually impossible" for Salters to obtain a fair trial in Fort Sackville. A Fort Sackville Police report states the Salters was Palmer's "gay lover."

Court documents reveal that Montgomery stated in his change of venue request that "media accounts concerning this cause have contained an undue number of extra-judicial statements by the prosecutor, the press, and others relating not only to the progress of the investigation, but conclusions by said prosecutor and others calculated to prejudice the defendant."

Prosecuting attorney Dallas Ellerman rejected Montgomery's statement, saying, "I have never, ever made any kind of statements in this case concerning the facts or the defendant."

Chapter Seventeen

August

By August, the congregation of Wabash Valley Baptist Church, and by proxy the rest of the community, began to steer clear of Daniels' Family Buffet. Loyal customers who had eaten with us for generations simply quit coming to the restaurant in a show of allegiance to Pastor Daryl, or to avoid perceived association and support of the restaurant and my family. Grandma Dixie had been right all along: owning a family business meant having the community involved in your everyday life. There was no way to keep folks at bay.

My parents began to receive letters in the mail admonishing them for allowing me to manage the restaurant, and in doing so, trying to "convert Trace Thompson, an impressionable seventeen-year-old Christian boy, to homosexuality." Hate mail—mostly anonymous, some with signatures—began arriving at the restaurant. One woman even wrote a poem:

Daniels' Family Buffet was divine,
Its atmosphere, great food, and desserts
Gave our town a wonderful place to dine.
But like Eden, the apple, and the snake,
The sins of your son have destroyed Daniels'
Bringing upon it God's wrath in his wake.
Send Grey away, wherever to his kind.
Return to Christian ways,
While you still have time.
—A Loyal Customer NO Longer

We were getting stacks of hate mail, enough to be bundled with a heavy-duty rubber band. The Wabash Valley Baptist Christians were pissed. Answering my phone was not an option; it would likely be an angry, former customer cursing. "Go to hell!" one caller shouted. I replied, "I don't have to. I'm already there."

The restaurant began receiving calls too, and similar mail.

All of us, my family and our employees, were trying to work through the uproar. None of us were feeling particularly well. But my dad was looking especially rough. We never knew what each day would bring and were fearful each day that Dad would not survive another sunrise.

That first Wednesday morning of the month, a few minutes after eight a.m., my home phone rang. It wasn't until later that morning that Mom told me she thought Dad was having one of his good days and that's why they went to the restaurant early. She had wanted to gather up time cards and get started on payroll; they had planned to leave before the restaurant opened.

Rarely did I answer my home phone. I didn't care to be told I was a fag and I would burn in hell. But I answered it, and I heard my mother's voice screaming frantically through the receiver: "Come here! Now! Something's happened to your dad!"

"What?" I asked.

"Get here now!"

I ran across the lane and woke Cameron, home on summer break from the university, and told him to throw on some clothes; we had to get to the restaurant.

Only minutes after Mom's phone call, Cameron and I pulled into the restaurant's parking lot amidst the flashing lights of an ambulance, fire rescue, and two fire trucks. *What the hell happened? Why this kind of response?* It seemed all of Fort Sackville's emergency medical personnel had arrived. Their presence alone would send tongues wagging all over town. I could imagine the gossipmongers: "CJ Daniels' gay son has ruined the business; CJ's had another heart attack. Probably got his bank statement."

The EMTs were gathering their gear, rushing through the front door.

I pulled around back, parked, and Cameron and I entered through the back kitchen door and ran through the kitchen into the office. My mother, standing along the back wall of the office, was crying hysterically. Dad was gray and motionless on the floor in front of his desk. The EMTs began resuscitation. He wasn't breathing. He had no pulse.

I yelled to Mom across the commotion, "What happened?" There'd never been so many people jammed inside the restaurant office.

"He's dead!" she cried. "He turned in his chair, his eyes rolled back, then he fell. He was so heavy. I tried to turn him on his back. I screamed 911. Then I called you."

"We got 'em," one of the EMTs announced.

My dad jerked.

"He's back. He's back with us," said the medic clasping the defibrillator paddles. He'd brought my dad back to life. In that moment it seemed there was no solid ground. I didn't know how to stand firmly in this new world. Nothing was what it had been.

The EMTs loaded my dad on the gurney. As they rolled him out of the office, an oxygen mask strapped to his face, he saw my brother crying. Dad tried to grab Cameron's forearm, but the medics were in the way and moved too quickly as they guided the gurney between tables and chairs. Mom, Cameron, and I followed behind. Dad couldn't speak. His eyes said, *I'm sorry,* as they wheeled him out the front door, then hoisted him into the ambulance. Cameron helped Mom into the back so she could ride with Dad.

"Cameron, get my car and follow us. Grey, you stay here," she said before the driver shut the doors. They sped off to Mercy Memorial.

I knew Mom would call when she knew something.

Cameron and I watched the emergency vehicles leave, the ambulance racing down Highway 41. My world was a vacuum collapsing within itself, like a Styrofoam cup taken to the depths of the ocean. So far, this morning had been the summer's nadir.

To an outsider, my Mom's words from the back of the ambulance would seem odd, considering moments earlier Dad was dead. Yet to me it was completely logical, understandable. For three generations the restaurant had been priority number one.

Cameron took off in Mom's car; I walked back into the restaurant. Outside the office door, our employees lingered, uncertain of what had just taken place. Their lives had become a pressure cooker too. All of us were exhausted. This turn of events added to our collective anxiety.

"Let's get back to work. We still have to open this place at ten thirty," I said. I didn't know from where that calm voice had come. I recognized it as mine, yet it sounded militant. Compassionless. All business. Slowly, the employees returned to their duties.

At the hospital, the cardiothoracic surgeon told my mom that Dad's right lung had stopped functioning, had become entrapped. A plaque had enveloped it. The lung could no longer expand, thus forcing his left one to overcompensate. The stress was too much for his heart. Adding to this, fluid had collected between his lung and chest wall, in the pleura. The fluid would be drained, but he was going to need surgery to remove the plaque. "It'll be like peeling an orange," the surgeon said. The operation required removal of the fifth rib on his right side in order to access the lung. Surgery was scheduled for two days hence. We knew surgery meant Dad would again spend months recuperating at home, his recovery capricious. It was the same surgery he'd undergone only a year earlier on his other lung.

A week later, during an afternoon break from work, I went to my parents' house. It was an opportunity to escape, if only for a few hours, the reality of fewer customers and declining sales. Even Old Man Atkinson, who was still showing up every day at ten thirty a.m., noticed we weren't as busy. "I knew you'd run this place into the ground when your daddy turned it over to ya. It's gonna die when he does. If not sooner," he said to me as I headed for the door.

Mom and I decided to sit outside on the front porch step to enjoy some fresh air. We kept the door cracked behind us so we could hear

Dad in case he needed something. He'd been discharged from Mercy Memorial the day before.

I loved the front door of their house. It was a nine-foot arched mahogany door with leaded glass. Its matching sidelight panels collected sunlight in a prism of color. After remodeling the gabled house a few years earlier, they had the yard professionally landscaped, its various annuals and perennials growing, blooming in the shades of the seasons. Sitting there looking at Mom's orange butterfly weed and yellow black-eyed Susans under the window of my dad's home office—ones like Grandma Augusta, my Mom's mother, once had in her yard—I realized it was the only moment of quiet we'd had together all summer. It was also an opportunity for us to talk.

"I get it," Mom said.

"What do you mean?" I asked.

"I get it. I understand my mother. You realize I'm almost exactly the age she was."

"I don't understand."

"You saw your dad's prescription bottles lined up on the bedside table—the heart medication, lung medication, Ambien, Lortab. The bandages. Antiseptic. His nebulizer. That rehabilitation thingy he uses to strengthen his lungs—inspiratory muscle training, they call it. All of it. He even said our bedroom looks like a goddamn hospital room."

"What are you saying?"

"I mean, I *get* it. The house in Hartwell, the one I grew up in. *My* dad's bedroom. The front one, where you and I used to sleep when you were little, when we'd stay with Grandma Augusta. It looked like a hospital room after *his* surgery. *My* mother had to take care of *him*. And raise my brothers, sister, and me. You're able to take care of yourself, but I still have Cameron to get through school. I still must help you run the restaurant."

After Dad's massive heart attack several years earlier, it had taken him a long time to bounce back from surgery. Then a year ago he'd had his first lung surgery. After *this* operation he looked and felt even worse than last time. And he'd lost a massive amount of weight and muscle.

"After my dad died, I felt guilty for not helping my mother more in caring for him," she said. "I get it now. I understand the pressure she was under. Why she acted the way she did. I'm the age she was." She paused, took a deep breath, and let it out slowly. "I don't know if he can survive this. If *I* can survive this."

I'd heard the story before. My grandpa Cecil McGregor had been a coal miner all his life. His dad had been one too. The Red Ember Coal Mine operated a few miles south of Hartwell, off Highway 67, near Beehunter, Indiana. My grandpa was pit boss. He worked for James Stackhound. My house on Kelso Creek Road across the lane from Mom and Dad—the one in which Rio had lived with me part of the time before our breakup, the one in which I still lived—had been Mr. Stackound's house. He had built it and raised his family there. When I was in grade school, before Cameron was born, my parents bought acreage next door to him and built their own house. The year I began managing Daniels' Family Buffet, Mr. Stackhound died and I bought his house from his estate.

And now Mom was telling the story again. She remembered that day in 1952. "A day like this," she said. "The doorbell rang. My brother Konner and I were in the living room fighting over Lincoln Logs. I heard Mom open the kitchen door, a quick, whispered conversation, and then she screamed."

Mr. Stackhound had come to tell Grandma Augusta that Grandpa Cecil had suffered a terrible mine accident. He'd been rushed to Mercy Memorial. His right leg had been crushed under a rail car, one that lowered miners into the earth's murky, underground corridors. Her dad had come home from the hospital after a month, his leg amputated at the thigh, a wooden prosthetic in its place. Their medical insurance only covered thirty days of hospitalization. He would need long-term rehabilitation. Recovery would have to be at home. He was homebound for a year.

I began to see the similarities.

"You have to remember all four of us were still living at home," she said.

My uncle Mathew was the oldest, then Aunt Kerry, Mom, and Mom's baby brother Konner. The house had two bedrooms and one bathroom. There were bunk beds positioned in what was supposed to be the dining room. Mathew's room was an enclosed front porch. Theirs was a seven-gabled prewar home, unlike my parents' four-bedroom, three-bath house, with a soaring fifteen-foot dining room window—a crystal cathedral, Grandma Augusta use to say. The horrific results of my grandpa's mining accident put my mom's family in serious financial distress. Having a husband to tend to and children to raise kept Grandma at home, unable to seek employment.

"That winter, Mr. Stackhound made sure coal was delivered to heat our house free of charge, which helped some during Dad's recovery. Dad was a company man, not union. He wasn't getting a paycheck. Mom had to get what meager assistance she could from social security benefits to see us through. We ate bean soup and cornbread almost every day."

"Are you afraid we're not going to eat? We own a restaurant, for Christ's sake. We eat there," I said, trying to lighten the mood.

"Kerry's bedroom became Dad's recuperation room. The whole feeling changed. I used to sleep there with her—big feather pillows, a cozy pink chenille bedspread. There was a metal lamp shaped like a tulip that sat on the nightstand. It was my favorite. When Dad moved in, everything switched. Mom had to keep layers of protective rubber pads over the mattress. She used white sheets so they could be bleached. The tulip lamp was replaced with a bedpan, urine sugar test strips, Tucks pads, and a small stainless steel spoon she would insert in my dad's rectum to help with his bowel movements."

My mom said the daily, familiar sounds of the house had ceased. "It was as if our home stopped breathing, its lungs entrapped too," she said. "Mathew and Kerry took over most daily duties, watching us kids."

She and her brother Konner were too young to help.

She spoke of her dad's bandages, blood blisters, his black-and-blue leg stump that looked like a burnt log. The often grotesque, humiliating recovery he had suffered. The morphine.

Grandma Augusta once told my mom that Mr. Stackhound said Cecil McGregor was one of the best pit bosses he'd ever employed. A year later, my Grandpa McGregor returned to work, but he was never fully himself.

"Things sort of went back to normal until 1965," Mom said. "*That* August the bottom fell out from under our world." Mom again told the story of how Grandpa McGregor had suffered a stroke while driving home from the coal mine. He was killed in the resulting automobile accident. Mom and Grandma Augusta were gardening among Grandma's butterfly weed and black-eyed Susans when the civil defense sirens sounded in Hartwell, alerting the town's two squad cars of trouble. Mom said she and Grandma Augusta sensed something terrible had happened to Grandpa.

"What, do you think the bottom's falling out from under us now?" I asked. "Is that what you're thinking?

"I don't know. It's just this all seems so familiar. That's why I said, *I get it*."

My conversation with Mom that August afternoon remains with me still, collected like sunlight in the windows of my parents' front door and refracted in multicolored prisms on the front porch floor.

GAY LOVER FOUND NOT GUILTY
IN PALMER MURDER CASE

By Foster Lawrence
Fort Sackville Sentinel staff writer

FORT SACKVILLE, Ind. — Riley Salters, 22, of Greenfield, Ind., and a former law enforcement student at Fort Sackville Community College, was found not guilty in the mysterious death of a Fort Sackville teen.

The charges against Salters stemmed from the mysterious May 3, 1986, death of Robbie Palmer, 18, of Fort Sackville, Ind., following an alleged homosexual gathering in Fort Sackville. Salters denied moving Palmer's body from a house in Fort Sackville and dumping it in a drainage ditch on Highway 41 South near the Knox Road exit, where Palmer's body was discovered by two young boys on three wheelers May 17th.

Defense attorney Eli Montgomery said, "Justice has prevailed, and this not guilty verdict effectively ends the prosecution's witch hunt and antigay harassment surrounding my client. Mr. Salters is innocent. His sexual orientation and his attendance at the party have no bearing on Robbie Palmer's death."

Fort Sackville prosecuting attorney Dallas Ellerman had hoped for a guilty verdict and that the maximum sentence for each charge be imposed. "This is an egregious error in judgment, a miscarriage of justice. The law and facts of the case have been blatantly ignored.

"Mr. Salters is a homosexual who attended a homosexual sex party. He knows how Robbie Palmer died. He disposed of the body."

Salters related the events of the night of the party on May 3, 1986, during cross-examination by Ellerman. He confessed to Fort Sackville police that he and Palmer were lovers and admitted he performed a sexual act with Palmer in the upstairs bedroom of the house located at 25 E. 1st Street.

The house was gutted by fire a few months ago. A Fort Sackville Community College student died in the blaze. The investigation is ongoing.

Salters said he and Palmer later left the bedroom and went outside to sit on the porch steps.

He passed out, continued Salters, and when he awoke he found Palmer's body beside him. Salters said he knew the Fort Sackville youth was dead because his body was cold and he was not breathing. Salters said he panicked and left immediately.

"I had never seen a dead person before, but you just know. When I woke up and realized he was dead, a shock came over me. It washed over me. I was placed in a situation I had no control over," commented Salters.

Ellerman asked Salters why he panicked, and the defendant replied, "I was afraid someone had tried to set me up."

Slaters explained that he was an outsider in Fort Sackville and knew only one person well—Palmer. Salters also admitted he panicked because he did not know why Palmer had died.

When asked by Ellerman why he did not notify the authorities about Palmer's death, Salters said he was afraid. "I knew my family would disown me if they found out I was gay."

Salters' immediate family was not present during the trial.

During closing arguments, Salters's attorney Eli Montgomery said the testimony of the witnesses for the prosecution indicated incompetence of Indiana law enforcement officials investigating Palmer's death. He also said the news media and local press implied his client was guilty of the crime of homosexuality, not the crime of obstruction of justice.

"He was scared and afraid and made an error in judgment."

Prosecuting attorney Dallas Ellerman concluded his closing argument by saying that "Salters's error in judgment is symptomatic of amoral, atypical, deviant behavior.

"We have more questions here today than we have resolved. This is one of the greatest cases of obstruction of justice I have ever seen. Salters threw Robbie Palmer's dead body into a drainage ditch for the turtles and fish to eat and rot. Robbie Palmer was not garbage. No one, no man, is garbage. Society has been greatly offended in this case. One question can be and should be answered today: is Riley Salters guilty? Yes, yes he is."

Salters was unavailable for comment.

Chapter Eighteen

September

September arrived. The summer had been long and hot, I was looking forward to a cooling-off spell. Dad was struggling to recover from his surgery, and each day he seemed to feel a little bit better, but I knew he would never fully regain his strength. It was Labor Day weekend, and Saturday at the restaurant was slow. Families were outdoors enjoying their last slice of summer. Cameron was home, and at his urging I took the day off and spent it at home, alone. I'd grown tired of people. Since he had offered to watch the restaurant, I thought a nap on my sofa in the study near an open window would be just the remedy I needed. And it was just after I had settled in that I received Trace's third letter—the mailman slipped it through my front door's mail slot.

I'd spent the summer months battling declining sales at the restaurant and community gossip circulated maliciously by Wabash Valley Baptist Church, the Thompsons, their friends, and Pastor Daryl. The struggle was taking its toll. Perhaps Trace's letter, I thought—or at least some of it, considering where he was—might have some good news. By my account, he only had about a month remaining. He'd be home soon. Everyone in my world, it seemed, was desperate for good news.

Dear Grey,

I want you to know that now you can share my letters with whomever you please. I'm asking you to share them. I've figured out how to solve my illness. My parents arrive today, and I'll be in my bath. They'll think I'm running late. I've chosen an honorable death—an alternative to the tyranny of my

> *parents, Pastor Daryl, and Victory House. My choice is the preferred method of the ancient Romans. I will end my suffering like Seneca. My name will not be written on the chalkboard in the Resurrection Room. My name will not be the whispered words of my "brothers in Christ" praying to God for my death and peace that passes all understanding. My story will not be that of a "backslider."*

Trace's parents' visit was the first since they'd dropped him off five months ago. Since it was Labor Day, he'd been granted a pass to spend the holiday weekend with them. It would be his first excursion away from Victory House. His mother and father were arriving at five p.m. on Friday to pick him up, and they were going to Spring Valley Retreat, an outdoor ministry owned by several evangelical congregations in southeast Minnesota. Director Mike had told Trace the retreat was about four hours from Fergus Falls, so Trace needed to be ready to go when his parents arrived. I found this out after Myrna Boil cornered Mom in the restaurant and told her every sordid detail. "As I was told," she said, "by Pastor Daryl from his private conversations with the Thompsons, Grey needs to know what he's done. The Thompsons want Grey to know."

I imagined Trace in the bathroom: I could picture the claw-foot iron tub, the white tile floor, and the white porcelain toilet, its water tank mounted on the wall above the seat, and a matching pedestal sink with a chrome-mirrored medicine cabinet framed above the faucet.

In the bathroom Trace is barefoot and bare chested. The floor feels cold beneath his feet. He folds his T-shirt, placing it neatly upon the toilet seat. He unbuckles his belt, then slips out of his blue jeans and white Fruit of the Loom briefs, folds them, and then rolls his brown leather belt into a tight circle, placing it on top of his T-shirt. Standing naked, he wears only his gold necklace and cross, fashioned to resemble Christ's crown of thorns. His buttermilk-pale skin and blond hair give a yellow contrast to the white Victorian paleness of the bathroom.

He walks to the tub and sits on the edge, turns on the hot and cold water, and adjusts the ancient chrome handles while placing one hand beneath the flowing water to gauge the temperature. After plugging the tub drain with the rubber stopper, he crosses the room to the bathroom door to check and see that it's locked. Steam rises from the tub, fogging the mirror as Trace returns to the tub and slips in.

At first the heat of the water stings, but his body slowly adjusts. The old cast-iron tub is three-quarters full as Trace leans forward, slowing the faucet to a trickle—he doesn't want it to overflow. Reclining, he looks at his body, his thighs, knees, and feet under the water. He considers the seventeen years he spent sculpting and molding it with sports he never wanted to play. He thinks about his voice, which he also sculpted and molded, but did enjoy improving. He thinks about his dreams of Broadway. He was supposed to be a dancer. His arms, torso, legs, and feet—with proper training—could have been a dancer's body. He has the voice. Trace studies himself, liking what he sees. He begins humming his favorite hymn, "Just As I Am." The song Pastor Daryl didn't let him sing on Easter Sunday.

"Trace!" the voice on the other side of the bathroom door shouts. It's Keenan, checking on him. "Trace, are you in there?"

"Yeah."

"Okay. Director Mike was wondering if you're getting ready. He was looking for you. He wanted me to remind you to be on time."

"I will."

"Okay. See you in a bit."

Trace sits up and slips off his necklace. Sinking back into the warm water, he holds the cross between his right forefinger and thumb. He was so happy the night he won the Festival of Lights soloist competition. Everybody's eyes were on him. Pastor Daryl was so proud. Trace remembers the small gift box and the silver paper in which the gift had been wrapped. He's worn the cross ever since. "This cross of thorns is to remind you, Trace, of what Christ did for you, for all of us. May you wear it willingly and walk mighty in His light," Pastor Daryl said. Trace positions the cross of thorns so it is inverted. Turning his left wrist upward, he slices his artery lengthwise, the first squirt of blood startling him. *It doesn't hurt*, he thinks. Not like he thought it would. Scraping his knees on the asphalt as a little kid hurt worse. He digs deeper, two more times, to open the vein wide. Then, placing the bloodied cross between his left forefinger and thumb, he turns his right wrist up and slices open that artery as well. This time the squirt of blood doesn't shock him. *My left hand isn't as strong*. It takes four tries to dig the artery open. *I can't believe it doesn't hurt*.

Bending his head, he slips the necklace back around his neck. The crimson cross of thorns nestles into its usual place on his chest. Relaxing back, he slips his wrists into the water, its warmth soothing his wounds. He watches his seventeen years of life flow from him quickly, all the pain gone, nothing left but the warmth and tenderness of the water's embrace.

Twenty minutes later Trace's heart stopped. The tub began overflowing—the cherry-colored water spilled and flooded the tile floor, then seeped beneath the locked bathroom door. The dark carpet in the second floor hall was saturated when the doorbell rang.

Trace's parents had arrived.

Myrna, glowing with the tragedy of it, told Mom that Mr. and Mrs. Thompson stepped into the front foyer and were greeted by the director.

"Welcome," Director Mike said. "It's so good to see you. Trace is excited about his weekend."

"We're excited to see him," Mr. Thompson said.

"Has he been well behaved?" Mrs. Thompson asked. "Keeping his room clean? Picking up after himself?"

"Yes. Absolutely. He's a fine young man. And he's made wonderful progress," Director Mike said.

"Great news," Mr. Thompson said. "We're looking forward to spending time with him at the retreat and hearing about his experience, about what he's learned."

"I think you'll find God has changed his heart." Director Mike motioned toward the adjoining room. "Have a seat in the parlor. I'll get him."

"Oh, Mike, do you mind if I go? I'd like to surprise him," Mr. Thompson said.

"Not at all. Do you remember which room is his? It's the last door on the left, nearest the bathroom."

Mr. Thompson nodded, then turned and ascended the staircase, while Mrs. Thompson and Director Mike stepped into the parlor and sat down. Keenan met them with glasses of iced tea.

Upon reaching the second floor hall, Mr. Thompson stepped onto the soaked carpet, his Rockport shoes sinking beneath his heavy step. He stood there a moment, shifting his weight from foot to foot, pressing his shoes into the carpet. Turning to face the staircase, he called out, "Hey, Mike! I think you've got a water leak."

Mike appeared at the bottom of the stairs. "Excuse me?"

"I think you've got a water leak. The carpet is soaked."

Mrs. Thompson appeared behind Director Mike, holding her glass of iced tea.

"A leak?" Mike asked doubtfully.

"Seems so. It's quite of bit of water from the looks of it."

Mike hurried up the stairs with Mrs. Thompson following. Soon all three were standing next to one another, shifting their weight back and forth in their shoes, pressing water from the carpet.

"This is strange," Mike said. "There are no water pipes on this end of the house. Only the bathroom at the end of the hall."

Mr. Thompson stopped shifting. He looked toward the closed bathroom door. Panic overcame him. He ran down the hall, his khaki pant cuffs soaking up the red-tinged water. Upon arriving at the oak door, he pounded his fist on the ornate, carved wood while trying to turn the doorknob with his other hand.

"It's locked!" Mr. Thompson said. "It's locked! I thought there were no locks on the doors. Trace! Trace! Are you there! My God, the door is locked!"

Mrs. Thompson dropped her iced tea. The glass, cushioned by the wet carpet, rolled toward the steps, then under the banister, and plummeted downward, shattering on the wood floor of the foyer below. "Trace!" she screamed.

In a moment, Mike was behind Mr. Thompson. He tried forcing the knob. Mr. Thompson pounded harder with both fists. "Trace! Trace! Unlock the door!" Other men who'd been going about their evening chores, preparing for dinner or doing yard work, heard the commotion and began appearing at the top of the steps. Mrs. Thompson stood as if frozen, gripping the staircase's second-floor newel post, her knuckles white. She watched as Director Mike and Mr. Thompson began using their bodies in an attempt to break down the bathroom door. On the third try, their body slams ripped the frame from the plaster-and-lath wall. Mr. Thompson and Mike fell on top of the door as it crashed upon the bathroom's tile floor. From the end of the hall, Mrs. Thompson saw her son's head turned toward her, resting on his right shoulder, his eyes open and fixed in a stare above the overflowing claw-foot tub. Standing on the landing behind Mrs. Thompson, Keenan caught her as she collapsed unconscious into his arms.

It had happened. There was nothing I could do. Although I finished reading his letter, Trace was dead. I was numb, cemented to my sofa, my mind blank.

Don't be angry with me or feel sorry for me. I have chosen this. I'm okay with it. My family is not like your family. They would have never been okay with me being gay. You're so lucky to have people that love you for who you are. I don't feel that. Mother and Father, even Pastor Daryl, always expected something from me. I was never going to have the opportunity to be myself. I'm a disappointment to them and to God. But I'm not disappointed in myself. I'm proud that I have the courage to end this. Please, Grey, don't be disappointed in me. I really wish we could've become friends. I would've liked having you in my life. I never had a brother. I kind of think of you as my big brother. Thank you for everything you did for me. Once I'm on the other side, I'm going to ask God to forgive me and then I'm going to ask if I can be your guardian angel. I'm going to protect you.

With love.
Your little brother,
Trace

I heard my front door open. A moment later, Cameron appeared in the doorway of my study, trying to catch his breath, his face red and sweaty.

"Trace committed suicide," he said.

I laid the letter in my lap and looked at my little brother standing there, visibly shaken, waiting for my reaction.

"I know," I said. "He just told me."

Chapter Nineteen

September

For years the transition of seasons from summer to autumn witnessed a surge in customer counts at the restaurant. This was the first year the count dropped significantly.

This particular Saturday night was the slowest I'd seen yet. Many of the regulars simply didn't show up. Early on that evening, I began cutting servers, bussers, and kitchen staff. At the height of what should have been our evening rush, I employed a skeleton crew. Two servers were able to manage the entire front of the house—an impossible task only a few months earlier. Rosabelle and Mae were stopping in more frequently in spite of the fact that Daniels' didn't serve cocktails—and Rosabelle was breaking her *I don't serve, I want to be served* dining rule.

Doc Vonderbreck seemed to have switched his daily dining habits also. He was coming in during his lunch break and in the evenings after working in his horse barn. "I always knew you were full of shit, Doc," I said as I approached his table. "But tonight you even smell like it."

"Ah, good ol' country living. It's good for ya. Horse shit on your boots and dirt under your nails says a lot about a man," Doc said.

"Yeah, it tells 'em you need a bath and clean boots."

"I take my bath on Saturday night. It's a ritual. Once a week, whether I need it or not," he said. "Going to after I leave here." Looking around the somewhat desolate dining room, Doc asked, "Where are the usual suspects? Business seems a little slow."

"I don't know, Doc. Something is up." He could read my facial expression and see the concern in my eyes.

"Grey, it's gonna be okay. Sometimes folks just like to let others know who's in charge—or at least act as if they're the ones in charge. It'll all turn out. Hell, when I went through my divorce I lost longtime patients. But I gained others. Folks will find their way back."

"I hope so, Doc. The numbers aren't good. I don't know how long we can keep it up."

"Y'all been around too long. You're not going anywhere," he said.

"Words of wisdom," I said. "But right now I have to get back in the kitchen and give our cook a break. She's got the whole thing to herself."

"All right buddy, take it easy and don't sweat it. Daniels' Family Buffet will rise again!" Doc said with a wink and a smile.

"Yeah, just like the South," I said.

As I walked away from Doc's table, I noticed some unfamiliar faces, new customers that seemed to also be showing up more frequently, but tonight it wasn't enough to make up for the loss of our regulars. Maybe Doc was right—my family and I just needed to batten down the hatches until this current storm passed.

After closing that Saturday night, I stayed to study the day's receipts, or the lack of them. I had no plans and decided to spend the silent hours catching up on what little bookkeeping there was. The numbers were not good; in fact, they were terrifying. The restaurant was failing fast. And I could not get Trace's suicide out of my mind.

The employees had gone home for the night and I was alone in the empty restaurant when I heard popping sounds coming from the back exterior wall. I got up from the desk chair, left the office, and headed toward the back service and employee entrance. As I walked through the kitchen, I spotted the yellow mop bucket filled with dirty mop water and the mop propped in a nearby corner. *They never empty the mop bucket. I've got to remember to do that before I leave.*

When I got to the door, I heard glass breaking, as if soda bottles were being thrown against the brick wall. I looked through the door's peephole but saw no one. My keys were in my pocket and the back door was locked, but it could be opened from inside by its emergency crash bar. Opening the door, the air curtain's fan began to whirl, and I stepped out far enough to look around.

In that moment, a glass beer bottle shattered on the exterior wall beside me. Startled, I jumped out of the way, dodging the blast, unaware that I had stepped away from the door. A muscular arm wrapped itself tightly around my neck. I heard the restaurant's back door slam shut behind me. While the muscled arm constricted my airway, I was kicked behind the knees and knocked to the pavement.

As best I could tell, there were three of them, shadows, two of similar height, standing in front of me in the dark parking lot. The one holding me seemed biggest, his breath beating the top of my head. I could smell rotgut liquor on him. I was sure they were local guys. I knew their kind. Perhaps they'd been drinking all day in the cab of a pickup truck or SUV while driving country roads, then later in a Main Street bar. I was certain they were young, the type that dressed up for church on Sunday after raising hell on Saturday night. "Queer baiting" was a game for them. They hunted in local parks, near the Wabash River, or on the campus of Fort Sackville Community College. Like buck hunting, out-of-towners were an easy eight-point score for them. A local was tougher to get; when found, he might garner fourteen points. Theirs was the same game once played by their fathers and grandfathers when hunting *niggers*. These hunters judged their prey by their alien physical characteristics or perceived differences in dress and demeanor. I'd been linked to Trace's suicide, my hometown was talking, and these good ol' boys were taking advantage of the town gossip to act and secure their bragging rights.

They wore black beanies, dark shirts, blue jeans, boots, and work gloves. Their shadowy farm-boy bodies, thick and stocky, were most likely beef- and corn-fed, developed in the melon fields south of town.

I had never been punched like they punched me. Forced to kneel by the Big Shadow, his arm holding me in position, his knees pressing my legs to the ground and his body pushed against my back, holding it erect, he laughed while the other two shadows began taking turns.

I felt their first blows to my face and head. "You like being on your knees, don't you, faggot," Big Shadow said. My ears and eyes filled with blood. *Why did I walk outside?*

After a round of punches, the shortest shadow stopped and walked to a parked truck while his twin shadow took swipes at my face, and each flinch of my body seemed to make him more elated, more sure of himself. Short Shadow returned with an open beer bottle. "Open your mouth and deep throat this, cocksucker." He forced my mouth open and shoved the bottle in. My teeth scraped the long glass neck and paper label, and the warm beer churned in my throat, burning my esophagus. I couldn't breathe. When he withdrew the bottle, I threw up on him and myself. "You fucking faggot. I thought queers swallowed," he said, and punched me in the jaw. He dropped the bottle; it rolled next to my leg.

"Don't touch his puke. The fucker probably has AIDS," Big Shadow said. His arm released me. I threw up again, then broke free. I grabbed the bottle by its neck and busted it on the pavement; the glass shattered, leaving a sharp, jagged bottleneck. I brandished it like a knife.

"Oh, the queer thinks he's going to cut us," Big Shadow said.

"Just leave me alone," I said.

"Oh no, fag. You're going to learn your lesson. You're going to wish you were never born."

"Look, I don't know what you want. I don't have anything to give you. If you just leave, I won't do anything. I won't say anything." All the while I kept taking swipes at the three of them, the broken bottle my only defense.

"You should have stayed away from Trace," Short Shadow said, the one that tried to force the longneck beer bottle down my throat.

"He only worked here," I said.

"We know you tried to get your faggot hands on him," he said.

I kept waving the broken bottle at them. "I never touched him. I was trying to protect him. I was trying to keep Daryl from him. We just talked."

"Well, you see where talking got you," Big Shadow said.

Short Shadow and his twin charged me. I cut Short Shadow's right arm.

"Fuck! He cut me. The faggot cut me. You're gonna die now, queer."

In that moment I felt the car keys in my pocket. There was no way I could unlock the back door of the restaurant and get in before getting caught. I could make it to my car though; it had a remote keyless entry. All I had to do was approach the driver's door, and the remote in my pocket would unlock it. If I could get in and lock the door, then press the ignition's start button, I could escape.

I kept them at bay, summoned every bit of strength I had, and then sprinted across the lot to my car. The car beeped as I approached. It worked! I got in, locked the doors, started the engine, and sped across the parking lot toward the Highway 41 on-ramp. In the rearview mirror I saw the cloud of dust left in my wake and the shadows dashing toward their truck. They were going to follow me. Local folks often gave me hell for buying "one of those Japanese cars," but in that moment I was grateful for my Infiniti G-35 and its remote. It had saved my life.

I sped south on Highway 41, pushing my car as fast as it could go. I saw the truck's headlights behind me; I could see through the mist that they were still a decent distance away. Then it began to rain. I flipped on my windshield wipers. My face was covered in blood. It was in my eyes, my nostrils had filled with the smell of topsoil from their work gloves. I tasted earth, and with each gasp of air I sucked and swallowed my own blood. I reached into the center console and pulled out my stash of fast-food napkins. I wiped the blood from my eyes and tried to blow my nose. Nothing but more blood came out. The sinus pressure stung. It didn't seem like my nose was broken, but it ached. My face was throbbing. I could feel every pulse of my racing heartbeat behind my eyes.

I threw the bloody napkins onto the passenger floorboard. I had to lose the truck. Their headlights were getting closer. The highway was desolate; I'd only passed one car, and it was in the northbound lane on the other side of the median. *Fuck!* I thought. I'd left my cell phone on the office desk. Highway 41 was for the most part straight and flat. The shadows would be able to follow me; I needed to lose them. The rain wasn't helping matters. Knox Road exit was approaching. If I could take the turn like Daryl had in his dad's vintage Corvette that summer day all those years ago and head toward other country roads, I'd have a better chance of losing them. I hesitated for only a moment. My car could do it—it could take the curve. I was approaching 120 miles per hour. As the exit neared I slowed down a bit, but I was still driving over one hundred miles per hour when I took the curve. That was it. My tires shrieked, metal scraped against pavement, a kind of carnival ride inertia pinned my back against the driver's seat. And then everything went black.

I awoke to morning sunlight and EMTs placing me on a stretcher. An oxygen mask covered my nose and mouth; its air was dry and cool. Red lights flashed in my eyes. One of the men called me by my name. He told me to hold on. I slipped away again.

Farmer Stone is the reason I didn't die in that melon field near Highway 41 on Knox Road. Every morning at sunup, he headed to town to eat breakfast, run a few errands, and then return to the farm. He saw my battered car flipped upside down in his field. He stopped his truck, jumped out, and ran to it. Just a few feet away I lay unconscious in the soft sandy soil. I'd been ejected from the car. I had rocketed headfirst from the driver's seat. I had not been wearing my seatbelt. The impact of the car's first flip popped the windshield and hurtled me through the opening. Someone or something was watching over me. Had I been strapped inside the car, I would be dead. Farmer Stone, Pastor Daryl's dad, called 911 from his cell phone. It was the farmer of stones who saved my life.

Although it had rained that night, I was caked in blood. The EMTs said I had lain there, most likely in and out of consciousness, all night, and that I was lucky to have been lying on my right side. I had vomited several times. Had I been on my back, they said, I would have choked to death. And lying curled into the soil and being somewhat sheltered by my overturned car may have prevented hypothermia.

Being hoisted onto the gurney and loaded in the ambulance is a hazy memory, as are the first few hours I spent in the emergency room at Mercy Memorial Hospital. I was asked by EMTs, then the attending emergency room physician and nurses, what had happened, but I was unable to gather my thoughts. I kept telling them I forgot to empty the mop bucket, I got in a fight and hit my head, and I had a bad headache. I remember Doc Vonderbreck showing up. I was told later that I smiled when he appeared by my bedside. He said I looked as if I'd won the fight, and that the mop bucket must surely be in worse shape. He ordered a CT scan, and a while later I was taken to a dimly lit room, placed on a scanning table, and told to lie still. A voice over the intercom told me to relax. The table began to slide horizontally, and it seemed I was floating into a huge powdered doughnut hole that made an enormous, whirling hum. Afterward, I was back in the emergency room.

When the test results came back, my parents were told I'd suffered a blunt force trauma to the head, causing an open fracture and a cerebral hemorrhage. The pressure against my skull and brain was increasing from the bleeding. The CT tech and emergency room doctor insisted I be prepped for surgery, my head shaved, so they could temporarily remove part of the bone and allow my brain to expand. Once the swelling subsided—possibly over the next forty-eight to seventy-two hours, they said—I would undergo surgery to replace the bone.

Doc Vonderbreck said absolutely not. "Get him out of here," Doc said. My parents, still in shock, did not comprehend his demand. "Tell me you want him transferred."

"What?" Dad asked.

"Tell me you want him transferred. Doc Floyd is the neurosurgeon, and that drunk son of a bitch will kill him."

"Transferred where?" Dad asked.

"Get him to Evansville. Call Mitchell's Ambulance, and we'll get him to Deaconess. Let them do additional tests there. These assholes don't know what they're doing."

My parents trusted Doc Vonderbreck, just as I had trusted him years ago with my secret.

"We want him transferred," Mom said.

"Yes. Transfer him," Dad said.

Like a badly damaged film, the next image I have is of Mr. Mitchell loading me into his ambulance and driving away from Mercy Memorial. I came to inside another powdered doughnut hole to the hum of another CT scan at Deaconess Hospital.

My first forty-eight hours at Deaconess were a blur. I stopped vomiting. The neurosurgeon there placed me in ICU to monitor the swelling of my brain—he would only open my skull as a last resort. My parents and brother were the only family members allowed to see me, for ten minutes every two hours. Once my brain swelling began to subside, I came around. I stayed in ICU for ten days. After the first forty-eight hours, my family was allowed to stay in my room. Mom, Dad, and Cameron rarely left, and never all at once.

My memory of the attack and the wreck returned in fragments, like putting together the pieces of a shattered mirror. The "accident" had been reported, and Mom and Dad called the Fort Sackville Police Department on several occasions to follow up. Each time they got the same answer: there would be an investigation once I was feeling better, perhaps once I was home recovering.

My dad was enraged. He thought the police were trying to avoid an investigation.

"How can we investigate when he doesn't remember?" Dad was told by the police chief, a deacon at Wabash Valley Baptist Church. "There is speculation he may have been driving under the influence. We found broken beer bottles behind the restaurant," the police chief said.

"Goddamn it, Grey was not under the influence of anything but fear. He was fearful for his life; he was beaten by three guys behind the restaurant. He wasn't drinking. He was not on drugs. The hospital sent you the blood test results," Dad said.

"I haven't received those medical records. They're not in his file. So this is still being considered a DUI, and charges may be filed," the police chief said.

"File the fucking charges and I'll see your ass in court," Dad said and hung up.

I'd only ever seen Dad that pissed off once in my life.

Lying there in my hospital room listening to my parents and Cameron chatting quietly, I recalled the last time Dad had been enraged, when he'd felt cornered, and a seismic power shift had occurred between Grandpa Collin and Dad. It was during my freshman year of high school, on a dark evening after Mom and Dad left Grandma Dixie's bedside. Grandma Dixie's youngest sister Kay Ann, a nurse at the Indiana University Medical Center, was staying the night to care for her. Grandma Dixie's health was failing fast from stage-four lung cancer. On their way home, my parents decided to pick up fresh doughnuts from Sal's Bakery on Oak Street for the morning's breakfast. When they pulled out of the bakery's lot, they saw Grandpa Collin's truck racing down the street, flashing his headlights at the car ahead of him. All my parents could see was a woman's head behind the wheel. Mom and Dad, keeping their distance, followed them. Dad said he knew the moment both cars turned south onto River Road that his dad was meeting her—Jackie, the other woman. When both cars turned right onto the gravel lane of Dumes Pond, Mom and Dad went straight. Feeling they were a safe distance away, Dad parked alongside the road and then walked back toward and down the lane to the pond. He saw his dad and Jackie sitting in the cab of his father's beat-up blue GMC truck.

The next night, after the diner closed—the employees gone, having finished their duties—Dad confronted Grandpa Collin. It was Dad's day off. Typically he stopped by the Diner after closing to check the day's receipts and to catch up on the day's events. As always, Dad parked in the side lot and entered through the back door. Walking across the dining room, he spotted Grandpa Collin tallying stock invoices at the table next to the cash register, the one Grandma Dixie sat at when manning the register during her lunch- and dinner-rush shifts. Dad stopped at the waitress station, poured himself a cup of coffee, and joined Grandpa Collin.

"Dessa and I were with Mom last night. You should have been home with her. Kay Ann thinks she could pass any day now," Dad said.

"I had to work last night. Somebody has to run this goddamned place. We can't all take days off. Besides, those inside rounds needed to be cut and prepped for Swiss steak today."

"Were you here late? You should've said something—I'd have come to help. Or done it this morning."

"No. You spend time with your mother."

"What time did you get out?"

"What the hell is this, a cross-examination? I don't know what time I left," Grandpa Collin said, looking over the rim of his eyeglasses.

Dad paused.

"I saw you, Dad."

"What do you mean, you saw me?" The adding machine began totaling numbers. "Damn it, CJ, I'm trying to get these figures together." Grandpa Collin hit the erase key and began again.

Dad sipped his coffee.

"Dessa and I saw you following that woman. I saw you with her at Dumes Pond."

Grandpa Collin stopped, his fingers poised midair. He looked up from his adding machine, leaned across the table, and said, "You and Dessa didn't see anything."

"Yes, Dad, we did."

Grandpa Collin slammed his fist on the table, sending invoices sailing to the floor. "Goddamn it, I'm telling you, you didn't see anything. You're sticking your nose where it don't belong."

"Dad, do you remember what you did in this diner when I was thirteen years old—one of the nights I was here with you after closing?

It was late. Two cars pulled up in front and parked. You went to the kitchen and got your gun. Before you went outside, you walked me to the front door of the vestibule, gave me the keys, and told me to lock it behind you. I'll never forget it. You told me those men were there to kick your ass, that if it looked like you were winning I was to keep the door locked. But if it looked like you were losing, I should unlock the door. Do you have any idea how fucking scared I was? I watched you pull a gun on those men."

"What in the hell's that got to do with anything?"

"You've been fucking around with waitresses and other men's wives your entire married life. Could you please, just once, stop? Let Mom die with dignity?"

Grandpa Collin stood up and walked around the table to my father's side with his fists clenched. Dad stood his ground.

"Listen, you little son of a bitch," Grandpa Collin said, his back erect and legs planted. "My marriage to your mother is none of your goddamn business. You understand me? You need to remember: this is *my* restaurant, and your mother is *my* wife. If you don't like *my* world or what I do in it, you're welcome to get your ass out."

Dad wasn't sure if words would turn to fists. It had before. He remembered being eighteen years old and fighting his father in the front living room of their house on Ridge Road; he remembered his mother screaming for them to stop; he remembered his father's punch to his gut, the final one that sent him into a fetal position on the living room floor; he remembered his dad laughing, calling him a pussy, his father's footsteps retreating, and the front door slamming behind him.

The next day, Dad joined the Navy.

In the restaurant that night, Dad backed away from Grandpa Collin, but was unable to turn away from him. Later, Dad said it was the first time he really saw his father for who he was—just a flawed man. That same night, Grandma Dixie died in her sister's arms.

My mom, just as upset at the lack of interest, the apathy the Fort Sackville Police Department and its police chief Dallas Ellerman Jr.—his father Dallas Ellerman Sr. had been the prosecuting attorney in Robbie Palmer's murder—showed toward my claim. Mom tried to refocus her anger on my care and recovery. She asked Dad to do the same. I lay in my hospital bed listening to them arguing. There was comfort in this. It reminded me of being a little kid and eavesdropping behind closed doors when they were upset about restaurant finances, employees—or Grandpa Collin.

"Someone attacked *our* son on *our* property," Dad said. "It's a violent . . . criminal attack. He was trying to escape in the car. The police are supposed to protect people! Investigate! Ask questions! Look for evidence, for Christ's sake!"

"CJ, I know. I get it. But right now *our* priority is to make sure Grey is okay. That he survives this. When he's out of the woods, then I'll be angry," Mom said. "Then we'll go after whoever did this."

My parents were scared, but I wasn't. It was as if I had no troubles, cares, or worries in the world. For the first time I didn't feel anxious. Something or someone was taking care of me. My worst fears had been realized, and I'd survived them. I remember thinking about how I felt. Was it peace?

Just then, Mom and Dad stopped talking. They turned to look toward the door. I turned my head too, and watched Rio walk into my hospital room. I hadn't seen him since Miami Beach in June.

DEFENSE ATTORNEY IN PALMER MURDER VICTIM OF VANDALISM

By Foster Lawrence
Fort Sackville Sentinel staff writer

FORT SACKVILLE, Ind. — Eli Montgomery, defense attorney in the recent Robbie Palmer murder trial, and his family were the victims of vandalism in the early morning hours.

Fort Sackville Police were called to the Montgomery house in historic Old Town Fort Sackville at 2:12 a.m. after the home's upstairs bedroom windows were shot out.

Police also discovered that Mr. and Mrs. Montgomery's vehicles had tires slashed and windows busted.

Several threatening epithets were spray-painted on the front porch.

The Montgomery home is the former and historic residence of Indiana Governor M. Scott Jameson.

Montgomery's youngest daughter received lacerations to her face and forearm from flying glass from the bedroom window. She was rushed to Mercy Memorial Hospital and remains in stable condition.

An armed officer has been placed in front of her hospital room.

"This illustrates that even in our peaceful community, some folks choose to try and frighten others into submission," Montgomery said.

Montgomery was defense attorney for Riley Salters, the former Fort Sackville Community College law enforcement student and gay lover of Robbie Palmer.

Palmer's decomposed body was discovered in May of 1986 in a drainage ditch on Highway 41 South near the Knox Road exit after he had attended a party rumored to be "homosexual in nature."

Salters was found not guilty in the charge of obstruction of justice.

"Whomever disagrees with the outcome of the Palmer trial has decided to use scare tactics, intimidation, and violence against my family to make their point. It won't work. I will not be terrorized in my own home," Montgomery told reporters.

Robbie Palmer's alleged murder and trial have fueled antigay rhetoric and violence throughout the community.

Anonymous sources claim Salters's recent not guilty verdict has exacerbated the situation.

When asked to comment, prosecutor Dallas Ellerman said, "It is no surprise that Mr. Montgomery is receiving backlash from the Fort Sackville community.

"The community is offended by the Palmer proceedings and does not feel justice has been served. I do not condone violence, but I can honestly say I'm not surprised by this turn of events.

"Unscrupulous, amoral behavior is not welcome in Fort Sackville. The community will not tolerate it."

Fort Sackville police are investigating. They ask that anyone with information please contact the department. An anonymous tips line has been set up and can be accessed by calling the police department.

Chapter Twenty

September

Rio walked into my hospital room carrying a small vase of Tropicana roses. He had remembered their coral color was my favorite. We'd once built a rose garden along the exterior wall of our garage on Kelso Creek Road. He smiled, sat them on the windowsill, then hugged Mom, Dad, and Cameron.

"I think we'll leave you two alone," Mom said. And for the first time since I had been hospitalized, my entire family left the room together.

"What are you doing here?" I asked.

"I came to see if you were okay," Rio said. "I tried to come earlier, but they wouldn't let me in. They said visitation was restricted to family members only."

"You drove up here from Miami Beach?"

"I left as soon as your mother called me and told me about the accident." Rio leaned in and kissed me lightly on the lips. My lips were dry and parched, and his were moist and soft.

"Whoa. I wasn't expecting that," I said.

"Not had a kiss in a while?" Rio asked.

"Not a kiss from *you*."

"It's nice to see I haven't lost my touch," Rio said, feigning an attempt to lift the sheet and look under my hospital gown.

"No, you haven't," I said, playfully knocking his hand away. "That's what I need—a nurse coming in and seeing you in the room trying to get into my gown."

"Darling, remember, I know you. You've had other men get under your gown plenty of times," Rio said.

"Whatever," I said. "Are you staying in Mount Vernon? At your mom's? What about your job in Miami?"

"It sure doesn't seem like you're having any problems thinking. You're still able to grill me pretty good," Rio said. I giggled. It was nice having Rio in my hospital room. It seemed like the first time I'd laughed in a year. He made me feel better. I didn't feel so alone.

"Yes, I'm staying at Mom's. And yes, my job in Miami is fine. But I'm not worried about any of that. I'm here for you. I'm worried about you. So what have the police said?" Rio asked, sitting down on the edge of my bed.

"Apparently they're not doing anything other than charging me with DUI and reckless endangerment. They're waiting until I get home to arrest me. They don't believe that I was getting beaten up behind the restaurant. The police chief said there's not much they can do since there were no witnesses or security cameras."

"What? You're fucking kidding me!"

"No. They're going to let me tell them my story. They saw the broken bottles, but there seems to be no evidence linking any of it to anyone other than me. And they're trying to only link the beer bottles to me since I totaled my car."

"Are your parents going to contact someone else? The FBI? Isn't there somebody they can sue?" Rio asked.

"If the police chief isn't interested in investigating, do you really think someone else is going to check it out? The county sheriff and the Indiana State Police are only concerned with the car wreck. The restaurant parking lot, since it's in town, is apparently under the Fort Sackville Police Department's jurisdiction. As stupid as it may sound, I'm kind of relieved. I was always fearful something would happen, and now it has. I have no reason to be afraid anymore."

"This is bullshit, Grey. Someone almost killed you. There's got to be something we can do."

"I suppose I could press charges, but against who? I don't know who they were. I couldn't really see what kind of truck it was. I don't remember seeing a license plate. Nothing. Besides, it's not worth it.

Nobody's going to do anything. I ended up in practically the same field ditch as Robbie Palmer. They didn't do anything to whoever tried to kill . . . I mean, killed him. It'll end up being a tale full of sound and fury resulting in nothing, just like Robbie's murder investigation. Mom, Dad, Cameron, and I have been talking. I really want to move to Miami Beach. I hate Indiana. Mom and Dad are thinking of locking up the restaurant for good. We're all tired. The employees are tired. We don't want to fight it any longer."

"Seriously? You're ready to move? What will your parents do, sell the restaurant?" Rio asked.

"I think they're going to try," I said. "And if it doesn't sell, Dad says the way he feels at this point, since all this, he'd let the bank have it." I paused a moment to lift myself against the pillows behind me.

"You know, Rio, I didn't realize it but Dad's medical bills have practically wiped them out. Dad's health insurance cancelled him several years ago after his first heart attack. He can't get insurance now. They've been paying his medical bills with their savings and money from the restaurant."

"Holy shit."

"It's all been fucked up for some time now. More than I ever knew."

There was a long pause. Rio and I held each other's gaze. He leaned down and kissed me again.

"Well, I'm here. And I'm not going anywhere."

"I'm glad you're here," I said.

"We'll get through this. It's all going to work out for the best. Listen, I need to go. I've got to pick up Mother from her hair appointment. I dropped her off and then came here. How much longer are you going to be in here?" Rio asked.

"Another week or so. The doctor thinks I need to stay a little longer."

"Well. I'll come by tomorrow. I'll bring you lunch. You want a Stromboli from Turoni's?"

"I'd die for some Turoni's."

"Grey."

"What?"

"Don't say the word *die*."

"Oh. Sorry. I guess I better watch that."

Rio got up from my bedside and walked toward the door.

"Rio," I said.

He turned to look at me.

"Thanks for the roses."

"You're welcome," he said. "I'll see you tomorrow."

"See you tomorrow." I watched him walk out the door. For the first time in a long while, I felt Rio and I had a future.

Chapter Twenty-One

September

The day after Rio visited, I had another surprise visitor: Farmer Stone. My parents had been in the room earlier but had stepped out for lunch, and Cameron had class at the university. I had been expecting Rio, so when Farmer Stone appeared my surprise, I'm sure, was evident.

"How're you doing, son?" he asked as he stepped uncertainly into my room.

"I'm all right," I replied, bewildered.

"Are you sure? Are the nurses and doctors taking good care of you?"

"I'm glad to be in my own room. My neurologist is pretty cool. He owns a Ferrari and parks it out there in the lot for me to look at." I motioned toward the window with my head. "We talk cars when he comes to visit."

"I think you need to stay away from fast cars. You're lucky to be alive."

I paused a moment. It was the first time the enormity of what Farmer Stone had done struck me. It rushed over me and I couldn't control my emotions. I began to cry. Mr. Stone walked toward me, took off his John Deere cap, and sat in the chair beside my bed.

"Son, I didn't come here to upset you," he said.

"I know. I just don't know how to thank you. You saved my life."

"Well, I like to think that God just put me in the right place at the right time. You can thank Him," he said.

"I do. But you're the one that found me. You're the one that called the ambulance."

"Just consider yourself lucky that I never miss a breakfast." He smiled. "Listen, I came here to ask you something: is it true there was some trouble behind the restaurant that night?"

His eyes were steady and clear, and I could sense that he was not out to hurt me. He truly wanted to know. Perhaps he even wanted to help. He had saved my life; I figured I'd answer any question he had.

"I don't know who they were. There were three of them. They beat me up."

"Any reason why?"

"I suppose it had something to do with Trace's suicide. And that . . ." I paused. I had promised myself I'd be honest.

"And what?" he asked.

I'd made my mind up as I lay there in my hospital bed after the beating, after the accident, that I wasn't going to hide anymore. Not from anyone. I had almost died. Nothing and nobody could hurt me any longer. Life was too short. It could be gone at any minute. The accident had taught me that. I had nothing to lose. I was tired, my body hurt, my head ached, and trying to keep up appearances had exhausted my soul; it had been split in half for far too long.

"Mr. Stone, I'm gay. They were beating me up because I'm gay. And because, I guess, they think I made Trace gay," I said.

Farmer Stone didn't say anything. He just sat beside me, his cap in his lap, scratching his dull gray hair with his forefinger. He took a deep breath and exhaled. "Son, I understand that. What I'm asking is, do you think my son Daryl had anything to do with those guys behind the restaurant?"

"I don't know. I'd like to think he didn't. But I really don't know."

Farmer Stone looked at me for a long moment then turned his gaze to the floor.

"You know, I knew what you boys were up to in high school," he said hollowly.

"What?"

"You and Daryl. I knew what you boys were up to."

"What do you mean?" I asked.

"You know what I mean," he said. "Parents always know. That is, if they accept the truth. I suppose some parents choose to see their children a certain way. Some may deny it. But in their heart they always know. Daryl's mother and I always knew," he said.

"Did Daryl ever say anything to you about . . . how he felt?"

"Heavens no, he'd never do that. Daryl doesn't know who he is. He's been lost for a long time. I've given that boy everything he ever wanted. I suppose I screwed up. Some of the biggest fights his mama and I ever had were about him."

"If you don't mind my asking, is that why she left you?"

"Could be. There are a number of reasons, I'm sure."

Farmer Stone sat in silence, then he turned to look out the window. "You say that doctor of yours has got himself a Ferrari, huh?"

"Yes, it's to the left, near the entrance. It's black. You can't miss it."

Farmer Stone stood up from the chair and walked to the window. When had he become an old man? His blue jeans and brown Carhartt jacket seemed to hang off his body. He'd lost weight and muscle, though he still appeared strong and rugged, his skin like leather hide from working the melon fields all his life. His masculinity had scared the shit out of me, his sort of alpha-male superman aura. But the man standing at my window admiring my doctor's Ferrari seemed a steadier, more compassionate and concerned version of the Farmer Stone I knew as a teenager.

"Oh, yes. Shoo wee, that is mighty pretty. I bet she cost him a pretty penny, and I bet your stay here is paying for it," he said with a dry chuckle. "You remember that time I caught you and Daryl driving my Corvette?"

"Yes, sir. How could I forget? You were really pissed."

"No, I wasn't. Not really. I just acted like I was. Secretly, I was happy to see Daryl had the gumption to strike out and do something like that. In a weird way, I was sort of proud of him. I had to keep appearances though, be the concerned father."

"Well, you sure did a good job. I know you scared me half to death," I said.

"Daryl always did have a mind of his own. He reminds me a lot of my own daddy. You can't talk to him, you can't tell him anything. He's stubborn. Has his way, and that's the only way." There was a distant look on his face, as if he were staring at his own past through the window. "I've always tried to protect Daryl. I guess I allowed him to become that way."

I wanted to say something nice about Daryl—the moment felt like I should. But I couldn't think of anything. What I did say, though, was, "Daryl isn't the way he is because of you, sir."

Farmer Stone continued to stare out the window. "You know, you weren't the only one to come swimming out at the farm."

"Sir?"

"You and Daryl. Swimming. I saw you boys. You weren't the only one. Robbie Palmer came out a time or two also," he said.

"He did?" The thought of Robbie Palmer going swimming at Daryl's had never occurred to me. Neither one had ever said a word about it. How did I not know that Daryl had invited Robbie out to swim?

"I never knew that Daryl and Robbie hung out. Other than on the golf team," I said.

"Daryl's good at keeping secrets. He only tells folks what he thinks they need to hear. I suppose he gets that from me. My daddy told everything he knew—I remember growing up wishing some days for him to just keep his mouth shut. So I always did. I guess Daryl kind of does the same—keeps his mouth shut, I mean. His older brother doesn't. James is just like my old man, tells everything he knows. That's why I'm glad he spent most of his time at the university in Bloomington. Had James known Robbie had been to the farm, word would have gotten out."

"Mr. Stone, are you saying Daryl had something to do with Robbie's murder?" I asked.

"You know why I sent Daryl to Liberty University?" he asked.

"Well, since you said you thought Daryl was gay, I suppose it was to make him straight. Maybe a Baptist college would save him?"

He turned from the window and looked at me. "I don't give a goddamn if someone is gay or straight. I might just be an old redneck farm boy, but I got sense enough to know you are what you are."

"I didn't mean to upset you, sir. I just kind of figured that was the reason."

"You're right, I did it to save him—but not from being a homosexual. I did it to save him from Fort Sackville. When Daryl left that party, he saw a car with Hancock County plates and a Fort Sackville Community College law enforcement program bumper sticker parked down the street from the house. The engine was running, and two guys were sitting in the front seats. Daryl told me that when he drove past he thought the guy in the passenger seat kind of looked like Robbie. The windows were tinted, so he couldn't be sure. He didn't want to stop to see. He'd already been there almost an hour and was worried locals would see him. I knew what that town would do if they found out Daryl was gay. I knew what they'd do if they found out he was at that party the night the Palmer boy died."

"Daryl really was at the party?"

"Yes. Yes, he was. He got called before the grand jury to testify, and I knew if he stayed around after the indictment was delivered, his name would surely come up. I called my buddy at Liberty, and along with a substantial donation to the athletic department, I got Daryl on the golf team there and out of Fort Sackville. I was hoping he'd find himself while he was there. I'm beginning to think they just fucked him up more."

"Does Daryl know how Robbie died?"

"He swore to me he didn't. He says Robbie was drunk and called him. Said he wanted Daryl to come to the party, that he needed a ride home. Daryl said he didn't really want to go, but he didn't want Robbie to get in trouble. So he went. But by the time he arrived Robbie was nowhere in sight. Daryl figured he was in one of the bedrooms. He said he waited around for about an hour but Robbie never appeared, so he left."

"He never saw Robbie?"

"Apparently not. I told Daryl he could tell me anything, that I'd protect him. He swore he was telling me the truth. I asked him how in the hell then did Robbie end up in a ditch on *our* land? Daryl swore he didn't know. He told the grand jury the same thing. He's my son, Grey. I had to believe him. I *had* to protect him."

My mind felt overloaded. The dull ache from the accident and now this news. It was hard to believe that Farmer Stone was standing in my hospital room, telling me his family's secrets.

"Why are you telling me this, Mr. Stone? Did you know Daryl came to my house that night? He was kind of drunk."

Mr. Stone turned from the window to look at me. "Yes, I did. And I don't know why I'm telling you, son. It's a burden I buried deep inside a long time ago. I didn't come here to have this particular conversation. I just wanted to check up on you. Seems God had other plans for me."

"Do *you* think Daryl had something to do with those guys beating me up?"

"I just don't know." Mr. Stone again turned away. "Yep, that is a mighty fine car sitting there." Finally, he came back to the chair by my bed.

I could sense that Mr. Stone was questioning everything Daryl had ever told him. He was not convinced that Daryl didn't have a hand in the dumping of Robbie's body, or even in instigating those shadowy figures behind the restaurant—the ones that wanted me dead too.

"Listen, son, did your folks tell you I came down early on to visit? When you were in ICU?"

"No sir, they didn't."

"Well, I did. I had some drivin' force in me needing to talk. I'm glad I came down. I got to meet and sit with your friend Rio."

"You met Rio? He was in the waiting room?"

"Yes sir, he was. A mighty fine fellow, very smart, and someone that cares about you. He and I had us some nice conversations." Mr. Stone got up from the chair, put his cap back on his head, and took a step toward my bedside. "You need to let that guy love you. I know, sounds odd coming from a redneck farmer like me, and I sure wouldn't go around tellin' folks I had this conversation with you. But you do. Love is an awful hard thing to come by in this world, and it's clear that young man loves you."

"Mr. Stone, I have to say this is making me kind of uncomfortable."

"I suppose it is. And I suppose it seems odd coming from me. I had a basketball teammate in college; his name was Walter. He was gay. Spent his whole life hiding it from almost everyone, including me. All I know is he was my friend. That's all that mattered to me. And when he died a couple of years back and I went to his funeral up near Chicago, his partner came up and introduced himself. Said that Walt always talked about me and the fun times we had in college and playing ball. He said he was happy to meet me finally, and that he was sorry it was on such a sad occasion. I thought a lot about Walt on the drive home. It would've been nice to spend time with him and his partner, to get to know them. But I didn't. I found out there at the funeral they'd been together for over forty years, longer than my wife and me."

"Mr. Stone, thank you. Thank you for everything you've done. For saving my life and for being nice."

Farmer Stone shook my hand and then walked toward the door. As he opened it, he turned back. "You know, in college I studied Matthew Henry. Do you know who he was?"

"No. I don't."

"He was an English minister during the 1600s. I memorized his words, his thoughts about Matthew 7:1. You know that scripture?"

"That's the *judge not lest ye be judged* one, right?" My battered brain was still able to recall my Sunday school Bible studies.

"Yes, that's it. Matthew Henry said, *We must judge ourselves, and judge our own acts, but not make our word a law to everybody. We must not judge rashly, nor pass judgment upon our brother without any ground. We must not make the worst of people. Here is a just reproof to those who quarrel with their brethren for small faults, while they allow themselves in greater ones.* I remember the first time I read it. I was barely nineteen years old. It's stayed with me since. I've always tried to live my life by it. I tried to teach my boys that."

Mr. Stone paused a moment; his gaze drifted downward to the floor. He held his stance as if in a daydream.

"Mr. Stone, are you okay?" I asked.

He looked up, turned his gaze toward me, and with a somber expression said, "Just remember, son, it's none of our business what other folks think or say about us. Take care of yourself. And you be nice to Rio." And with a tip of his John Deere hat, that tiny gesture, Farmer Stone was gone.

DUI AND RECKLESS ENDANGERMENT CHARGES DROPPED IN NEAR FATAL CAR ACCIDENT

By Jacob Pittman
Fort Sackville Sentinel staff writer

FORT SACKVILLE, Ind. — Charges were dropped Monday morning against a Fort Sackville man by local and state authorities, police said, after the county sheriff's department and Indiana State Police found no evidence to warrant an arrest.

Grey Daniels, 37, of Fort Sackville, Ind., was ejected from his 2005 Infiniti G-35 south of Fort Sackville near Highway 41 in the early morning of September 13.

According to Fort Sackville Police investigators, Daniels was allegedly driving "in excess of 100 mph" when he lost control of his sports car exiting onto Knox Road.

ISP investigators said they are "unable to determine Daniels' rate of speed at this time." No charges will be filed. His BAC was normal.

Daniels' car flipped numerous times before resting in a melon field.

The land is owned by Stone Melon Farms and Trucking. It is the same site where a local teen's decomposed body was found 21 years ago.

Darrius Stone, 68, the farm's owner, discovered Daniels lying unconscious near the overturned car.

Grey's father, CJ Daniels, owner of Daniels' Family Buffet,

told reporters his son was beaten behind the restaurant in the early morning hours and was trying to escape his assailants.

"He was trying to outrun them and lost control of his car. There were broken beer bottles all over the back parking lot. They were trying to kill him," CJ Daniels said.

Fort Sackville police chief Dallas Ellerman Jr. said the accusations are "unsubstantiated."

"There is no evidence to suggest that Daniels was fleeing for his life. There were broken beer bottles behind the restaurant. It appears someone had been drinking that night.

"Daniels wrecked his car south of town. It's not rocket science. It is another example of someone making the tragic decision to get behind the wheel of a car after they've been drinking."

When told Daniels' BAC was normal, Ellerman said, "I've not seen that file. Our investigation is ongoing."

Grey Daniels remains in critical but stable condition at Deaconess Hospital in Evansville, Ind. He was not available for comment.

Chapter Twenty-Two

October

I was released from the hospital a week after the DUI and reckless driving charges were dropped, given instructions to rest, to take it easy, to avoid lifting or climbing on anything, and most importantly to not fall and hit my head. My monthly checkups were scheduled with Doc Vonderbreck, with a follow-up appointment in six months with the neurosurgeon at Deaconess. I was happy to be at home and sleeping in my own bed. Rio decided to stay with me. He took care of me and worked from the house via phone and e-mail. Mom had her hands full with Dad and the restaurant.

A few weeks later, she cooked a family meal for all of us, including Rio. Mom never cooked; we always ate at the restaurant. Dad was sitting at the head of the dining table with Mom at the other end. Cameron sat across from Rio and me. Eating in the dining room meant it must be big news.

"I spoke with a real estate agent in Evansville two days ago," Dad said. "Your mother and I have done a lot of talking and soul searching. We've decided to sell the restaurant."

No one spoke. Not a word was uttered. Dad's words had erupted, then began to settle, floating down like volcanic ash accumulating on the dining table.

"Are you serious?" I asked. Had their talk about closing the restaurant become a reality?

Mom continued, "We've looked at everything. This family has sacrificed too much for that restaurant. It has to stop. The accident was our wake-up call."

Mom referred to my beating as *the accident*. She couldn't bring herself to say the word *beating* or even think of it in those terms. I was not upset by their decision. Rio remained quiet.

"Well, it's about time," Cameron said. He never had any interest in the business and avoided it at all costs. Growing up, neither one of us was ever forced to work the business like Dad was.

"We as a family have a huge responsibility toward our employees. We've been made well aware of the community's priorities, their loyalty. Our employees are the ones we have to take care of. Your mother and I are cashing in our IRAs and giving each of them one month's severance pay. We're shutting the place down."

Sitting there at the dining room table with my parents, Cameron, and Rio, I tried to process Dad's announcement. *Shutting the place down?* I thought

My mind was whirling with the gravity of it all, the history of the Daniels family and the two restaurants. Our lives had been ruled by it. I sensed my hometown community—the customers—had no clue of the sacrifice, the bloodshed, the tears and betrayal my family endured—often at the hands of Grandpa Collin—in order to keep appearances up and the restaurant profitable. Fort Sackville only saw the houses and the cars, my family's possessions. They could not begin to comprehend that our souls had been sold that day in November of 1951, when Grandpa Collin bought the Diner from Lo Campbell.

Looking at my family and Rio sitting at the dining room table and weighing Dad's announcement, I thought about the year *I* first began managing Daniels' Family Buffet after dropping out of college. The year the restaurant became *my* life too.

I opened Daniels' Family Buffet most Saturdays, working the morning and afternoon shift until five p.m., when Dad arrived for the evening shift and to close. All his life Dad worked in the restaurant; his only reprieve was the four years he served in the Navy during Vietnam. Dad said to me once, "Fighting in Vietnam was safer than working for your Grandpa Collin." When Dad returned to Fort Sackville after the Navy, he returned to the restaurant only temporarily, with plans to find something better. He says he did find something better—my mother—and then he was given me, and then an extra treat, Cameron. Before Dad knew it, he had a family to support. Daniels' Diner, then Daniels' Family Buffet, became his life, just as it had been Grandpa Collin's life. And when Grandpa Collin retired due to a health scare and Dad bought Daniels' Family Buffet from him, for the first time the restaurant was truly Dad's. Over the course of a couple of years while Mom stayed home to raise Cameron and keep the restaurant's books, together Dad and I made small, incremental changes. Business picked up as Grandpa Collin watched from the sidelines.

Two years after Grandpa Collin retired, the restaurant prepared to celebrate its fortieth anniversary and receive an award from the Fort Sackville Chamber of Commerce honoring Daniels' for its local philanthropy and community involvement. Two weeks before the big celebration, on a Saturday morning, as soon as the restaurant opened, Grandpa Collin came in to sit and drink coffee with the Coffee Club Clan—the CCC boys, we called them—and later have lunch with the kitchen staff.

I was sitting at the office desk on the phone taking a catering order, the door open, when I saw Grandpa Collin join the employees after leaving the CCC boys' table. The employees ate lunch while Grandpa Collin drank his coffee and smoked one cigarette after another. This day, however, the employees were not their usual lively selves. Grandpa Collin kept looking into the office, watching me. I sensed something was up. When the employee lunch break was over, he left.

Later, after finishing the stock order and my lunch, I walked into the kitchen and saw Eloise sitting at her stainless steel prep table cutting onions. She was crying.

"Take a break, Eloise. Looks like those onions are getting to you." Her eyes were bloodshot, tears streaming down her cheeks.

She didn't respond.

"Eloise, are you okay?"

No answer. I pulled a chair from the corner near her and sat down.

"What's going on?" I asked again.

"I don't want to get involved."

Eloise had worked for my family for as long as I could remember. She'd begun working at the Diner in high school, a few years before Grandpa Collin bought it. When he closed the Diner and opened the Buffet, she followed, although initially she was upset he'd pulled her from waitressing to put her in the kitchen. She was one of my family's best employees. Eloise was a fixture, like the green-band Buffalo china and chrome napkin dispensers.

"I don't understand what you mean," I said.

"Please, Grey, I need to finish these onions."

I kept pushing for an answer.

Eloise slammed her knife on the prep table, the sound of steel against steel echoing off the walls. The other employees stopped for a moment, looked our way, then returned to their tasks.

"Grey, you always were a stubborn little shit," she said.

I smiled. "Yeah, so? You've told me that before."

"Oh, I have, have I?"

"Yes, I remember it clearly. When you first started working in the kitchen."

Along the outside wall of the Buffet's kitchen, at chest level, was a swinging disposal door that allowed access to the dumpster below it. The opening was large enough to throw number ten cans, smaller boxes, produce scraps, and other items directly into the receptacle outside, instead of walking out the back delivery door and around the building.

"I asked you what that swinging door was for," I said, pointing to it. "You told me it was to toss stubborn little boys into the dumpster, ones that asked too many questions."

Eloise laughed. "I said that?"

"Yes, I remember it well. I didn't know if you were joking or not. You used to scare the shit out of me. You've scarred me for life."

"Well, I've known a few people in my day I'd have liked to throw through that door. Today your grandpa is one of 'em."

"What's going on?"

"He's pissed. Business has picked up. People are saying the food is better than ever. They're talking all over town, saying your mom and dad have brought new life to the place."

"Yeah, I'm sure he's mad."

"Listen, I've known your family a long time, everything about them—more than you know, I bet. If I didn't like y'all, I would've never stayed, especially after Collin took me from waitressing, which was grossly unfair, and stuck me back here. But he's causing trouble with the others."

"What others?"

"The other employees. He was sitting out there this morning saying awful things about your mother. Saying Dessa was a gold digger; that she married CJ for the restaurant money; that we might as well get used to never seeing anymore Christmas bonuses or vacation pay. That Dessa, if she hasn't already, would spend all the money."

"You're not serious."

"He's got them all riled up."

"Did you say anything?"

"I don't want to get involved in your family's drama. I need my job. It's not my place, Grey."

"Eloise, first of all, nothing is going to happen to your job. Secondly, everyone is getting their annual Christmas bonus as well as vacation pay. That kind of stuff's not changing."

"He was saying some awful hateful things about Dessa."

"Look, Dad and I'll talk to everyone. In the meantime, you can tell them that Grandpa Collin is just trying to stir up shit. You're right, he's pissed about talk around town. I'll call Dad and we'll get it worked out."

I stood and returned my chair to its corner.

"Take a break, will ya? Your face looks like hell."

"Well, thanks a lot. You don't look too damn good yourself."

I leaned in and gave Eloise a kiss on the cheek. "Maybe we can get you on the serving floor for a few shifts," I said.

"Stop that!" she said, swatting at me. "I don't need any more shit from anyone today. I'm set in my ways now. Too old."

Returning to the restaurant office, I closed the door and called Dad.

"Eloise says the employees are upset. They really aren't saying much to me," I told him.

"I'll be right over," he said.

Even though I'd been general manager since Dad and Mom bought the restaurant, I hadn't yet totally earned the trust of our employees. I was still the boss's son; some thought I was a mole. Mom was at home raising my little brother Cameron. Dad was the one they trusted because they'd worked under him for so many years. When Dad arrived, he went directly to the kitchen to speak with the staff.

Just before noon, Grandpa Collin returned to have lunch with the remaining CCC boys. I went to the kitchen and cornered Dad.

"Grandpa Collin is back," I said.

My dad's face turned red; the vein in his forehead began to throb. With a determined gait, he left the kitchen and headed directly to Grandpa Collin in the dining room.

From my position standing behind the buffet near the kitchen door, I watched as Dad stopped Grandpa Collin in the middle of the dining room, before he could reach the CCC boys. The dining room's Saturday hum fell silent. The sound of glasses clinking and utensils scraping plates ceased. Waitresses stopped in their tracks; customers sat motionless.

"Why are you saying that shit to my employees? Spreading lies," I heard Dad shout, his finger waving in Grandpa Collin's face, then pointing toward the kitchen. "Why are you talking about my wife, about my family, that way?"

Something changed. Grandpa Collin suddenly looked like an old despot, desperate for former glory—an old, disheveled man who looked somewhat like the vagrants he once fed at the Diner's back kitchen door. Dad's face and neck were as red as butchered meat. Everyone was watching. Had the power between them finally shifted?

Grandpa Collin turned and walked toward the front door. Dad followed. Outside, they stood near the front windows. Dad's jugular looked as if it might rupture. Grandpa Collin, his right fist clenched, tried to take a swing, but Dad's arm shot out and stopped his father's fist in motion. The power had indeed shifted.

"I'll be damned if I ever step foot in this restaurant again!" Grandpa Collin shouted. We could hear him through the glass.

Grandpa Collin got into his car and sped off, his tires sending a cloud of loose sand and dirt flying behind them.

He never did return to Daniels' and never spoke to Dad again.

Two weeks later the restaurant celebrated its fortieth anniversary without him. December arrived and the employees got their Christmas bonuses, vacation pay, plus a glazed ham for their holiday dinner tables.

Not long after the argument, Grandpa Collin was rushed to Mercy Memorial Hospital with abdominal pain. Tests revealed an abdominal aneurysm. Mom told me he'd developed it from harboring so much anger and hatred over the years. He underwent surgery immediately to correct the problem, but never fully recovered. For a week after the surgery Dad spent every night at his bedside, but Grandpa Collin would not speak to him. He refused to acknowledge Dad sitting there. When Aunt Charlene would come—she and Dad sat in shifts—Grandpa Collin would speak with her and look right through Dad as if he didn't exist.

For over sixty years Grandpa Collin smoked. Although his abdominal aneurysm was corrected, his lungs were unable to survive the surgery. The night Grandpa Collin died, Dad was sitting by his side. Grandma Dixie's sister Kay Ann, the nurse, was convinced Grandpa Collin's paper-thin lungs had been destroyed by too much oxygen pumped into them during the operation.

"Doc Vonderbreck is a professional," Mom told Aunt Kay Ann. "He would *never* make the mistake of allowing someone to give too much oxygen to one of his patients."

Now, after almost sixty years in business, my dad was closing the restaurant. I couldn't imagine it not being in business—this Fort Sackville institution that had fed the community for so many years. Was the oppression, the pain, the struggle and sacrifice over? *What is Dad thinking? What must he be feeling? Is he relieved?* I wondered. The restaurant had been his entire life, all of his life. He said he was closing Daniels' because we as a family had sacrificed too much. The beating I'd taken was his wake-up call. And yet he too had taken a beating—first abused by the hand of his father, and then by his father's legacy.

"The real estate agent is going to contact a commercial broker at their sister office in Indianapolis and enlist him to help sell the property," said Dad. "This Sunday will be our last day." He smiled. His body language became uncharacteristically light. Suddenly, the weight of his illness was no longer present. Usually Dad struggled for breath—an exhale, then a wheeze. With this news, his wheeze disappeared. "We're scheduling an employee meeting for Sunday evening. We're going to close early so we can speak with everyone. Nobody breathes a word until then."

Dad didn't want to give the employees advance notice. He didn't want anyone trying to change his mind. He would have the payroll checks cut and ready to hand out. One month's pay, he thought, would be enough to hold them over until their unemployment kicked in. For the half-dozen long-term staff, he'd spoken with the director of food service at Fort Sackville Community College, who happened to be his second cousin, and found positions for them in the food court there. If they wanted to work for the college, they would get health insurance and some benefits—a perk for them since Daniels' Family Buffet was never able to offer benefits to its employees. The Fort Sackville Community College food court would be a better job. Mom and Dad had planned everything.

"So I guess this means I can move to South Beach?" I asked with a shaky smile.

"Your mom and I are going to help you. Miami Beach is where you belong," Dad said.

Wait. Are they serious? I thought.

I looked at Rio. He sat motionless, staring at his plate. I could tell he felt uncomfortable being a part of our conversation. He wouldn't look at me.

"Rio, you're awful quiet," I said.

"This is business between you and your family. Perhaps I should go back to your house and let you all finish talking," Rio said.

"Rio, you're a part of our family," Mom said. "We want you here."

Rio looked up from his plate toward Mom.

"Mrs. Daniels, I . . ."

"Dessa, Rio. You call me Dessa."

"Dessa, I think the world of your family. And I am so happy that Grey is okay. But I think I need to go," Rio said.

"No. Don't go," I said, grabbing Rio's hand. "I want you to stay."

A tear fell from Rio's eye.

"Rio," Dad said, leaning forward, "you obviously care for one another a great deal, and I can't imagine what Dessa and I would have done these last few weeks if you hadn't been here. I agree with Dessa—you are just as much a part of this family as any of us. You don't need to go. I'd like for you to stay."

I hadn't counted on my parents being so forthcoming. I knew they liked Rio. They always had. But something must have taken root when they watched him care for me during my recovery. Now they were saying so out loud, right there at the dining room table.

"You both are so kind. Thank you," Rio said, looking at my dad. Rio looked me in the eyes. "Move in with me," he said. "You can. Now you have nothing holding you here. You can find a job in Miami Beach. We can live together. Build a life. We can start over there."

My hope for the future exploded in my chest as I realized the impact of his words.

"Are you serious, Rio?" I asked.

"I've never been more serious in my life," Rio said. "We can go together. We can have the life that you and I wanted so long ago."

The reality of not having the restaurant in my life, in my family's life, began to take hold for the first time. None of us would ever be tethered to it again. After Sunday, all of us would be free. We could begin living the lives we wanted. My dad, for the first time since his father bought the Diner sixty years ago, would never have to do another day's work there. I didn't know if I was happier for me, or for him.

My mind was whirling. Rio could tell. He didn't speak. He kept looking into my eyes.

"Okay," I said. " Yeah. Let's do it. Let's go!"

I leaned into him and wrapped my arms through his. We kissed right there at my parents' dining room table.

"Oh, Jesus. Really? You guys can't do that at your house?" Cameron asked.

"Cam, you leave them alone. They've been through a lot," Mom said.

Rio pulled away from our kiss and my embrace. Smiling, he said, "Yeah, Cam. We've been through a lot. And you better watch out, or I'm going to come over there and give you a kiss."

"I don't take my brother's sloppy seconds," Cam said, returning the smile.

"It's settled. Your mother and I have an appointment tomorrow at ten a.m."

"But wait," I said. "What are you and Mom going to do? Where will you go?"

"You don't worry about your mother and me. We're going to start living our lives and enjoy whatever kind of retirement we end up with." Dad looked at Cameron, "And your brother is going to keep his ass in college, get a degree, and then a job."

"I knew this would all come back around to me," Cam said grumpily, then smiled.

Chapter Twenty-Three

October

After the employee meeting on the last Sunday we were open, Dad posted a sign on the front door of the restaurant.

> *It is with gratitude that the Daniels family and employees of Daniels' Family Buffet offer our thanks for fifty-eight wonderful years serving Fort Sackville and the surrounding communities. Sunday was our last day in business. Thank you for your patronage.*
>
> *If anyone asks, we've gone fishin'.*

The next day the real estate agent put a *for sale* sign in the front yard of my house on Kelso Creek Road, and a week later she hung a huge *for sale* banner on the side of the restaurant. Without a doubt, everyone in Fort Sackville knew that the Daniels family was no longer in the restaurant business.

No customers called.

No customers sent letters.

No customers asked questions.

Fifty-eight years died on the vine all at once.

Two days after the *for sale* sign went up at the restaurant, Mom, Dad, Cameron, Rio, and I were sitting at the kitchen table at my parents' house when I spotted two faces, Rosabelle and Mae, peering in from the exterior side of the kitchen's sliding glass doors. They'd brought a home-baked and sliced honey-glazed ham, green beans, and fresh canned tomatoes from Mae's garden. In Fort Sackville, the only time food was ever taken to someone's house was when someone died. Which is what my family was experiencing—closing the restaurant was indeed a death in our family.

Rosabelle's life had not been easy. Her family was one of the largest, most successful orchard families in the county. But when she met Mae and they moved in together, she too paid a price. She compromised. Rosabelle loved Mae very much, but never were they as a couple able to express their love publicly, even something as simple as a kiss or holding hands on an evening stroll through their neighborhood. Nor were they able to hug in front of a camera for the local paper in celebration of their union. All the precious yet seemingly minor, almost insignificant moments that heterosexual couples take for granted, they could never share. No, life for Rosabelle and Mae was not even separate but equal. They were, for all intents and purposes, second-class citizens. Rosabelle often brought to my mind the hymn "Onward, Christian Soldiers" from my Sunday school days at Wabash Valley Baptist Church. That was Rosabelle: a Christian soldier. Her policy was a simple life lived with a smile, kindness, compassion for others, plus a cocktail or two and a cigarette. She understood what bigotry looked like, along with avarice, greed, and the wrath of others, and how some folks used religion as a weapon, trying to veil their actions as goodwill and saving souls. So it was in her nature to show up at Mom and Dad's door with Mae, bringing nourishment for *our* stomachs and *our* souls. Mom invited them in, and we sat in comfortable companionship, sharing the meal.

Four days later, Mr. Mitchell, the ambulance driver, showed up on my front step.

Mr. Mitchell had been the one who drove me to Deaconess Hospital in Evansville. He also owned a local moving business and U-Haul franchise. He had been a successful businessman most of his life. His was a lifelong Fort Sackville family. They did not live extravagantly; they had a comfortable home and a nice life. They had worked hard for all of it. But a few years back, Mr. Mitchell was charged with a felony related to his ambulance service. Several patients under his care had their wallets and jewelry stolen while they were being transported to Mercy Memorial. At the time, Mr. Mitchell had several employees, including a nephew who'd been in trouble for drugs. Dad said Mr. Mitchell used the equity in his business and all his retirement investments—"every dime he had," Dad said—to reimburse the victims for their losses. The charges were eventually dropped. Mr. Mitchell even tried to get his nephew into a rehabilitation program, but the young man skipped town, never to be seen again. Many in Fort Sackville had a hard time letting Mr. Mitchell move on. He and his family were regular customers at Daniels' Family Buffet, and during his entailment, when the Mitchells ate in the restaurant, Dad allowed them to sign their guest checks. Dad kept them in a file in the office, and at the beginning of each month Mr. Mitchell stopped in and paid his bill. Dad said he'd known the Mitchell family all his life; they were good people. The restaurant employees were advised to pay absolutely no attention to town chatter or those folks that, with their gossip and petty jealousies, convicted, sentenced, and shunned Mr. Mitchell even though he'd been acquitted of the charges.

When I went to the door, I found Mr. Mitchell standing there, firm in his flannel shirt, his Wrangler blue jeans tight around his thick legs. He was a tall man, broad shouldered with a wide back. Years of moving furniture had molded his frame.

"I knocked on your mom and dad's door. They didn't answer. Are they home?" he asked. Mr. Mitchell was one of the most physically fit men in town, and he had a peaceful, quiet strength. I never heard him utter an unkind word to anyone. And no one, it seemed, ever said an unkind thing to his face. I don't know how he had managed to be so unobtrusive and ignore the community's ostracism. Somehow through it all, *he* had kept *his* business going.

"No, I don't know where they are," I replied.

"Look. I don't know what's going on," Mr. Mitchell said. "I'm hearing all sorts of stories, and you're really the one I need to speak with anyway."

"What's that?"

"It's none of my business really. But I heard you're moving to Miami Beach. Is that true?"

"Yes."

"When are you going?" he asked.

"Well, I plan to leave sometime around the first of December." I paused. "I'm sorry, Mr. Mitchell, but with all due respect, I don't know what any of this has to do with you." I had become suspicious of everyone in Fort Sackville.

"Your family's been good to my family over the years. You've always used us for moving restaurant equipment and such. Hell, your dad's ambulance trips to Mercy Memorial alone have kept my books in the black." He cracked a smile, and I laughed at Mr. Mitchell's attempt at humor. It was true. It seemed for the last several years Mom was calling 911 every few months when Dad would have one of his spells.

"Listen, I want to help you out. You let me know when it is you want to load up and head south, and I'll have a truck here and my guys ready to work. Free of charge. All you'll have to do is pay for the gas to get you to Miami Beach, and you can return the truck there."

It hadn't quite hit me that I'd be driving a U-Haul to Miami Beach. At least Rio would be with me.

"Mr. Mitchell, I . . . Thank you . . . But really, you don't need to do that."

"I insist. In fact, I won't take no for an answer. You just call the office once you have dates, and we'll do the rest."

And with that, Mr. Mitchell turned, stepped off my front porch, and walked back to his pickup truck, got in, and drove away.

Rio walked up behind me. "Did I just hear what I think I heard?"

"Yeah, you did. Mitchell's Movers are moving me to Miami Beach for free."

Chapter Twenty-Four

November

A few days after Mr. Mitchell's surprise visit, Rio and I made plans to spend the evening with Rosabelle and Mae at their house.

Mae met us at the front door. She gave each of us a hug and then swept us through the foyer, past the living room and into the kitchen. Standing there was Rosabelle, busying herself and putting finishing touches on the meal she had prepared or, as she often said, a meal she "slaved over the telephone ordering."

Rio and I took our seats at their yellow-and-white vintage 1950s kitchen table centered with cheese and crackers on a turquoise Fiesta platter.

"You boys want a cocktail?" Mae asked.

"Absolutely," Rio said. "A rum and Coke, please."

"What'll you have, Grey?" Mae asked.

"I know what Grey wants," Rosabelle piped in. "He wants a titty-pink cosmo. I already started fixing 'em when I heard the doorbell ring. The shaker is chilling as we speak."

"I always did suspect you could read minds, Rosabelle," I said.

"Darling, don't think for a second I'm gonna let you leave town without toasting to your good fortune with a martini or two—or three," Rosabelle said. "I am thrilled to see you and Rio together." She poured the chilled vodka concoction into two frosted martini glasses and passed one to me. "There's still enough to top each of us off in a moment. And I got a whole bottle of Kettle One in the cabinet for more."

Rosabelle and Mae's kitchen was the center of their home. Most of their entertaining was done there, with folks sitting at their kitchen table. The white cabinets and appliances, the sunny yellow walls and matching speckled linoleum floor made the room inviting, warm, and welcoming. It was large enough to accommodate several guests standing about, and the Formica table sat six; but at the same time it was an intimate space, personal, filled with Rosabelle's and Mae's distinctive and vibrant touches. Their kitchen was a wedded version of their personalities.

On their refrigerator they kept amusing and wacky magnets collected from their travels, as well as small magnetic framed pictures of those they loved. I spotted a picture of me from one of their Christmas parties and made a mental note that when Rio and I were settled in South Beach to snap a photo of us, perhaps on his penthouse terrace at sunset, and send it to Rosabelle and Mae. There was also a picture of Eric Sims. Eric Sims was a local hair stylist and close friend to Rosabelle and Mae. Aside from doing their hair, he worked at Rosabelle's during the holidays to pick up some extra cash and help during the peak season. Rosabelle often said she had no idea how they could ever make it every year without Eric's help. He had a flare, a style that made Rosabelle's a winter wonderland of holiday trappings with opulent and ornate Christmas trees—the envy of all who entered. It was not uncommon for those women married to Fort Sackville's wealthiest to walk in and purchase directly from the sales floor a fully trimmed Christmas tree decorated by Eric. Some women would buy a new tree every year and hire Eric to recreate the display in their home. Everybody, especially the local country club women, loved Eric—that is, until Eric became one of Fort Sackville's first "infected." I remember the day well, not long after my twenty-fourth birthday.

Every Sunday, Daniels' Family Buffet received the local newspaper to sell, a bundle wrapped in yellow strapping delivered and dropped inside the restaurant's front entrance vestibule. As part of my morning opening routine, after I prepared the cash drawer and took it to the register, I'd retrieve the bale of newspapers and carry them to the cashier's desk, cut the strap, and arrange them for sale to customers.

That particular Sunday morning, there on the front page of the *Fort Sackville Sentinel* was the headline in bold print: *AIDS HITS FORT SACKVILLE.* The picture was a shadowed profile of a man sitting on the side of his clinic bed near a window. Although the person interviewed in the article chose to remain anonymous, I recognized Eric's profile. Eric had AIDS.

Eric had moved to the Damien Center in Indianapolis, a coordinated care facility supported by local Episcopal and Catholic churches, in order to receive treatment and battle the disease. Although this was in the early 1990s, the residual local AIDS panic from the 1980s lingered in southern Indiana. Eric left his family, friends, and business in order to fight for his life. If I could recognize his profile in the paper, I knew the rest of the community could too. And they did.

Later that day, while I relieved the cashier during her lunch break after the noon rush, one customer approached to pay for his meal, looked at the front page, then said to me, "The faggot got what he deserved." Myrna Boil, the organist at Wabash Valley Baptist Church, said to her dining companion as she pointed to Eric's picture with her manicured nail, "It's God's punishment."

I was dating Rio at the time. We'd met only a few months prior. In spite of the fact that Rio and I were becoming comfortable in our relationship, the newspaper announcing Eric's news reaffirmed my instinct concerning my hometown. I knew it would be wise for Rio and me to keep our relationship a secret in Fort Sackville. Otherwise, customers might turn their attention on me. Homosexuality, even in the early '90s, was, in Fort Sackville, synonymous with AIDS. Local chin-wags would undoubtedly turn from speculation and "did you hear CJ Daniels's son is gay?" to "Grey Daniels—AIDS patient."

"I miss Eric," I said quietly.

Mae, standing beside the kitchen sink, her eyes first focused on me, turned her attention to Rosabelle. Rosabelle pulled out the chair at the head of the table and sat down with her martini, a bewildered look on her face.

"Yes," Rosabelle said, and turned in her seat to look at the picture.

"That was taken at the gift shop one Christmas after closing. A few months before his diagnosis. As long as I live, I'll never forget that phone call," Rosabelle said.

Mae interrupted. "Rosabelle and I lay in bed that night and just cried and cried."

"Just after that article about Eric, Greg Louganis announced he was HIV positive. That really threw me for a loop," I said.

"Well, this is certainly an odd way to start a going away party," Mae said.

"To old friends," I said, raising my martini glass. "And to new relationships." I got up from my chair, stepped around the table to Rio, and gave him a kiss. "I'm just not sure he knows what he has signed up for, taking me on full time. In his house."

"I have no fucking clue," Rio said with a grin.

Chapter Twenty-Five

November

Two weeks before Rio and I left Fort Sackville, before Mr. Mitchell showed up with my U-Haul and his guys to load it, Mom and Dad signed the contract to sell the restaurant property. Rio and I worked diligently, along with my brother Cameron and one of our longtime servers, to clean up the restaurant, since the building would stand empty and unused, its contents sold at auction. The real estate agent had told Dad that no restaurant would be interested in a building so large. "The best staging would be to empty the place of everything," he said. "Potential commercial buyers must be able to see an empty box. They want options for a thirteen-thousand-square-foot building. No doubt they'll want to subdivide it," he said. "Just get it prepped with that idea in mind."

So in those remaining weeks we cleared Daniels' Family Buffet of everything: kitchen equipment, cooking utensils, stainless steal prep tables, pots and iron skillets, tables, chairs, the cash register, coffee makers, coffee cups, the green-band Buffalo china we'd used since the beginning. Personal items and pictures were temporarily stacked in the office.

I was alone in the office while taking a break when I began to flip through the picture frames that once hung on the wall near the restaurant's exit, now stacked in front of the filing cabinet drawers. I spotted one of my family not long after Dad bought the restaurant from Grandpa Collin. We all looked much younger and almost giddy with expectation. My father's hair was coal black, my mother looked rested and vibrant, my brother was just a little boy in elementary school, and

I looked much thinner. For the restaurant's fortieth anniversary we'd remodeled and purchased a new outdoor sign, and we were sitting on the edge of a flatbed trailer; strapped behind us was the restaurant's new twenty-by-forty boxed sign. After the picture was taken, Seymour Advertising raised, mounted, and secured the sign atop a sixty-foot pole and connected electricity. That first night the illuminated sign with its green background and yellow lettering signaled that Daniels' Family Buffet had transitioned to the second and third generation. Since 1951, the restaurant had been my family's legacy in Fort Sackville.

That autumn was sunny and warm. Our restaurant was built on the highlands of the former Bonhomme Apple Orchard, above the valley in which Fort Sackville lay. And from my perch on the flatbed, I could see across Highway 41 the white steeple of the Wabash Valley Baptist Church, the four Gothic courthouse towers, and the sycamores safeguarding the Wabash River like silver-green sentinels. My father's journey had been a long one, and that day, the mounting of the sign was a cherry on top of his hard-earned sundae.

The anticipation throughout Fort Sackville of my father's stewardship was palpable, and no one was more excited than my family. I remember the smell of that day, like burning leaves, the exhaust of the crane lifting the sign. I watched as the welder's sparks fell to earth, his electric-blue flame a star burning hot and bright.

Standing now in the restaurant's cluttered office, I flipped through the other pictures. I saw Robbie and Daryl at the golf tournament; I saw the black-and-white framed photo of a very young Eloise standing behind the lunch counter at Daniel's Diner taking a customer's order; there was another of me as a little boy sitting with Mom and Dad at my favorite table near the jukebox; and another of Grandma Dixie sitting near the cash register reading a romance novel.

I heard the back kitchen door delivery bell ring. Brucken's Auction House trucks had arrived. My family's restaurant had become photographs in frames. A year had passed since Pastor Daryl first returned to Fort Sackville, and just months since Trace had committed suicide. *It wasn't supposed to end this way.* I let the framed pictures slip from my hands, and with a soft thud they slipped into place against the others. I walked out of the office, shutting the door behind me, and headed toward the ringing delivery bell.

After Daniels' Family Buffet was emptied and cleaned and the personal photographs and memorabilia stored at Mom and Dad's, the restaurant was ready to sell. At my house, Mr. Mitchell's guys packed my U-Haul. I had lived in Fort Sackville all my life. The plan was for Rio and me to leave Sunday midmorning after having breakfast with Mom, Dad, and Cameron, and then stop in Mt. Vernon to say goodbye to his mother before we began our trek south. I knew the road ahead would be difficult, but at least now I would have a chance at the life I had always wanted.

After breakfast, Rio and I said goodbye to Mom, Dad, and Cam.

"Do you want to drive through Fort Sackville one more time and take one last look?" Rio asked.

"You're joking, right?" I asked.

"I'm serious. I want to go by that old Chinese restaurant where you and I had our first date. I want to get a picture of us out front."

"Seriously?" I asked.

"I think you and I both know it's going to be a long time before we ever come back here—if we ever come back. I know a lot of bad shit has happened, but a lot of good stuff happened here too. It would be kind of nice to have a picture of you and me out front to remind us," Rio said.

I drove the U-Haul through town to Second Street and parked it opposite the old China Palace. It had gone out of business not long after Rio and I had our first date and had been abandoned since. The sign was still hanging on the side of the building. Rio took out his new iPhone, and together we stood in front of the storefront while he did his best to position the phone to capture us in front of the sign.

"There, you see," Rio said, showing me his phone screen. "When we're old and gray we won't remember that we took this picture of our first date all these years later."

I laughed. He was right. I was glad he'd insisted we take one last look.

We got back in the truck and headed toward Highway 41.

"You know, since we're doing this, I'd like to stop by the old Daniels' Diner building one more time," I said.

"Sure," Rio said.

Grandpa Collin's first restaurant on Fairground Avenue also stood empty now. It had for years. The abandoned building had been bought and sold several times. Rio and I parked our U-Haul on the street in front. I reminded Rio that Daniels' Diner was the restaurant I kept warehoused in my earliest childhood memories, and how it had been a bustling business, often requiring that Grandpa Collin lock the front door during the lunch rush, only allowing customers to enter as others left.

Together, Rio and I approached the entrance and peered through the dusty front window, using our hands to clear the glass as if it were frosted by the cold winter's day. He could not imagine it. But I, ignoring its sagging, pressed tin ceiling and the trash left behind by midnight vandals, could see the waitresses in their white starched uniforms as they carried daily plate specials on green-band Buffalo china—and I could almost smell the vegetable soup.

Daniels' Diner used to serve beef vegetable soup on weekends. Mom and I would meet Dad there for lunch every Saturday. On this particular October afternoon, when Mom opened the Diner's front door, its distinctive *whoosh* released the pressure of its almost airtight glass vestibule, allowing the sundrenched air, parked outside with our car on Fairground Avenue, to follow us inside. Then, as Mom and I stepped through the vestibule's second interior door, the spicy scent of Saturday's soup of the day welcomed us. I was six years old and loved the welcoming aroma.

We stopped next to the cashier's counter. There my grandma Dixie Daniels sat manning the register, reading a Harlequin romance. The steam from her neglected cup of coffee rose in a conjugal vortex with the smoke from her nearly neglected Winston cigarette, its scorched tobacco dangled, poised to fall into the black well of an ashtray. There was red lipstick on the cigarette's filter, and green guest checks were speared in place by an inverted six-inch nail on a small block of wood next to the cash register. In her mind I'm sure she inhabited some exotic locale that had nothing to do with cash registers and customer checks.

Suddenly, she looked up from her book. "Grey! Dessa! I didn't expect to see you today. CJ said you were out shopping." Grandma Dixie placed her paperback on the table next to her coffee. She stood as I dashed behind the counter to give her a hug and a kiss.

"We are," Mom said. "We're going shopping for a Halloween costume today. Grey insists Tressler's will sell out before he gets the one he wants."

Pulling from our embrace and looking into my eyes, Grandma Dixie placed her hands on my shoulders and asked, "Who's it going to be this year? A hobo? Casper? Frankenstein?"

"I'm not telling," I said. "It's a secret."

A customer approached the counter. "Well, I suppose I'll have to be on the lookout for a strange creature standing on my front porch," Grandma Dixie said with a chuckle.

Mom stepped away from the counter, allowing the large customer to approach.

"Been busy, Dixie?" the customer asked.

"Yes," she replied. "This gorgeous day has everybody out. How's everything with you, Dallas?"

"Can't complain. Got a full belly," he said, rubbing his stomach. "Nothing like Daniels' to fill a body up."

Leaving the cashier's counter, as Mom and I walked to our table, I heard the cash register's familiar refrain: first, a finger punching keys; then, the rip of a guest check speared through by the nail and added to the stack; the *ka-ching* of the cash register's bell, followed by the final thud of the cash drawer springing open. There was a sense of security in its everyday, every-sale repetitiveness: *punch*, *rip*, *ka-ching*, *thud*. *Punch, rip, ka-ching, thud.*

In the kitchen behind the lunch counter, visible through the order-up window, stood Grandpa Collin, his head tilted forward, offering a clear view of the pale yellow nicotine streak ascending his gray pompadour. His hair resembled the arched back of our neighbor's old gray-and-yellow tom when he prepared to strike. A Depression-era street kid, Grandpa Collin had smoked his first cigarette at age ten.

Mom and I had come to meet Dad to get money for my Halloween costume. Saturdays at the Diner were more steady than busy, so Dad would have time to eat with us. He was sitting in a chair pulled up beside the back booth with the Coffee Club Clan. They were a constant on Saturdays, like the beef vegetable soup.

Dad heard our voices, stood, and returned his chair to a neighboring table. The CCC boys waved to Mom. She smiled and nodded. Dad joined us, and together we sat at my favorite table, nearest the jukebox.

"So, you two are out running around today," he said, giving my head a quick rub with his hand.

"We're going to get my costume," I replied.

"He insists on the Wicked Witch of the West," Mom said under her breath.

I was wild for the movie *The Wizard of Oz*. Every spring since my first memory of Grandma Dixie and me singing "We're Off to See the Wizard" until she died during my freshman year in high school, we'd watch the annual April broadcast on NBC with our usual trappings: Jiffy Pop popcorn and ice-cold eight-ounce bottles of Coca-Cola. The green-skinned Wicked Witch fascinated me—I often rode my mom's broom through the house pretending I could fly. And I was captivated by the tornado, especially since spring was tornado season in southern Indiana.

"Boys don't dress up as witches," Dad said.

"Why not?" I asked.

"Girls dress up like witches. Boys dress up like monsters. What about Dracula, Frankenstein, or a skeleton?" he asked, wearing a look of concern that confused me.

"There's no use arguing," Mom said. "I've already explained it to him. He insists on the Wicked Witch."

"We have to hurry up, before they sell it!" I cried.

"He's dead set," Mom said, her eyes communicating something with Dad that was beyond my comprehension.

My father sighed, his face registering resignation. To him, I imagine, it wasn't worth an argument. During my dad's childhood with his sister, Grandpa Collin had raised them with a harsh hand. As a boy about my age, Dad, after refusing to eat spinach one night, was humiliated in front of his older sister and her neighborhood friend when Grandpa Collin grasped the spinach from Dad's plate with his bare hand, then, while holding the back of my father's head with his other, rubbed the greasy leafy greens into my father's face.

"Goddamn it, you eat what I tell you to eat!" he'd said, wiping his hand afterward on my dad's shirt. Grandma Dixie was mortified and rose to try to stop Grandpa Collin. While trying to pull Grandpa Collin away, he backhanded her, knocking her off balance into the china hutch, bloodying her nose. Recounting the story to me, Dad said the only sound he remembered were the dishes rattling on their glass shelves.

Mom, Dad, and I finished our lunch, then he walked us toward the cashier's counter. He lifted me level with the cash register and let me hit the *no sale* key: *punch, ka-ching, thud*. The cash drawer sprang open.

"How much do you need?" he asked.

"Ten dollars," I said.

"Ten dollars! Is it custom-made?"

"CJ, you let Grey take what he needs; it's been a good day," Grandma Dixie said. She winked at me and playfully slapped Dad on his arm.

"All right, ten dollars. It better be one hell of a costume for that kind of money. No wonder the Tresslers live in the Heights."

"Thanks, Dad." I gave him a kiss and slammed the cash drawer shut. Grandma Dixie returned to her book.

Once outside in the autumn air, the faint smell of burning leaves wafted above us. I stood next to the passenger door of our tan-and-brown Pontiac Grand Prix waiting for Mom to unlock, fingering the crisp ten-dollar bill in my pocket.

Once inside the car, I said, "Grandpa Collin didn't come say hello."

"Well, it *is* a good day, isn't it?" Mom said smiling, starting the engine, then placing the gearshift in drive.

The Diner's phantoms dematerialized. Rio stepped away from the window. "Are you ready to go, Grey?"

"Yes. I'm ready."

"Do you want a picture?" Rio asked.

"No. I like the ones in my memory," I said. "It really is over, isn't it?"

"What?" Rio asked.

"The past. It's over," I said, standing there, facing Rio in front of the dusty Diner window.

"It is. We have each other now. And tomorrow, and the day after that, and . . ."

Midsentence I kissed Rio, right there on Fairground Avenue in Fort Sackville, for the entire world to see. No more would I think about the past, analyze it, dissect it. Rio was my present and my future. Before Rio, I'd never shared my life with anyone, and that moment standing with him as I peered into my childhood world was analogous to his peering into my heart. We returned to our U-Haul and headed down Fairground Avenue toward Highway 41.

On our way we passed Wabash Valley Baptist Church. Sunday service had just let out. It was almost winter and the day was cold but clear, and the sun was shining bright. Parishioners were gathered up and down the front steps of the church and in front of the open sanctuary doors. Standing just outside the middle section of doors was Pastor Daryl, shaking hands and receiving hugs from churchgoers as they filed out. I saw Mr. and Mrs. Thompson walking down the steps; Myrna Boil lumbered along behind them holding tight to the handrail; Daryl's wife Rebecca was at the base of the steps, trying to corral Isaac and Jacob and a few other children running wild. Life had not skipped a beat for Wabash Valley Baptist Church. I saw folks that for my entire life had been regular customers of the restaurant. I imagined their conversations. I knew how they spoke. I'd often listened to their talk in the restaurant. Perhaps the Ward family and the Cullen family, the small group gathered just beyond Pastor Daryl, were making plans with each other for Sunday dinner somewhere.

"Where are you all going?" Mr. Ward asks.

"I don't know, we're undecided," Mr. Cullen says.

"What about that cute little café on Main Street?" Mrs. Cullen asks.

"Honey, they're not open on Sunday, remember? We tried last week," Mr. Cullen says.

"Well, we could go to Arby's," Mr. Ward suggests.

"I don't want fast food," Mrs. Ward replies shortly. "How about Applebee's? You know, one just opened south of Terre Haute. We could go there."

"But that's an hour's drive," Mr. Cullen says.

"What other options do we have?" Mrs. Ward snaps back.

"I don't know," Mr. Cullen says, "I sure wish there was someplace a body could get some good ol' southern Indiana home cooking. There just aren't any decent restaurants in this town anymore."

I drove our U-Haul toward Highway 41, took the exit, and headed south. Rio and I were beginning our new life.

END

Acknowledgments

It is said the spot in the center of one's chest, just behind the breastbone, above the heart but below the throat, is where our instinct lies; some call it the voice of God. It takes practice and patience, stillness and being with one's self, in order to hear it, to really listen. I think, at one time or another, everyone has felt the presence of his or her own voice within, heard its plea offering internal guidance. Too often, perhaps, it is ignored.

When I lived in Miami I often walked during the evenings in my upper eastside neighborhood. It was an opportunity to clear my head and my heart, to think and reflect. Many times during these walks that internal, hidden *voice* said to me, "Just write. Writing is your answer." When I finally decided to listen to my true voice and pursue my craft, a new and vibrant world opened its door to me. My guide, the first soul I met on my journey, was the indomitable Kaylie Jones. Our meeting was not serendipitous, it was arranged by the Universe. And for that I am eternally grateful. She has been steadfast in her support and mentorship of me, committed to my work and to our journey.

Kaylie and I have lived very different lives: she was born and raised in Paris, living her adult life in New York; I was born and raised in southern Indiana, living my adult life in Miami. Yet, it seems, there is something about the Midwest, its soil and spirit, which dwells within her heart and is most likely coded in her DNA from her father and his family. The Midwest was something she and I had in common.

Kaylie Jones changed the trajectory of my life. And because of her, most of the names listed in gratitude below—teachers, authors, friends, and cohorts, folks I met and admire, people who kindly gave the gift of their time and talent in order to help me follow my voice, and who are now forever a part of this extraordinary journey—each of them tracks back to one quiet Monday night in March of 2010 at Books & Books in Coral Gables, Florida, when Kaylie swept past me before her reading, yet stopped to say hello.

It is with tremendous gratitude and love that I thank the following people for their time, talent, consideration, and guidance: Justin Kassab, Taylor Polites, Susie Merrell, Suzanna Filip, Mark Childress, Casey Telesk, all the writers in the Kaylie Jones Books collective, and Johnny Temple and the folks at Akashic Books. Thanks to the Stony Brook Southampton and Manhattan MFA faculty and my cohorts, including Dan Sarluca and his wife Lauren, as well as Janice Maffei, for their unyielding hospitality and for opening up their homes to me, and to Lou Ann Walker for publishing my first piece in the *Southampton Review*.

I also want to thank my friends and former coteachers Janas Byrd and Jacqui Pinilla for their unwavering support, my friend and former principal Shelley Stroleny for her steadfast guidance, and all of my former colleagues at G.W. Carver Middle School in Miami.

Most certainly I want to thank my family for their love: my mother Canda Burton Winkler, my father Charles "Chuck" Winkler, and my brother Charlie Winkler. I absolutely could not have made the journey without them. And my chosen family members—Andrea Kaskus, Margaret A. McGiffen, Toby Roberts, Kevin Axsom, and Marsha Wood—I say thank you for always being there and for allowing me to use your homes for my very own summer writing retreat.

Some of the newspaper articles in the novel are inspired by true events. The characters, names, businesses, incidents, locations, and events have been reimagined and fictionalized for dramatic purposes. I wish to thank the archivists and employees of the Knox County Public Library, the *Vincennes Sun Commercial*, the *Evansville Courier and Press,* the Evansville Vanderburgh County Public Library, the Lawrence County Public Library, and the Robinson Public Library for their generosity of spirit and unyielding assistance as I conducted my in-house and online research.

Finally, I would like to thank all of the former employees and customers of my family's restaurant, Charlie's Smorgasbord. For many, many years we captured lightning in a bottle. And, I am certain, the legacy of Charlie's will forever dwell in each of your hearts as it does in mine.

J. Patrick Redmond

Esther Bloom Photography

J. PATRICK REDMOND was born and raised in southern Indiana and recently returned to his home state after sixteen years of living in South Florida and teaching for the Miami-Dade County Public School System. He holds a BA in English from Florida International University in Miami and an MFA in creative writing and literature from Stony Brook University in Southampton, New York. He is a contributing blogger for the *Huffington Post*, and his writing has appeared in the NOH8 Campaign blog, the *Southampton Review*, and in the *Barnes & Noble Review*'s Grin & Tonic. He is also the 2012 recipient of the Deborah Hecht Memorial Prize in Fiction. *Some Go Hungry* is his first novel, and when asked about it, Patrick says, "It's about God, guns, gays, and green beans." Additional information is available at jpatrickredmond.com.